ARKHAM HORROR

It is the height of the Roaring Twenties – a fresh enthusiasm for the arts, science, and exploration of the past have opened doors to a wider world, and beyond…

And yet, a dark shadow grows over the town of Arkham. Alien entities known as Ancient Ones lurk in the emptiness beyond space and time, writhing at the thresholds between worlds.

Occult rituals must be stopped and alien creatures destroyed before the Ancient Ones make our world their ruined dominion.

Only a handful of brave souls with inquisitive minds and the will to act stand against the horrors threatening to tear this world apart.

Will they prevail?

Also available in Arkham Horror

ARKHAM HORROR™

SHADOWS
of PNATH

JOSH REYNOLDS

ACONYTE

First published by Aconyte Books in 2023

ISBN 978 1 83908 205 4

Ebook ISBN 978 1 83908 206 1

Cover art by Daniel Strange

Distributed in North America by Simon & Schuster Inc, New York, USA

Printed in the United States of America

9 8 7 6 5 4 3 2 1

ACONYTE BOOKS

An imprint of Asmodee Entertainment Ltd

Mercury House, Shipstones Business Centre

North Gate, Nottingham NG7 7FN, UK

aconytebooks.com // twitter.com/aconytebooks

For Katrina, and the other folks at FFG.
Thanks for letting me visit Arkham again.

PROLOGUE
Comte d'Erlette

Henri-Georges Balfour, the Comte d'Erlette, descended into the crypt where the bones of his ancestors, esteemed and otherwise, had lain for centuries. Or rather some of them, at least. The earthly remnants of his great grandfather, Francois-Honoré, had never been recovered, after that worthy's untimely end. Another debt owed his family by the worms of the earth.

Sometimes it seemed to Henri that he'd spent his entire life collecting what was owed on behalf of the loved dead, rather than seeing to his own desires. Still, one did what one must when it came to family. He lit a cigarette, more to cut the smell in the crypt than anything. The air was thick with a rank, animal odor.

The crypt extended for some distance beneath the grounds of his ancestral estates near Toulouse, stretching from the vaulted cellars of the family home to the very banks of the Garonne. Once, the tunnels had served a dual purpose – burial and smuggling. Now, they were all but forgotten by everyone but the current Comte d'Erlette. Which was just the way he preferred it. Secrets were power, and Henri had plenty of both. But he desired more.

He paused on the bottom step, smoke circling his head like a crooked halo. His gaze swept the darkness. There was no sign of movement, no hint of an ambush. He smiled thinly. "Light it up," he said, softly.

Behind him, one of his bodyguards struck a railroad flare, filling the antechamber of the crypt with a hellish red light. The sudden flash of infernal radiance illuminated a scene of charnel devastation. Broken bones were scattered everywhere, as if cast aside in haste – or frustration. The man with the flare cursed in Turkish. Then, in French, he said, "I warned you, Comte."

"So you did, Selim," Henri said. Besides Selim, there were two others. All three were hard men, inculcated in the ways of the horrors that prowled the inner earth. They had hunted such creatures in Turkey and Abyssinia before coming into the employ of the Comte d'Erlette. It was because of that experience that he'd hired them.

He needed men who knew what lurked in the dark; men who had faced the terrors of the night and emerged the stronger for it – who would not flinch from the tasks he required of them. Most importantly, they were men who knew how to trap the sort of creature now prowling about his family crypt.

Henri took in the disorder and clucked his tongue in disapproval. "Such a mess. One might think you are unhappy with your accommodations, young sir."

A growl echoed from the shadows that bunched at the edge of the red light's reach. An animal sound, but with the hint of words. Henri's smile widened and he stepped down, kicking aside the skull of one of his ancestors as he did so. "Is this how you repay my hospitality? With such desecration? Were I another man, I might take insult. As it is, I am merely disappointed. I was told your folk were polite, at least."

The growl deepened, becoming a bone-deep rumble packed with unpleasant promise. Henri's smile didn't waver, though he felt his bodyguards tense in anticipation. He gestured, calming Selim and the others.

Henri took a drag on his cigarette and expelled the smoke in the direction of the sound. "Growl all you like, young sir, but we both know that is all you can do. That is all you will do, until I say otherwise. Until I get what I want."

The growl rose in volume. The sound was edged with hunger; a raw, primal need. Henri frowned. It had been nearly a week since he'd caught the beast. A week it had been trapped in this crypt, unable to leave. He'd made sure of that. At the time, he'd considered the remains of his ancestors to be a necessary sacrifice. Everything he'd read about them said that they could survive indefinitely on the most meager of scraps. But now, he was starting to wonder if he'd underestimated his captive's hunger.

He tapped ash onto the floor and expelled smoke from his nostrils. "If you'd simply acquiesced to my request, we could avoid this unpleasantness. All I have read concerning your folk portrays you as a pragmatic people. Surely you see that aiding me is in your best interests?"

Something scraped against the stone floor of the crypt and he detected a heaving motion, as of something rising to its feet. Bones clattered as the unseen creature began to prowl along the edge of the flare's glow, moving on all fours. Its stink wafted anew toward him, and he wrinkled his nose in disgust.

He caught the flicker of its eyes; they reflected the light like a cat's, and he couldn't help but feel a chill as they fixed on him. He swallowed the sudden twitch of fear, knowing that to show even a moment's weakness would be to cede the advantage to his captive. That he could not do. He needed the creature broken; obliging. Else his chances of achieving his goal were slim to none.

The shadow rose; bipedal now. It stared at him, still growling. But it made no effort to step into the light. It found the glare of the flare painful, Henri thought. He took a step toward it, waving aside the wordless sound of protest from one of his guards.

"You are mine," Henri said, in a flat tone. "There is no help coming, no way to escape. I have barred your kind from my lands with the old methods. Your only option is to do as I say. Or you can rot here in the dark, until your bones join those of my ancestors."

The growl became a snarl; again, the hint of words. Obscenities, perhaps. That such a creature would curse at him in such a fashion brought a laugh bubbling up from Henri's throat. That laugh was almost his undoing.

It came at him a moment later, lunging out of the dark with pantherish speed. It was big, but slim. An adolescent of the species, having not yet attained the full, foul growth of its kind. Henri fell back with an undignified squawk as claws meant for tearing open caskets and prying off tomb-lids tore the buttons from his waistcoat.

Henri fell onto the stairs, yelling for his men. They reacted with commendable speed. Pistols cracked, and his attacker sprang back and scurried away, into the deeper darkness of the crypt. Heart pounding, Henri allowed himself to be drawn to his feet.

"Did you hit it?" he panted. "Selim, is it injured? If so, I will take it out of your hide!"

"No," Selim said, with obvious disappointment. The big

man looked at Henri. "We should kill it. I told you, there is no bargaining with... those folk."

"Anything can be bargained with," Henri snapped. "One must simply find the correct lever with which to open negotiations." He looked down at his waistcoat and stifled a curse. The creature had left the prints of its paws on the fabric; black stains of congealed grave mold and bone marrow. It was utterly ruined, and would need burning.

He took a calming breath. He'd lost his cigarette somewhere in the fall, so he lit another. The flare was spitting and dimming. He stared into the darkness, silently daring his captive to try again. But it was gone. It would be back, of course. It had nowhere else to go.

There were only two potential exits, and one was sealed and marked with certain sigils that creatures like his captive could not bear to be in close proximity to. That left the door at the top of the stairs, which led into the wine cellar of his ancestral chateau. It was the only possible route of escape, and the creature watched it like a tiger trying to fathom how to escape a circus wagon.

Henri allowed Selim and the others to escort him back upstairs, to safety. The door was barred behind them, and the Sign of Koth reapplied to the ancient wood. A guard was left on duty, just in case. Henri was not so confident in his mystical defenses as to wholly disdain mundane precautions. In some circumstances, a man with a gun was just as effective as a magical sigil. Occasionally, more so.

Upstairs, Henri found someone waiting for him in his study. Alerted by the servants, he made his way to the room and entered to find a familiar face sitting on a chaise-lounge, a short, sallow man, dressed all in white.

"Monsieur Swann," Henri said to his visitor, in English. He gestured and Selim closed the doors behind them, ensuring some privacy. "It has been some time since you last darkened my doorstep. What brings you to Chateau d'Erlette?"

Chauncey Swann rose to his feet, hat in hand. "I bring you the greetings and well-wishes of the Silver Twilight Lodge, Comte," he said, in badly accented French. Henri gestured sharply.

"English, please. Your French is an offense to God and myself."

Swann grimaced. "No one ever complained before." Swann was a professional acquisitionist – a collector of things obscure and eldritch. It had made him wealthy, if not wise. If you needed something, Swann could get it. Even if getting it meant breaking laws... or people.

Henri had employed Swann on more than one occasion to acquire certain items of interest, though of late the American had worked solely on behalf of one individual in particular. An individual with interests similar to Henri's own.

"You are American, and allowances must be made for children and idiots. Why are you here, Swann?" He loosened his neck tie. "Your employers and I are not on the friendliest of terms." In point of fact, Henri thought the Silver Twilight Lodge a stain on the demimonde. A loose association of petty occultists, grasping politicians and smug power-brokers, all seeking to make use of the unknown for their own ends. But whatever he thought of their membership, their leader, Carl Sanford, was a man of great influence, even in Europe. Henri had found that out to his chagrin, more than once.

"Times change, Comte, and hard feelings with them." Swann twisted the brim of his hat in his hands nervously. "I've been sent to make something of a rapprochement, you might say. A gesture of goodwill on the part of Mr Sanford."

"And what might this gesture be?" Stripping off his waistcoat, Henri made his way to the drinks' cabinet in the corner. He tossed the ruined garment to Selim and poured himself a drink. He didn't bother to offer one to Swann. He doubted the acquisitionist would be staying long enough to enjoy it. Swann's master had long been seeking a way to place Henri under his thumb. No doubt this gesture was just another of Sanford's ploys to gain Henri's trust.

"We know where she is."

Henri stopped, drink halfway to his lips. He set it down and turned, eyes narrowed. "To whom might you be referring, Monsieur Swann?" he asked, his tone low and dangerous. Swann licked his lips nervously, gaze darting toward Selim.

"You know who."

Henri studied the other man with a hooded gaze. Then, deliberately, he poured his guest a drink. "Tell me," he said, as he added ice.

"Alessandra Zorzi is in Paris."

Zorzi. The name ricocheted through Henri's head like the echoes of a gunshot. He offered the glass to Swann. Swann accepted it with a nod of thanks. He took a sip and elaborated.

"Don't know why. Sanford don't know why either." Swann gave him a sly look. "But he thought maybe you'd like to ask her yourself."

Henri moved past him, to the large windows that overlooked the overgrown stretch of his estates. He'd never been a believer in manicured lawns. He much preferred the wild growth of flowers and trees. "I almost had her in Marrakesh, you know? A half-step behind. I lost her trail after that." The ghost of a woman's laugh echoed in his head. That was, perhaps, her most unforgiveable crime. She had laughed at him. He could stand any pain but that.

"She went to Arkham," Swann said. "Massachusetts."

"Ah." Henri turned and bared his teeth at his guest. "That explains that. What did she steal from Sanford? Nothing valuable, I hope."

"She didn't steal nothing, at least not that I know of," Swann said. "But she was… well." He shrugged. "She was a bit rude to Mr Sanford is all." He smiled thinly. "You know how he feels about that kind of thing."

Henri nodded. "I do. A man after my own heart." He knocked back his drink and smiled. "Paris, you say?"

CHAPTER ONE
Les Deux Magots

"What do you think of Paris so far, then?" Alessandra Zorzi asked, before blowing a thin plume of cigarette smoke into the cool evening air. Zorzi's tablemate dabbed her lips with a napkin, before dropping it onto her recently cleaned plate.

"Food's good," Pepper Kelly said, as she sat back in her chair with a contented expression. "Coffee's okay. No one knows how to drive though." She was a young woman, with thin, boyish features and a spattering of freckles across her nose and cheeks. She wore a battered flat cap, and loose clothes that made her resemble a roustabout or dock worker.

Alessandra laughed. "I shall pass along your comments to the board of tourism." Idly, she let her gaze sweep across the nearby tables. They sat outside a café in Saint-Germain-des-Pres, enjoying an early evening aperitif. Or at least Pepper was enjoying one. The younger woman was akin to a fire in constant need of fuel. If there was food, it soon found its way into her belly. Alessandra, on the other hand, could happily subsist for hours on nothing more than an expresso and a cigarette.

In contrast to her companion, she was dressed for autumn

in Paris, in a pair of red wide-leg trousers, a modest top and a long, fur-lined jacket the color of dying foliage. Her hair was long again, and messily piled atop her head, held in place by several silver Chinese hairpins. While it was technically illegal in France for women to dress with such flagrant disregard for gender norms, Alessandra suspected that their foreignness lent them a certain amount of leeway in regards to public censure. She was Venetian after all, and Pepper, American. Decadence on one hand and barbarism on the other.

She took another drag on her cigarette and let her eyes continue their wandering. She took in their fellow patrons of *Les Deux Magots*, looking for familiar faces. It never paid to get too comfortable, especially in Paris. It was still enemy territory after all.

Some of that was her fault, perhaps. She'd made her share of mistakes; gotten involved with the wrong sorts; crossed a few Rubicons, so to speak. But that was in the past and she was attempting to turn over a new leaf.

She'd lived the life of a gentlewoman thief for nearly thirty years, specializing in the acquisition and redistribution of esoteric paraphernalia. She'd stolen books of occult knowledge, rare artifacts and even a crystal skull, once. But those days were behind her, or so she assured herself.

It was difficult to change the habits of a lifetime, of course. Thievery was in her blood. The idea of returning things she had previously stolen was anathema to her. Yet here she was, on the mostly straight and often dangerously narrow. At least she wasn't alone. She glanced at her companion and smiled.

She'd met Pepper a year previous, during her last visit to the States and a dreadful little town in Massachusetts called Arkham. She'd been hired to steal a mummy of unusual provenance from the local museum. Things had taken a turn for the strange, but she'd survived – largely thanks to Pepper's assistance.

In return, Alessandra had offered to teach the younger woman how to do something more lucrative than driving a cab. Just because she was no longer a thief didn't mean she couldn't pass along her wisdom, as her own tutors had done for her. The problem was that Pepper was an inattentive student at best. As if reading her thoughts, Pepper sighed, and played with her napkin. "Is something wrong, Pepper?" Alessandra asked.

"Bit homesick is all, Countess. We ain't been back to the States in almost a year." Pepper tipped back her hat and gave Alessandra a hangdog look. "It's not that I ain't grateful, you know? You taking me all over the world, teaching me the lingo, it's been great. But I miss Arkham." She frowned. "I miss my cab, stupid as that sounds."

Alessandra smiled gently. "It does not sound stupid at all." She reached into her clutch, sitting on the table, and retrieved a pack of cigarettes from beneath the heavy shape of her Webley revolver. She offered the pack to Pepper, who took one after a moment's hesitation. "It is the same with myself and Venice. It is home. Wherever else I wander, whatever sights I see, *La Serenissima* still holds me here." She tapped her chest. "What is the American saying? Home is where the heart beats, yes?"

"Where the heart is," Pepper corrected.

Alessandra waved this aside. "My point stands. It is the central point around which your everything orbits. All roads lead to Rome, you understand?"

"I thought we were talking about Venice."

Alessandra laughed and took another drag on her cigarette. Though she'd made her offer to Pepper on the spur of the moment, she found that she enjoyed playing mentor. "If it helps, there is a bit of American history here. The Treaty of Paris, which ended your revolution, was signed at a hotel nearby."

"Yeah?" Pepper frowned and leaned forward to plant her elbows on the table. "Ain't that something? How do you know that?"

Alessandra leaned forward, a sly look on her face. "Why, I was once hired to steal it," she said in a stage-whisper. Pepper's eyes widened and Alessandra sat back, laughing lightly. Pepper flushed.

"Ha-ha, real funny."

Alessandra smiled at her. "I did not say it was a joke."

Pepper squinted at her. "Are you funning me, sister?"

"Only a bit." Alessandra took another puff on her cigarette. "Would you like anything else to eat before we go, or are you satisfied for the moment?"

"I can always eat, but I know we're on a schedule," Pepper said, a trifle defensively. "You sure your pal is gonna be there this time of night? I've known a few artist types, and every one of them likes to clock out and get tight as owls come dusk."

"Znamenski is different. He claims to work best at night. If he is to be found anywhere, it will be his studio."

"I still can't believe he agreed to hand over the whatchamacallit…"

"The Zanthu tablet," Alessandra said. It was, or had been, part of a set of a dozen pieces of blackened jade, discovered by some expedition or other. The majority of the set was at an institute in California, but a few had made their way into the hands of private collectors over the years since their discovery.

"That's the gizmo," Pepper said. "What is it anyway?"

Alessandra expelled a stream of smoke into the air above their heads. "A tablet."

Pepper snorted. "I got that bit. But why's it special?"

"I do not know. I know only that Znamenski was willing to part with a formidable sum to purchase it."

"And now we're going to pay to get it back."

"Preferably," Alessandra said, with a slight grimace. Her financial situation was tenuous at best. She'd lived an expensive life; what was the point of having money, after all, if one didn't spend it? But she had some disposable assets in a safe deposit box at Tellson's, a bank in this quarter. It was a British bank, but she didn't hold that against it. It might take a few days to liquidate said assets, but she had nowhere pressing to be.

But that would only be a stop-gap, at best. Since she was no longer practicing her profession, she was burning through her assets at a greater rate than she'd anticipated. And since Miskatonic wasn't paying her for the artifacts she was recovering, she was soon going to need another source of income. That was a problem for tomorrow, however.

"We could just steal it," Pepper said, in a studiously innocent tone of voice. Alessandra looked at her and Pepper shrugged. "What? I got to put your lessons to use at some point, don't I?"

Alessandra made to reply, but paused. Something – someone, rather – had caught her attention. Pepper noticed. "What is it?" she murmured.

"We are being watched," Alessandra replied, in a low voice. She stubbed out her cigarette on her cup's saucer. "Two tables over. Disreputable looking fellow. Scar over his left eye. Tattoo on the inside of his right wrist."

Pepper blinked, pulled off her hat and, using it to mask her face, hissed, "You got all that from just a glance?"

"What is it I always tell you? Be aware of your surroundings. A moment of inattention and you could find yourself pinched by the peelers."

"The what?"

Alessandra smiled thinly. "You know… *piedipiatti*. Flat feet. The police."

Pepper frowned and darted a glance toward their observer. "So he's a bull?"

Alessandra blinked. "A what?"

"A cop!"

"No. But he is watching us. Nor is he alone." There were at least two others that she'd spotted, sitting nearby. None of three looked like the usual *Magots* crowd. It wasn't the way they dressed, so much as the way they held themselves. They were the sort of men for whom violence was the first and only answer to any question.

"So who is he?"

Alessandra sat back. "I have no idea. There are any number of possible explanations. Perhaps he fancies you."

Pepper shuddered. "Thanks but no thanks." She plopped her hat back on her head. "Maybe we should go ask, hunh?"

"I think not. Especially since we do not know what he wants or who he represents."

"Then what do we do, just sit here?"

"Actually, I was thinking we might go to the – what do you call it, the powder room?"

Pepper frowned, but only for a moment. Then she smiled and nodded. "Oh, I get you. The old dine and dash, hunh?"

"Not quite. I do enjoy this place, and I would like to come

back. Now, follow me." Alessandra picked up her clutch and rose unhurriedly, leaving a few sous on the table. Pepper followed her, hands thrust in her pockets. Inside, the café was packed. It was one of the oldest in Paris, and popular with the art crowd, both Parisian and expatriate.

The café took its name from the two Chinese figurines that adorned the far wall, gazing down at the patrons with expressions of serene mockery. Something about the duo had always set her ill at ease. Znamenski had once informed her that they were meant to represent magicians or alchemists; perhaps that was the origin of her distaste for them. She'd had enough of magicians for one lifetime.

She led Pepper into the back, moving with a surety designed to allay any questions before they were voiced. A brisk walk and a stern look could cow even the most vocal maître d'. A side door led to an alleyway, which led to the street.

From there, a quick walk in the direction of the cathedral, past the outside tables of the café, got them to Rue du Dragon. They paused next to a barrow offering an assortment of yellow jonquils, pale violets and Roman hyacinths.

"What do you see?" Alessandra murmured as she pretended to examine the flowers.

"Not the guy, if that's what you're asking," Pepper muttered, her cap pulled low. "Think he peeped us?"

"Maybe." Alessandra selected a jonquil and paid for it, thrusting it into her hair. "We shall find out directly, I suppose. Come. Znamenski's studio is in the Cour du Dragon."

She led Pepper through the huge gates that marked the entrance to the street. By tradition, the gates were closed at midnight and opened at dawn. It was only just after sunset, so they had plenty of time. They headed south down the narrow street, away from the river. Tall old houses rose to either side of them, and the sunken pavement was dotted with unsavory pools of rainwater. Children ran past in whooping mobs, pursuing one another along the stretch of road.

"Reminds me of Boston," Pepper ventured. "Parts of it, at least."

"I do not know that many Parisians would take that as a compliment," Alessandra said. The ground floors of the houses around them were occupied by second-hand shops and ironmongers. During the day, the street would ring with the sound of hammers. By night it was largely silent, save for the dim hiss of gas in the flickering lanterns that lined the street. The street was flanked by iron railings, protecting the shops from thieves.

Znamenski's studio nestled in the curves of the Cour du Dragon, just past a second-hand shop. A tidy little hole for a strange little man. A curved wooden door sat in a recessed archway, a bright splash of yellow paint at its center. The paint ran in strange directions, at once reminiscent of a flower and a wheel.

"What's with the decoration?" Pepper murmured. She looked around. "It's on all the doors, too. Weird, right?"

Alessandra, who'd once asked Znamenski about the symbol, but received no satisfying answer, shrugged. "A local custom, I am told. It is not important." She made to knock, and the door creaked inward at her merest touch.

Pepper whistled. "That ain't good."

"No," Alessandra said, "it is not." She felt a flicker of trepidation, quickly stifled, as she retrieved her revolver from her clutch, cocked it and nudged the door fully open. Inside, the studio was dark. As she entered, she heard the snap-hiss of a match being scraped to life as someone lit a cigarette. She froze, and Pepper nearly bumped into her.

"About time you showed up, Miss Zorzi," a woman's voice said.

CHAPTER TWO
Cour du Dragon

"Close the door," the woman said. She spoke in English. The accent was studiously nondenominational, which meant American. "No reason to alert the locals."

"I suppose not." Alessandra didn't lower her weapon, but gestured for Pepper to close the door as the stranger had asked. Something told her that it wasn't a trap – at least not the usual sort. "How did you get in here?"

"Through the door. Who do you think left it unlocked for you? Santa Claus?"

"How thoughtful," Alessandra murmured, looking around. Despite the gloom, she could tell that the studio was much as she recalled; a cramped space, cluttered with the debris of Znamenski's artistic career. Canvases lay stacked against the walls, or mounted on easels. Boxes of paint for mixing were piled in corners, and there were tarpaulins stretched over most of the furniture in a futile attempt to keep it free of stains.

"Where is Znamenski?" Alessandra kept her tone even, giving no sign of her unease or confusion. The woman had meant to rattle them, else why sit in the dark waiting for them to show up? Alessandra didn't feel like giving her the satisfaction, whoever she was. At least not until she knew more.

"Your artist friend is vacationing in Milan. He was very glad of the opportunity when it was presented to him. Something about wanting to avoid your sticky fingers." The woman lit a lamp, sitting on an end table beside her chair. A soft orange glow filled the room. "You were followed, I expect."

"Tell us something we don't know," Pepper said. Her hands were balled into fists and she was tense; ready to fight – or run.

"They work for the Comte d'Erlette," the woman said, not looking at Pepper.

Alessandra bit back a curse. There was a name she'd hoped to avoid hearing. "And you?" she asked, suspecting she already knew the answer.

"I work for another party." The woman reclined in her chair. In the glow of the lamp, her features had an unsettlingly innocuous cast. She didn't look like anyone; rather, she looked like everyone. Her clothes were of good quality, but utterly lacking in style – which was a sort of style all its own. A costume, Alessandra thought. A disguise.

"Who are you?" Alessandra asked. The woman was American, in Paris, trying to look inconspicuous. A criminal, then, or perhaps a spy. Not law enforcement, she thought. Nor was she obviously armed. That made Alessandra even more uneasy.

"A friend."

Alessandra's eyes narrowed. "Do you have a name, friend?"

"Trish," the woman said. She smiled. "And you are Countess Alessandra Zorzi. Professional acquisitionist."

"Good trick. Know my name too?" Pepper asked, pugnaciously.

Trish's smile didn't waver. "Philippa Kelly. Boston native. Late of Arkham, Massachusetts. Now, with no fixed abode.

How'd I do?" She spoke dismissively, as if the string of facts were of no more importance to her than any other bit of trivia.

Pepper blinked and glanced at Alessandra, visibly shaken. Alessandra lowered her weapon, her mind whirring. Things had taken an unanticipated turn and she was trying to catch up. "You are a veritable font of knowledge, Trish. Might I ask what you intend to do with it?"

Trish leaned forward. "That depends on you, Countess. The Comte isn't the only one interested in nailing your pretty hide to the barn door. You've got an enemies list that'd make Machiavelli blush. Sooner or later, they're all going to come looking for payback."

"And you can prevent that, can you?" Alessandra frowned. Blackmail, then. How tedious. "Not out of the goodness of your heart, one assumes."

Trish's smile was sharp and cold. "Good guess."

Alessandra glanced around. The studio was small; barely more than a hovel. Znamenski had an abhorrence of large spaces. It was why he'd chosen this place. That and one other, very important reason. She sighed and made a show of slipping her weapon back into her clutch. "What do you want?"

Trish stood. She was of a height with Alessandra. "Right to it, then? Fine. A book."

"I would be happy to direct you to the nearest library or bookshop," Alessandra began. Trish frowned.

"I thought you were going to play this straight, Countess. You want to make jokes, I can leave. Maybe the Comte's men will find you more entertaining, but I doubt it."

Alessandra gestured. "Tell me."

"*Cultes des Goules,*" Trish said, flatly.

Alessandra paused. "I know it."

"I bet you do. You stole it from the Comte d'Erlette little over a year ago, along with a substantial number of other volumes of occult significance. That one was special though – written by his great grandfather, I believe."

"If you say so," Alessandra said. Out of the corner of her eye, she caught a glimpse of Pepper sidling away from them. Trish either hadn't noticed, or had decided the younger woman was no threat. Alessandra forced a smile. The theft of the Comte's book was the precipitating factor that had sent her to Arkham in the first place, and she didn't much care to be reminded of it. "I do not read them, you know. I just steal them. I also do not keep them. So, if you were hoping I had it to hand, well, you are mistaken. Those books have been sold on since I acquired them, and likely more than once."

"But I bet you know to who," Trish said. "Or at least you could find out."

"And then what?"

"You go do what you do best," Trish said, in a low voice.

"You know, the Comte would pay well for that information," Alessandra said. Pepper was almost behind Trish now, moving slowly. Just the way Alessandra had taught her. She felt a spark of pride, but quickly quashed it. There would be time for self-congratulation later. She turned away from Trish, and stepped over to the side of the studio, where several canvases had been stacked.

The studio was messy; chaotic. By design, she suspected. Znamenski was a real artist, but he was also very aware of public perception. He arranged things so that visitors saw what they expected to see. It was one of the reasons she liked him.

She started to flip through the canvases, admiring the pale faces that decorated each. The same face, but from a slightly different angle each time. A familiar face, if one knew their history. *L'Inconnue de la Seine*. The death mask of an unidentified young woman, found drowned in the Seine some years earlier. Artists throughout France had found inspiration in the macabre remnant; Znamenski was no different, though his depictions bordered on the obscene. Too much yellow in the pallid texture for her tastes.

"You could try and sell the Comte's own books back to him, I suppose," Trish allowed, joining her at the canvases as Alessandra had hoped the other woman would. "I don't think he'd appreciate it, though. He doesn't seem like he's got much in the way of a sense of humor."

Alessandra smirked. "You have met him, then?"

"I have not had the pleasure," Trish said. She frowned, looking at one of the canvases. "God, these are awful. That woman looks dead."

"Znamenski would be pleased to hear it. And if you had met the Comte, you would not call it a pleasure. He is a bore and a prude, among other things."

Trish set the canvas down. "I'll take your word for it."

"You sold us out," Alessandra said. A guess, but an educated one. She could sense the walls of a trap closing in, though she could not make it out otherwise. How else had the Comte found them, after all?

"I can neither confirm nor deny that."

Alessandra looked at her. "Who do you work for?"

Trish tapped the side of her nose. "I tell you no secrets, you tell me no lies." She turned. "If you do as I ask, you will be protected. The Comte – your other enemies – none of them will ever be able to touch you." She paused. "Do you know the name Ruby Standish?"

Alessandra hesitated. "I do." As far as she knew, the name was an alias, used by a number of women over the years. The current owner was a precocious thief somewhere between herself and Pepper in age. They'd worked together once; it wasn't an experience she planned to repeat. Standish was flamboyant; impatient. Sooner or later, that would see her caught, and likely by someone worse than the police.

Trish nodded. "I've worked with Standish before. She'll vouch for me."

"That does not do me much good at the moment. As you said, we were almost certainly followed. If they are not waiting outside now, they soon will be."

"Then you'd better decide quick," Trish said. "You agree to find the book for me, I get you out of here and the Comte off your case. If you don't, well—"

She didn't get to finish that thought. Pepper had been busy while Alessandra kept Trish distracted. She'd snatched up a barren easel, and wielding it like an improvised bludgeon, she brought it down across the back of Trish's head with a crash.

Trish, unprepared for such an attack, went down like a sack of potatoes.

"You hit her," Alessandra said, bemused, as she looked down at the dazed woman.

"What'd you think I was going to do?" Pepper asked, tossing the broken easel aside.

"Tackle her; disarm her, maybe." Alessandra crouched and quickly searched Trish for weapons, papers or anything else of interest.

"Same difference." Pepper shrugged and dusted her hands. "Did you buy any of that applesauce?"

"Enough to know we are adrift in deep waters, and our boat

has somehow sprung a leak." Alessandra sat back on her heels, frowning. As she'd expected, Trish carried nothing of note. No papers, no identification, no weapons. She was smarter than that; practiced. A spy, then. Alessandra looked at Pepper. "In the parlance, we have been rumbled."

"Bushwa," Pepper said, but she didn't sound certain.

"I am afraid not. You heard her. I have no doubt she – or whoever she works for – is the one who told the Comte where we were, and where we were heading." Alessandra paused, but only for a moment. She motioned for Pepper to be silent, and then rose and went to the door.

Alessandra pulled the door open a crack and listened. At first, she heard nothing. Then, a muffled curse. Footsteps on the uneven pavement. Sound carried far in the Court of the Dragon. She considered risking a peek to see how many of them there were, but decided against it. They would be armed, that much she was certain of. She had her revolver, of course. But the odds were not in their favor.

She turned to find Pepper watching her anxiously. "What are we going to do?" the younger woman asked. Not frightened, but certainly worried. "Fight our way out?"

Alessandra forced a laugh. "Perish the thought. No, first we block the door. Then we find someplace to put our friend here."

"And then?"

"Then we go downstairs."

Pepper frowned. "Downstairs? This joint has a downstairs?"

"It does, though only myself and Znamenski know about it." She hesitated. "Well, and now you, of course." She snatched up a chair and jammed it under the handle of the door. Pepper found a closet and between them, they managed to get the stunned Trish into it. Alessandra used several spare paint rags to tie the woman's hands and feet, and stuffed a relatively clean one in her mouth. Trish had come to and started to struggle, glaring at them, but Alessandra stopped her with a look.

"I would keep silent, Trish. If you are not in it with the Comte, I cannot imagine he will be pleased to find you here. As I said, he is an unpleasant man."

She closed the closet as Trish made muffled protestations. "Now, come. Downstairs."

"What's downstairs, other than a cellar?" Pepper asked.

Alessandra smiled. "Our way out, of course."

CHAPTER THREE
Seine

Access to the cellar was through a trapdoor in the wooden floor. Said trapdoor was hidden beneath a Turkish rug and a pile of paint splattered canvases. As far as Alessandra knew, that pile was never moved save for one reason.

"A smuggler?" Pepper said, in disbelief. "I thought he was a painter?"

"He is. He is also a smuggler." Alessandra tossed the last canvas aside and lifted the edge of the rug. It was cleverly attached to the rim of the trapdoor, so that when the latter was lowered, the rug covered it automatically. "Painting is his passion," she continued, as she hauled the trapdoor up, revealing a square shaft of stone. "Smuggling is how he makes enough money to keep himself in absinthe and opium."

A wet, murky smell issued upward through the hatch. Alessandra, prepared for the odor, merely wrinkled her nose. Pepper on the other hand gagged loudly. "What is that smell?" she choked out.

"The sewers of Paris are not known for their sweet fragrance," Alessandra said. She gestured impatiently to the rusty iron rungs set into the stone shaft. "Down we go. You first." The Comte's men would soon be at the door. If it was anything like the last time they'd come for her, they'd try the door before attempting to kick it in.

"I'm not going down there," Pepper protested, but half-heartedly.

"Would you rather stay here?"

"Kind of."

Alessandra gave her a stern look and Pepper sighed. "Fine." She started down, accompanied by muttered curses. Alessandra hid a smile. Pepper was a tough cookie, as the Americans put it. But she had little experience to back it up. Alessandra was determined to show the young woman as much of the world as possible – especially the nasty, smelly bits. It was the only way she'd evolve from a tough cookie into a hard egg – another Americanism, and one she didn't quite understand, but was nonetheless fond of.

Once Pepper had safely descended, Alessandra followed, pulling the trapdoor shut behind her. It settled with a thump that she hoped hadn't been heard outside the studio. There was a simple deadbolt lock on the underside of the trapdoor and she quickly shot it into place. It wouldn't stop a determined effort to get down, but it would buy some time.

At the bottom of the shaft was a rickety wooden landing. It had been built sometime in the previous century, not long after Haussmann had razed and rebuilt portions of the city – or so Znamenski had claimed. The wood was soggy with seeping damp, and the iron bolts that held the whole edifice connected to the stone walls were slick with rust, but it was sturdy enough for all that. She could hear the insistent murmuration of the Seine rising from somewhere ahead, and felt the chill of the deeps rising up to greet them.

There was a lantern hanging from one of the support beams

and she took it down and lit it. It was full of oil, thankfully. Znamenski was no fool, and kept things in a state of readiness. You never knew when a commission would come along, after all.

As the light filled the space, it caught something white in the darkness – a moon face, staring, bloated and white. "Jeezum crow," Pepper exclaimed. Alessandra had to admit she was startled as well. She swung the light in a tight circle, illuminating more faces. Four in total, one mounted on each support post, their oval forms wreathed in yellow rags, their empty eyes locked on one another. "What are they?" Pepper asked, looking up at the faces.

"A death mask," Alessandra said. "Znamenski is obsessed with them. This one in particular. Many artists are."

"Who was she?" Pepper asked, softly, looking up at the closest mask.

"No one knows," Alessandra said, sadly. "She drowned in the Seine. One of many claimed by the river. Znamenski started out painting her, then I suppose he moved onto sculpture." Despite the grisly subject, the artistry of the sculptures was impressive. She'd been unaware that Znamenski had begun to dabble in the medium of clay.

Pepper reached up as if to touch the mask, and something about the simple act set Alessandra's hackles to twitching. She'd developed a new set of instincts since Arkham, to go along with the old ones. She caught the younger woman's wrist and shook her head. "Best not," she said, softly. Pepper gave her a quizzical look, but nodded.

"Anyway, we should be going," Alessandra continued and swung the lantern up, revealing a set of wooden steps that descended in a roundabout manner from the landing. At the bottom was a wooden jetty that extended out into the darkness, following the serpentine curve of the Parisian sewers.

"Really?" Pepper asked, doubtfully. She was still darting glances at the masks, and Alessandra was suddenly possessed of a desire to be far away.

"It is perfectly safe. French smugglers build to last," Alessandra said. "We have Napoleon to thank for these sewers, and his descendants. Haussmann as well. City still stinks in the summer, but what city does not?"

"Boston," Pepper said.

Alessandra snorted. "I beg to differ. Come, follow me." She led the younger woman down the steps and along the jetty. It had been built atop the old stone walkways, now worn smooth and slick by water and time. The dark waters of the sewer lapped at the wood, and an eye-watering stink rose from the noisome broth. She paused at the bottom and looked back. In the dim glow of the lantern's light, she could have sworn the masks had turned on their posts, to follow the intruders with their blank gazes.

"So, is this like an escape hatch or something?" Pepper asked, her voice loud in the quiet. "Like a secret tunnel, just in case the gendarmes come for your pal?"

"I told you – Znamenski is a smuggler. Like your bootleggers, yes?"

Pepper grunted. "Mostly they use the docks."

"Well, this is a dock. It just happens to be under the city." Alessandra glanced back at Pepper. "Znamenski uses it to bring in booze for the cabarets and guinguettes. They always need more than they can acquire legally, especially these days."

"So why do you know about it?"

She shrugged. "Znamenski told me as a favor. I – *hsst*!" She paused, straining to listen. The echo of cracking wood drifted through the tunnel. Pepper turned.

"Guess they found the trapdoor, hunh?"

Alessandra frowned. "I guess so," she murmured. And more quickly than she'd anticipated. Something else to thank the mysterious Trish for, perhaps. "Come, let us hurry."

"You still haven't told me where we're going," Pepper said, hurrying after Alessandra. "Is there another secret door around here? Back in Boston you can pretty much get from one building to another through the basements. We going to pop up under a café or something?"

"Something like that," Alessandra said. The wood shifted minutely beneath her feet, like vibrations in a spider's web. Someone was on the landing. Quickly she hooded the lantern and put a hand on Pepper's shoulder, stopping her. They stood silently in the dark for one moment, then two. Distant voices echoed along the curves of the sewer wall. Someone shouted and a pistol barked. Alessandra smiled. They weren't the only ones startled by Znamenski's masks.

"So, what's the plan?" Pepper hissed. "We just going to stand here?"

Alessandra lifted the hood on the lantern slightly, barely illuminating their faces. No light would reach the water, so there would be no reflection to give away their position. At least until their pursuers got closer. "Come on."

Two more curves and the end of the jetty came in sight. It terminated close to a curved arch of stone beyond which the river was a black stretch. The water that flowed beneath the arch was lower than it appeared from the exterior, due to a subsidence in the stones. It was just large enough to ease a boat through, unless there was flooding.

Alessandra hung the lantern on a support post and indicated a long tarpaulin-covered shape bobbing in the water. "There we are." Using a nearby boat hook, she dragged the tarp away to reveal the narrow form of a yellow-hulled motorboat.

"A boat?" Pepper asked, as Alessandra handed her the hook.

Alessandra nodded and smiled. "A 1911 Kitty Hawk to be exact. Courtesy of the Hacker Boat Co. of Detroit, Michigan." She made to climb down into the boat, but Pepper stopped her.

"You know how to drive one of these?"

Alessandra gave a short bark of laughter. "Of course! Who do you think taught Znamenski? Now climb aboard. It is time we were going."

"Where exactly are we planning to go in this thing?"

"Back to the hotel, I think. I could do with a bath." Alessandra started up the craft and was pleased to find it as easy as she recalled. The engine gave a low growl as it came to life.

"I don't recall the hotel being near the river," Pepper said, doubtfully. She was right of course. Their accommodation, the Hotel Lutetia, was only a short walk from *Les Deux Magots*, but Alessandra hoped taking a more roundabout way back might be sufficient to throw the Comte's hounds off their trail. Unless, of course, he already knew where they were staying – which he might very well.

But she said none of this. There was no sense in worrying Pepper. Instead, she shrugged and said, "A bit of a walk will do us both some good, I think." She heard a muffled shout and glanced back the way they'd come. Electric torches cut through the dark in wildly alternating patterns as their wielders raced along the jetty. "But first – the escape. Now stop dawdling and get aboard!"

The first shots rang out even as Pepper dropped into the back of the boat. Alessandra eased the craft away from the jetty, trying to ignore the hornet-hiss of gunfire. She deftly retrieved her pistol from her clutch as she spun the wheel, turned and leveled the revolver in the direction of the lantern. She fired – once. Luck was with her.

The lantern burst into a fireball that spread burning oil in all directions across the jetty. It was wet enough that it wouldn't burn for long, but it would hopefully keep them back long enough for her to guide the boat out of the sewers and onto the river.

The motorboat passed out into the night moments later, pursued by gunfire. They emerged at a low point between the Pont du Carrousel and the Pont des Arts. Canal boats slid by as Alessandra spun the boat in a tight circle, pointing it in the direction of Quai d'Orsay and the 7th arrondissement. There were a few stone quays there, where they could dock and vanish into the tangle of streets that lined the Left Bank.

Alessandra kept the craft steady and glanced back to see how Pepper was faring. The young woman clambered toward her, white-faced. "Never been on one of these," she shouted. "Didn't know they went so fast, either!"

"You learn something new in this business every day," Alessandra told her with a laugh.

"The Comte sure seems eager to get his hands on us," Pepper said, trying to steady herself as the boat skidded across the shifting surface of the river. "What'd you do to him, anyway?"

"Who says I did anything?" Alessandra caught Pepper's expression out of the corner of her eye and sighed. "Fine. I might have stolen a few trifles from his library."

"They're shooting at us because of a few books?"

"More like a few hundred, but yes."

Pepper goggled at her. "A few hundred!"

"It was not my finest hour, I admit," Alessandra said, a trifle more defensively than she'd intended. "But in my defense, he was very annoying, and I was being paid very well."

More than annoying, really – downright murderous, beneath that charming façade. The Comte d'Erlette was the worst sort of occultist; one with *ambition*. Once, she'd thought those ambitions were nothing more than pipe-dreams. But her recent experiences in Arkham had taught her differently.

Before that, however, she'd been hired by one of the Comte's victims – a business associate he'd dealt with harshly – to steal something that mattered, as an act of petty revenge. She'd settled on the library, recognizing the resale value of its contents. She'd spent more than a year winnowing her way into his confidence, all to gain access to the library. And when she'd judged the time right, she'd ferreted it all away.

"And now he's trying to kill us," Pepper said, holding onto her hat as they approached the Pont du Carrousel. "Wonderful."

"You have nothing to worry about," Alessandra began, then paused as she heard the growl of closing engines. She turned and cursed. Two motorboats arrowed in pursuit of their craft, cutting and weaving past the barges. The Comte was nothing if not prepared; perhaps he simply knew about Znamenski's operation. Either way, they were in trouble. She pushed the throttle to its limit. "Hold on, Pepper. Things are about to get very bumpy!"

CHAPTER FOUR
Dark Waters

Pepper held onto her cap as Alessandra gave the motorboat some gas. Her stomach leapt up into her lungs as the craft began to bounce along the surface of the water. She'd never been a fan of boats, or the water. She'd seen enough on the Arkham docks to know that it wasn't for her. But now here she was, holding on for dear life as her new mentor sped them along a twisty river, pursued by two boats full of mugs with bad intentions.

She wished she had a gun and not for the first time. But she didn't, so she'd just have to make do. She was good at that. She'd been making do all her life. When her mother had died, when her father had decided to move them back to Arkham and gone on the sauce... she'd adapted. You had to adapt quick in Arkham; had to learn what to see, and more importantly, what not to see.

Sometimes Arkham felt like the biggest goddamn city in the world, even though everyone called it a town. At night, the streets seemed to stretch forever and in all the wrong directions. Even Paris seemed small by comparison. The City of Lights was nice and all, but Arkham was Arkham. Her father had told her that once you were in Arkham's shadow, you couldn't escape it. Wherever you went, it'd be waiting.

The motorboat bashed over the water and her feet nearly left the deck. The suddenness of it chased all thoughts of Arkham out of her mind and brought her back to the present. Alessandra was busy keeping the boat steady, so Pepper decided to find something useful to do. Maybe there was something she could chuck at their pursuers.

There wasn't much in the boat. Just some tarps, a few tools and a steel lockbox. She used a screwdriver to jimmy open the lockbox. There was a flare gun inside. She grinned and snatched it up. That was more like it.

She popped a flare in and snapped the gun shut before making her way to the back of the boat. She braced herself against the rail and tried to take aim at the pursuing boats, but it was difficult. Finally, she managed to line up a shot and let fly. The flare struck the closest of the boats in the hull, bounced up and over the windshield. The boat veered as the driver panicked and she laughed.

Alessandra looked back and said, "Oh well done! Think you can get the other one?"

Pepper adjusted her cap, pleased by the praise. "Watch me," she said, with a grin. She braced the gun against the rail and made to take her second shot when her target suddenly accelerated and shot forward, nearly colliding with the back of their craft. She yelped and fell back, only just holding onto the flare gun.

"Are you all right?" Alessandra called out.

"Peachy," Pepper snarled, sitting up and firing. The flare sputtered and rolled through the air, striking the second boat and caroming off into the water. The boat edged in again, prow thumping against their rear hull and causing them to fishtail. Pepper fell back again and rolled across the back of the boat, cursing.

By the time she'd gotten her legs under her, the other craft was nearly alongside them. There were three men in it, all dressed like street roughs or dockworkers. All were armed, and she was forced to duck as one of them took a potshot at her with a revolver.

As she did so, she saw one of them take a running leap and cross the small distance between the two craft. He landed with a thump and gave her a fierce grin that had a glint of gold in it. He reached into his pocket and produced a butterfly knife. A quick gesture and the blade was out and racing toward her. She had no choice but to raise the flare gun and fire.

Her target avoided the whirling flare, but his pals in the boat weren't so lucky. They veered off, shouting and cursing. He watched them go with a perplexed look and then turned back to her. She charged, catching him around the waist and driving him back against the side of the boat. The knife went clattering from his grip and he sagged, wheezing. She let him have the old one-two, but he shoved her away. He was bigger; stronger. She had to keep him from remembering that.

She'd been in enough brawls in Arkham to know that the only fair fight was the one you won. She lunged for the lockbox as he grabbed for her. He caught the back of her jacket and she spun, bouncing the lockbox off his head. He pitched backward, still holding onto her, and she found herself yanked back against the rail and then – over.

A moment of vertigo, the lights of Paris spinning in a kaleidoscope around her. Then the moment of impact. Hitting the water at speed was like being punched from a dozen different directions at once. She found herself spinning in place, surrounded by darkness, unable to breathe, unable to think. Her thoughts rattled in her head like broken glass.

She blinked, trying to see, and almost choked on a lungful of water as something pale and ovoid rose up toward her out of the deep black. A face – a face like the masks she'd seen on the jetty, pallid and expressionless, save for the hint of an idiot's smile. Only it wasn't the dead woman's face, not really. It was someone else's, someone familiar.

It took her a moment to realize that it looked like Alessandra. The water became as treacle around her. The face rose, propelled on a coruscating column of river debris – rags and tin cans and yellowed newspapers. It encircled her like a snake, coiling about its prey, until that oh-so-white face was right next to hers, the lips moving, the half-shuttered eyes rolling in their sockets. She couldn't hear what it was saying, but she could feel it, way down deep in her gut.

It wanted to tell her something – to warn her. Or maybe to promise something. Then the face popped like a wet balloon and a hand shot through, catching her about the throat. The mug bared his teeth at her, bubbles seeping through the gaps. He was trying to throttle her. She clawed at his wrists and kicked out, catching him in the sternum with the toe of her boot. More bubbles exploded outward and his grip weakened.

She kicked him again and again, and then found herself clawing for the surface. She couldn't tell where her opponent had gone, and she didn't care. She needed air, and right now. She burst upward, gasping. She spotted her hat floating nearby and grabbed it, even as she started swimming toward a nearby stone quay.

When she reached it, she hauled herself up onto it, dripping and shaky. She coughed up river water, and felt nauseous. She looked around, but didn't see any sign of the motorboats. For a fleeting moment, she wondered if Alessandra had even noticed that she'd fallen off. Then a whole new set of worries intruded. She heard footsteps, and the tap of a cane, on the stone stairs leading up from the quay to the street. A pair of fancy shoes approached her, the cane tap-tapping.

Before she could get to her feet, the tip of the cane caught her in the hollow of her throat, but gently. She froze, and looked up at the cane's wielder. He was dressed like a swell, complete with a fur-lined overcoat and a fancy homburg. Youngish, but old enough to look like he meant business, with a neatly trimmed beard and moustaches. His gaze was hard and flinty. He said something in French, but she didn't catch it.

"Try again, pal," she coughed.

"I asked if she was employing urchins now?" he said, in English.

"Watch who you're calling an urchin, buster," Pepper said, making to rise though she wasn't sure her legs would support her at the moment. The cane pressed lightly against her throat and she paused.

"My name is not buster. Allow me to introduce myself: I am Henri-Georges Balfour, the Comte d'Erlette. And you are?"

Pepper frowned, but didn't reply. Mostly because she was still trying to gather her thoughts from being half-drowned. The Comte paused, then shrugged. "Ah well. It is of no importance. You are not my prey this night. I am after bigger game than one scrawny American woman in trousers. I – ah! And we speak of the devil, so that she might appear!"

Pepper heard a motorboat coming into the quay. She risked

a glance and saw Alessandra approaching, her face as pale as that of the thing in Pepper's hallucination. "Henri, this is between us," she called out, as she brought the motorboat to a halt. "Let her go."

The Comte extended his free hand toward her. "Ah, Alessandra, *mi amore.* You are as beautiful as the day we met."

"You always did know how to compliment a woman, Henri." Alessandra lifted her revolver and aimed it at him. Pepper forced a smile.

"You're going to get it now, bud," she said. He glanced at her and smirked.

"She is a barker, your pup."

"She knows a fool when she sees one," Alessandra said, glancing at Pepper. "Are you all right?"

"Still breathing," Pepper said.

"For now." The Comte gestured and Pepper heard the click of weapons being readied. There were half a dozen men on the quay and the steps leading up to the street. They were all armed and right now those guns were all trained on Alessandra. The Comte's extended hand curled into an accusatory gesture. "I want my book, Alessandra."

"Which one, Henri? You had so many."

"And you stole them all. Along with my heart."

"Be fair, Henri… you never had a heart to steal," Alessandra said. Her gun-hand trembled slightly as she glanced at Pepper. "Which book, then?"

"*Cultes des Goules,*" he said. "The unexpurgated version, written by my grandfather." He lifted his cane, forcing Pepper to rise to her feet. "I am aware that you have already sold it on, but I expect that will not prove an insurmountable obstacle for a woman as clever as you." When Pepper was upright, he guided her toward his men. She went grudgingly. She wanted Alessandra to just shoot the guy already, but the other woman clearly figured that wasn't the smart play.

"And if I find it for you?" Alessandra asked.

"Then our debt is settled. I will release your friend and you may go and vanish from my life once more." The Comte smiled thinly. "If you do not … well, I will make some use of her, never fear. There are any number of rituals which call for the blood of a young woman." His smile turned toothy and feral. "Waste not, want not, yes?"

"Perhaps I should just shoot you now," Alessandra said, in a flat tone. The barrel of her revolver twitched and Pepper swallowed.

"That gets my vote," she said, trying for bravado.

The Comte spread his arms. "Shoot me and my men will kill you and her. We can all cross the Styx on the same trip." He cocked his head. "We could use the time to catch up, eh? Talk about old times. What larks we got up to." He glanced at Pepper. "I think she would be interested to know such things, yes?"

Just as Pepper was beginning to wonder what that meant, Alessandra lifted her revolver. "Fine. I will find your damn book, Henri. But if you harm her, I will make it my business to send you to Hell … and you will not enjoy the journey, I swear this to you."

The Comte laughed. "I am certain you would try, my darling." He turned away with a dismissive gesture. "The book, Alessandra. I will give you, let us say, three days. No more, no less."

Pepper found herself herded up the steps to the street. She wanted to protest, to make a run for it, but something in

Alessandra's gaze had convinced her that it probably wouldn't be smart. There was a car waiting and as she was bundled in, she caught a last glimpse of Alessandra, her face expressionless.

As if it were nothing more than a pallid mask.

CHAPTER FIVE
Scarborough

Inside the café, Trish Scarborough sat on the bench of the public call box, trying to clear her head. It was still ringing from the sneaky blow Zorzi's sidekick had delivered. The kid had moxie, but not too much in the way of brains. Maybe that was why Zorzi kept her around. Sometimes you needed someone who'd cut the crap and throw a punch.

She touched the back of her head and winced. She looked at her fingers in the dim light of the café. No blood, thank God. It had taken her only minutes to work herself loose from Zorzi's improvised bindings and go out the window. Even then, that had been cutting it close. The Comte's men had busted down the door even as she was falling into the street. Luckily, they'd been too focused on the trap door – which they'd known about, interestingly – to pay the window any mind. She didn't think it was in anyone's interests for the Comte to know that there were other players in his game.

A waiter knocked on the outside of the box and gestured to the cup and saucer he held. She nodded, winced, and shoved the box open, accepting the coffee with a curt "*Merci*," before shutting it again. She'd been occupying the box since her escape, waiting for the phone to ring. She sipped at the coffee, enjoying the warmth. It helped with the ache in her head. A whisky would help more, but that could wait. She was still on the clock.

Trish considered herself something of a professional problem solver. Puzzles were her line, the more complicated the better. She'd always had a flair for them, even as a kid. It was one of the reasons she'd taken a job with the Cipher Bureau when the opportunity came her way.

The Cipher Bureau – or the Black Chamber, as some knew it – was America's cryptanalytic organization, responsible for the sanctity of the nation and the safety of its citizens, wherever they chose to make their home, and whatever sort of trouble they got into. Especially when it had bearing on national security.

The US government had a pressing need for clever people who could untangle knots and look innocuous while doing so. Her cover was as a commercial code analyst, and it gave her a reason to travel. She liked traveling, normally. This trip, however, was proving to be something of a headache, both literally and figuratively.

The phone rang. She watched it the way a mongoose watched a snake. One ring. Two. Silence. That was the signal that things had gone awry. They'd call back soon enough, and she'd find out where she was going next.

You had to learn patience, in this game. Jumping from one problem to the next was for amateurs. It only led to messiness – confusion. To solve a puzzle, you had to be observant; persistent. But the puzzles of late had become frustratingly bizarre. The sort of thing she'd once thought confined to pulp magazines. It was as if in the wake of the war, all the strange things of the world had awoken at once. The transatlantic wires hummed with odd whisperings. Theosophists, Anarchists, Rosicrucians and Bolsheviks; all of them bad news as far as Director Yardley and the Cipher Bureau were concerned.

Worse still, everyone was worried, not just them. From what she'd seen, every intelligence agency in the western hemisphere was chasing down weird leads and freak beats. There was something on the wind. Even the Bolsheviks were getting anxious. Little drops of unease, rippling outward through the secret, shadowed waters where fish like her swam.

Her eyes flicked back to the phone. Somewhere in the city, control was discussing her next move. She didn't know who they were – the Paris office was rotated regularly. They were just a voice on the wire, which was the way she liked it.

Trish worked best alone; she always had. Yardley knew that, and accommodated her. Some of her peers weren't happy about it, but she hadn't gotten into the game to make friends. She sipped her coffee and thought about Zorzi.

What they had on the countess was mostly hearsay. She'd never been arrested, or at least not anywhere that kept decent records. A lot of the background they had on her had come from what Trish considered to be less than reliable sources.

A lot of it had come courtesy of a file put together by an insurance investigator named Abner Whitlock. Whitlock worked for Argus Insurance, and had apparently tangled with Zorzi at least twice. He was competent, and his notes reflected that. Trish had interviewed him before crossing the Atlantic, just to see what he had to say.

Whitlock had been more reticent than she'd expected him to be from the tone of the file. Maybe something had changed.

Maybe he hadn't bought her cover story. Either way, he hadn't been as forthcoming as she might have hoped.

Still, she'd learned enough. She knew that Zorzi was in the family business. Her parents had been thieves, her grandparents; a line of villainy stretching back farther than she cared to contemplate. Zorzi claimed Venice as home, but that claim – like her name – was likely a fabrication. Trish, who was fond of Venice herself, understood somewhat. If you had to choose a place to be from, there were worse choices than Venice.

Someone came into the café, disturbing the locals. She looked up and frowned. Chauncey Swann sauntered toward her, a friendly smile on his face. "So, you really screwed the pooch, hunh?" he said, as she opened the call box. "I expected better from a professional like you."

"Your concern is noted, Chauncey."

"So, she sucker-punch you or something?" Swann asked, giving her a louche grin.

"Yeah. She did. She's a back-shooter, that one." He took off his hat and ran a hand over his slicked back hair. "I did try and warn your bosses, but I guess they didn't pass it along."

She didn't like Swann. He was too polished, too slick. He smiled like those varsity boys who'd tried to slide a hand up her dress at dances. Like he was owed all the wonders of the world, despite deserving not a one. She liked his bosses even less.

In her considered opinion, the United States government shouldn't be in bed with a group of oddball occultists like the Silver Twilight Lodge. Even if their member rolls were like a who's who of the American elite. It left a bad taste in her mouth, even if it was only a temporary arrangement. "She's in the wind," she said,

Swann dragged over a stool and leaned back against the exterior of the call box, his boater balanced on his knee. "That sounds like a you problem, not a me problem."

"It's an us problem, you sad excuse for a criminal," Trish shot back. "We lose her, we lose the book. I don't think your bosses will like that anymore than mine."

Swann frowned. "I'm not a criminal. I'm an acquisitionist."

"You're a thief, Chauncey. You're a thief who works for thieves."

Swann fixed her with a lazy look. "Yeah? Well, you're working with me, so what does that make you?"

"Stupid," Trish said. Swann laughed.

"Maybe. Lucky, though. You can't afford to underestimate the countess. She's sneaky, unprincipled and vicious. Even the nastiest guys in my line walk lightly around her. She's tangled with all of them, and come out on top every single time."

She finished her coffee and glanced around the café. They were being watched by the locals, mostly because they were speaking in English. Americans were thick as fleas in Paris these days, but they still attracted attention. "Noted. Did you come here just to tell me that, or do you have something useful to share?"

"Hotel Lutetia. That's where she's staying."

"I know that."

"Then why ain't you there?" Swann asked.

She looked at him. Swann talked like a layabout, but she knew he'd gone to Yale, and had enough political clout to choke a horse. It was a put on, like much of the way he carried himself. Swann was smart and cultured, but he played the buffoon. Made it easy to underestimate him. But the problem with playing a role like that was that if you weren't careful, it eventually stopped being a role. "I'm not there," she said, slowly, "because I'm here. I'm here because I'm waiting for a phone call."

Swann leaned forward and began to play with the brim of his hat. "Every second you waste, she gets further away."

"Then you follow her."

Swann shook his head. "I've done my bit. I stirred up the hornet's nest for you, just like your boss requested. The rest is on you, Scarborough."

"Then what is this? Just a checkup on behalf of your employers?"

"Just seeing how you're getting along retrieving our property."

Trish sat back. The book. Of course that was what he was worried about. The price for Carl Sanford's consideration in certain matters related to the US government. She didn't know much more than that, and was happy about it. Ignorance was bliss. It allowed her to do her job without any worries about the nature of their allies.

Sanford wanted *Cultes des Goules.* Specifically, the unexpurgated edition recently belonging to the Comte d'Erlette, and even more recently stolen by Alessandra Zorzi. Tracking a book like that was nearly impossible, unless you had the right connections, which she did not. Neither did Swann, apparently.

She gave him a hard smile. "You know, given how eager your bosses are, it's a wonder you haven't turned your immense talents to finding the damn thing."

Swann grunted and pulled out a pack of cigarettes. He drew one and tapped it on the pack. "You think they didn't? I looked for that thing for almost a year, and nearly got killed twice. There are bad people looking for that book." He paused, the cigarette frozen over the pack, and she saw a look in his eyes that might have been worry, or fear. "Well, people might be the wrong word, but you get what I'm saying."

"So that's why we're here. Because you failed."

Swann grimaced. "If you like."

"I don't. But here we are."

"Yeah." Swann lit his cigarette. "What's your plan, then? Just so we don't stumble over one another." He gave her another of his too-easy smiles.

"My plan is to wait for my phone call. Then, I'll follow her. If what you say is true, she'll be on the trail of the book soon enough. When she finds it … I'll be there." Scarborough looked back at the phone. It was going to ring, soon. She could feel it. She glanced at him. "Why do you want it, anyway?" she asked. It was a dumb question, but carefully so. A feint.

Swann left himself open, as she hoped. "You know better than to ask that." he said, teasingly. But as she'd suspected, he was too full of himself to leave it at that. He poked the air with the cherry tip of his cigarette – a Yale habit, she knew. "I will say this. Better my employer has it than a guy like our friend, the Comte d'Erlette."

"He's dangerous, then?"

"Oh, like you wouldn't believe, sister. Henri-Georges Balfour is a chewy nut and no mistake. Absolutely barmy, as our British cousins would say. The sort of guy you don't want to be on the wrong side of."

"Like the countess, you mean."

Swann gestured his assent, and took a drag on his cigarette. "Better her than us, am I right or am I right?" He flipped his hat around and deposited it on his head with an easy grace that made her hate him just that little bit more.

"You practice that move in the mirror, Chauncey?"

Swann grinned. "I try to stay away from mirrors. You never know who might be looking back." With that, he turned and sauntered away. She watched him go, and felt a prickle as she considered his words. She glanced at her reflection in the filthy glass of the call box and hurriedly looked away.

The phone rang.

She hesitated, then picked it up.

CHAPTER SIX
Hotel Lutetia

Alessandra stared at her luggage without seeing it. Instead, she recalled the look on Pepper's face as she was rushed up the stairs by the Comte's men. If there had been fear there, or betrayal, it would have been easier to take. Instead, there had been only trust in the younger woman's eyes. Pepper trusted that Alessandra had a plan.

But she didn't. Not a good one, at any rate.

After the Comte had made his demands, she'd sought out one of the small stone quays that intermittently lined the Left Bank and docked the boat. Someone would claim it; whether that someone was Znamenski or some opportunistic local didn't interest her. She'd made her way back to the Hotel Lutetia in a daze, bemused by the suddenness of the turn things had taken. There were too many questions and not enough answers.

She was angry, and at herself more than anyone. She'd known there was a chance that old sins might come back to haunt her – especially one as persistent as the Comte. She'd known and she'd come anyway. Worse, she'd dragged Pepper into it with her.

Mechanically, Alessandra continued packing. She'd already

bundled up Pepper's meager belongings in her worn military surplus kitbag; her father's, Alessandra suspected. Pepper had never volunteered that information, and Alessandra had never asked, not wanting to pry. She wished she had now. There were many questions she wished that she'd asked. She'd assumed that they would have time.

She paused and looked blankly around her room. The Hotel Lutetia was a byword for Left Bank luxury, and the room had all the modern amenities. Pepper had been very impressed, as Alessandra had hoped. She'd been even more impressed when she'd realized that she had a room of her own. It had cost a bit more than Alessandra intended, but the look on Pepper's face had made it worth it.

Alessandra looked down at the dress in her hands. Sequins and silk tore as she wrenched it apart in a sudden, violent spasm. She stared at the rags that were left behind. "*Vaffanculo*," she hissed, imagining the dress was Henri's sneering face. "*Figlio de puttana*." She tossed the rags to the floor. Adrenaline with no release surged through her, making her tremble. She wanted to hit something. To shoot and stab and punch until the problem was solved. That had been her mother's way.

But that wasn't a solution. Violence, however cathartic, was never a solution in circumstances such as these. It was only a gateway to more problems. Her grandfather had taught her that; murder was the resort of fools and cowards. In any event, violence wouldn't make the Comte blink. Henri-Georges was many things, but not a coward.

No. She would have to be smart. To play things like a thief. She'd outwitted the Comte once. She could do it again. But this time it wasn't just her life on the line. Pepper was counting on her; she was responsible for the younger woman. If she died …

Alessandra shied away from the thought and ran her hands through her hair, which was no longer pinned up thanks to the wind of the boat chase and her own frenzy. She began to pace, her mind whirring through the possibilities. She thought better when moving. Finding the book was no easy task. She had no way of knowing who'd bought it, or how many times it might have been sold on since. She had, in fact, made it a point not to know those things. It had seemed a sound professional decision at the time, but she was regretting it now. Then, many things that had once made sense no longer did.

It had all changed that first night in Arkham. That's what she told herself. But the truth was, she had always known the world wasn't what it seemed. Ever since the night her parents had died, in the Rue d'Auseil. At the thought, her eyes flicked to the window, and the sea of lights outside. For a moment, it was almost as if something passed between those lights and the window pane. A shadow, winging up and into the dark.

She turned away. Paris was the City of Lights, and thus had more than its share of shadows. Some were newborn, some thin – but others were old and deep, stretching back down the long road of years. The Rue d'Auseil was a shadow-street, a nowhere place. It was not on any map or in any guidebook. It was just a name, a whisper – a note, jotted in her father Ferro's untidy hand.

She had looked for the street, once. But only once. And then had done her best to forget it. Her grandfather had told her and her sisters nothing of what it meant, or what had occurred. Only that there had been an accident; unavoidable and tragic.

He had seemed so old, that day. So brittle. Hardly like the old lion of her father's stories. Then, it was said that no man was so broken as one who had outlived his children. But he had soldiered on, for the benefit of his granddaughters. Seeing them married off to fat old aristocrats and lean industrialists. All save his little lioness.

Alessandra closed her eyes. She had avoided thinking about her parents the entire time they'd been here, but now it came back to her. A different time, a different night, but the same sense of helplessness. The same fear.

But this time was different. This time, she could do something about it. She just had to think. To push the fear aside and find the cool well of logic that had sustained her all these years. Thieves, like all craftsmen, were creatures of logic. Calculation and extrapolation were as much a professional thief's tools as glass cutters and lockpicks.

She ceased pacing and forced herself to relax. To let go of the tension that had gripped her since she'd left the boat. The only way to help Pepper was to find the book. The only way to find the book was to start at the last place she'd seen it. And that was…

"Angoulême," she murmured. There was a private bookseller there she did business with – Mellin Thevet. Thevet had a talent for placing rare books with those who would pay well for them, and had often acted as an intermediary on her behalf. Thevet had disposed of most of the Comte's collection for her, netting himself a tidy commission in the process.

She hadn't spoken to Thevet since just before she'd absconded to Marrakesh; it was he who'd warned her that the Comte was on her trail. At the time, Thevet had managed to avoid the Comte's eye, but that might have changed in the year since. If it hadn't, and he was still in one piece, he might well be able to direct her to the buyer.

It was a slim chance, but slim was better than none, as Pepper often stated.

Alessandra took a deep breath and finished packing. She could catch an overnight train from Gare d'Austerlitz to Angoulême, in southwestern France. With luck, she would be there in the morning. Enough time to find a hotel, find Thevet… and then?

There was no telling where the search would take her. She only had three days. That wasn't nearly enough time. She couldn't take the chance of calling ahead. Henri-Georges was clever; diabolically so. He was having her watched, she was certain of it. He'd want to make sure that she'd left Paris. But he'd have people following her every step of the way, and no doubt they would have orders to try and snatch the book from her if she did manage to find it. There was no chance he would let Pepper go – or herself.

The French could hold a grudge as well as any Italian, and the art of revenge was considered a respectable one among men of the Comte's class. No, even if she found the book, she would need some form of insurance to make sure the Comte kept his word. But she would think about that on the train. The first order of business was catching a cab to the station. She wasn't planning to walk to the 13th arrondissement if she could help it.

She picked up her bag and Pepper's as well. She would store the latter with the hotel and retrieve it later… if there was a later. After a moment's further hesitation, she slipped her revolver into the pocket of her coat. Better to have it to hand and not need it, than to need it and not have it. Its weight was a comfort.

Alessandra took the elevator down to the lobby, and tipped

the attendant. The lobby was a monument to the Art Deco movement, all gentle curves and glass. The floor was covered by a mosaic of a ship sailing stylized seas. It was meant to evoke the hotel's namesake – Lutetia, the Roman trading post that was the seed of the Paris to come.

The attendants in their smart uniforms waiting by the front doors leapt to help her to the front desk, where she paid for the rooms for another week and saw to the stowing of Pepper's bag. As she waited for them to provide a receipt, she turned. The lobby was busy; tourists, mostly. The soft tinkle of piano keys echoed from the dining room, and the quiet hubbub of voices lent a pleasant air to her surroundings.

Out of the corner of her eye, she spotted a familiar face stepping through the revolving doors. Trish. The American woman swept the lobby with a cool eye, but Alessandra was standing just out of the radius of her eyeline. Trish was looking, searching, but doing a good impression of someone who wasn't doing either of those things.

Moving slowly, so as not to attract attention, Alessandra positioned herself behind a pillar and bent slightly, as if looking for something in her bag. She watched the American stride confidently through the lobby, straight to the bank of elevators at the far end. What was she doing here? Was she looking for her?

She'd wanted the book, the *Cultes des Goules*. The same as the Comte. She'd suspected they were working together, but it didn't seem that way. So, who was Trish working for? Not herself, Alessandra thought. The other woman had the put-upon air of a loyal servant; she was working for someone else. If not the Comte, then who?

Alessandra frowned and straightened as Trish vanished into

an elevator. She had a strong suspicion the other woman was heading for the rooms she'd just vacated. Looking for some clue as to where she was going, perhaps. When she found the rooms empty, the next obvious step would be to inquire at the front desk.

Alessandra hesitated, wondering whether she ought to confront the other woman and find out what her part in this truly was. But to do so was to risk wasting time that she didn't have. She had to be a miser, for Pepper's sake. But neither could she allow Trish to dog her steps, not until she had the luxury of time to confront her.

As the clerk returned with her receipt, Alessandra said, in French, "A friend is supposed to meet me at the train station this evening. An American woman. But you know Americans, no? Never where they are supposed to be. If she shows up here and asks, tell her I'll be catching the late train to Grenoble at Gare de Lyon." She passed the clerk a handful of francs, which he made vanish with startling swiftness.

A moment later, she was out the door and signaling for a cab. The misdirection would only buy her a bit of time, if that. But it would have to be enough. If she could get to–

She stopped. Someone was watching her. She could feel it, like the tip of a knife digging into the spot between her shoulder blades. She turned, scanning the nighttime crowd that wandered the boulevard. She saw nothing at first, but then, at the entrance to the metro across the street, she spied a hunched figure, wearing an ill-fitting coat and a wide-brimmed hat. Something about the way they slouched – crouched? – summoned up a familiar nausea. Yellow eyes gleamed in the shadows beneath the hat's brim.

Animal eyes.

A laughing couple passed between them, and when she could see the entrance to the metro again, her observer was gone. A cab slowed and she got in with ill-concealed alacrity.

"Gare d'Austerlitz, please," she said. "And hurry."

CHAPTER SEVEN
Paris-Bordeaux

Alessandra awoke to the dim clatter of the train along the southwestern track of the Paris-Bordeaux railway. Outside, the night still held tight to France and morning was only a distant promise. She'd been lucky enough to get a sleeper compartment; not large, but pleasantly sequestered. Or so she'd thought.

But something had awoken her from fitful dreams. Not a noise as such, but instinct – honed by a life on the edge of legality. She reached under her pillow and retrieved the revolver, cocking it slowly so as not to alert anyone listening to the presence of the weapon. The compartment was dark; warm. Too warm. Sweltering, almost. Or maybe that was simply how it felt. In her dreams, she'd been somewhere else, but she couldn't remember where. Already, the last tatters of the dream were fading. Maybe that was for the best.

She sat in silence, listening to the sound of her own heartbeat, the rattle of the track, the creak of the compartment. Her eyes flicked from one side of the space to the other. A soft sound, from the direction of the door. She slowly swung the barrel of her pistol toward it, and her index finger tapped the trigger. No sense shooting if it was just a common thief; sleeper trains were popular hunting grounds for a certain class of opportunistic criminal.

The sound ceased. Whoever was on the other side of the door seemed to be listening. Had they heard her stir, or the click of the revolver? Or had they, like her, sensed a change in the atmosphere? Either way, it was now a waiting game.

She'd thought – hoped – that she could at least make it to Angoulême without any trouble. But it seemed that had been a false hope. It wasn't Trish, or the Comte's men; she was fairly certain of that. The Comte would be following her, but interfering would only delay his desired outcome. And she'd seen no sign of Trish at Gare d'Austerlitz. She felt confident that the American woman wasn't on her train. So who was it?

Whoever they were, they were very good at being quiet. Or maybe…

She rose to her feet, and, still dressed in her pajamas, went to the door. She listened for a moment, and then jerked up the shade. The corridor was empty, save for the silver ripples of moonlight that spilled intermittently through the windows of the empty compartments. Cautiously, she flipped the lock and opened the door.

She caught a whiff of something musky and sour. An animal smell, like that of a wet dog. But no sign of anything. She heard a creak behind her and turned to look back into the compartment. Her eyes were drawn to the window. The shade twitched. Something that glittered like glass tumbled to the floor of the compartment. A thin whistle of passing air tugged at her ears, as if there were a crack in the window.

For a moment, she was back in Arkham, back in an unhitched train car, being confronted by a pale, twisted thing dressed in black. A thing with the face of a dead man, and a look of hopeless agony in its mismatched eyes.

Another bit of glass fell to the floor, bringing her back to herself. The shade bulged. Something long and thin slid from beneath the shade – black and sharp. The blade of a knife, she thought. But when it bent and began to pull up the lock on the window, she knew it wasn't a blade.

Heart thudding, she took a quick step to the window, pressed her revolver to the bulging shade and pulled the trigger. The sound was loud in the confines of the compartment, but not so much as it might otherwise have been. In fact, it was largely drowned out by a piercing cry, like that of a wounded animal. The dark thing that had been pulling at the lock vanished. She yanked up the shade, revealing a spider's web of cracked glass and the black blur of the passing countryside.

Something that might have been blood was smeared on the bottom portion of the glass. Wind billowed in, ruffling her hair and sending a chill through her. She drew up the window and risked a look out. The night air enveloped her, and she squinted in the gloom of the moon's glow, looking back in the direction of Paris. The boxy, serpentine length of the train extended away from her in a curving arc. She saw squares of light all along that length, but there was no sign of anything, or anyone, clinging to the side of the train.

Shivering, she closed the window and turned to find a porter at her door. Thinking quickly, she tossed her revolver into her open bag and slid it beneath the bunk with her foot even as she moved to respond to the porter's knock.

"Is everything all right, madam?" he asked, diffidently. "The other passengers reported hearing something strange."

Alessandra plastered an apologetic expression on her face. "I am afraid a branch – or perhaps a bird – struck my window. It appears to be broken."

The porter looked past her in apparent surprise. "A thousand pardons, madam. We shall get it blocked off for you immediately. Would you care to get dressed and wait in the drinks car until we are finished?"

Alessandra hesitated, but nodded. "That sounds delightful, thank you." While the porter hurried to get help, she dressed and made her way toward the head of the train, where the drinks car waited. She slid her revolver into her jacket before she went. She doubted whatever it was – whoever it was – would try again tonight, but better safe than sorry. She felt at once jittery and enervated. The thought that once again she was the quarry of something supernatural didn't sit well with her. She'd suspected the possibility was there, obviously, but suspecting and knowing were two different things.

The drinks car was all but empty when she arrived; unsurprising, given the hour. She looked around as she closed the door behind her, taking note of her fellow passengers. Men, mostly. But there was one woman, sitting at a table next to a window. She looked up as Alessandra entered, almost as if she'd been waiting for her. She made a surreptitious gesture and Alessandra paused. The woman gestured again, obviously summoning her. She was pretty, in an odd sort of way, and dressed richly. A woman of means, traveling on her own. Not so unusual these days.

Against her better judgment, Alessandra went up to her. "Yes?" she asked.

"Sit," the woman said, simply. As much a command as an invitation. Bemused, Alessandra sat. "A drink, Countess?" the woman purred. And it was a purr; a throaty, raspy rumble of contentment. The sound of it made Alessandra uneasy.

Alessandra paused, wondering if she knew the woman from somewhere. She kept her expression neutral. The woman's voice was odd. A slight emphasis on certain parts of each word made her accent hard to determine. She was not a native French speaker; not a native speaker of any romance language at all, Alessandra thought.

Up close, she was not so pretty. She was not ugly, but there was something unsightly about the way the sides of her jaws bulged slightly and the way the muscles of her neck flexed and contracted as she spoke. The way she kept her lips firmly over her teeth. The triangular shape of her nails. A curious affectation, that. Her hair was odd as well. It was coarse, thick; more like the mane of an animal.

"No, thank you."

"Mmm. Probably wise. Alcohol dulls the senses." The woman traced the rim of her glass. "For me, it is the only way I can endure the stink of these engines. And the thunder of them curdles the very marrow in my bones."

"Then why ride them?"

"Necessity. My name is Bera. Madam Bera."

"You seem to know who I am, so I will not bother to introduce myself." Alessandra studied Bera in the smoky light of the drinks car. She was well built, and vividly so, beneath her clothing. The clothes were stylish, but they couldn't hide the corded muscles in her wrists and arms. An athlete? Possibly a swimmer. Fitness was a religion with adherents in every country in Europe. But the woman didn't have that look.

Indeed, she reminded Alessandra of nothing so much as a tigress, crouched in a chair. Her eyes only added to this impression. Behind the smoked lenses of her glasses, they were a deep amber, almost yellow. She thought of the person she'd spotted leaving the hotel and shivered inwardly. Were they one and the same?

She was reminded of a previous employer – a man named Zamacona. Only Zamacona hadn't been a man at all, but something else. Something indescribable and malign. She'd found out his true nature almost too late, and had nearly been killed. Bera was not like Zamacona, she thought; there was a primal pungency to the woman that Zamacona had lacked. He had been an outsider. Bera, whatever else, was a thing of the world.

But what sort of thing?

Bera smiled. A mild, yet somehow grotesque expression. "We do know who you are. We know so much about you. Would you like to hear some of the things we know?"

"Who is we?"

"Us." Bera touched her chest. "My kin and I."

"And what do you want with me?"

"The book."

"I should point out that there are libraries in Paris, with books aplenty."

Bera's lip curled slightly. Alessandra caught a flash of sharpness and stiffened in alarm. The woman's teeth had been filed to points. No. Not filed. They were simply sharp. Like the fangs of an animal. "Do not play games with me, thief. Where is the book?"

"Which book? I am quite well read, and know of several."

Bera dug her fingers into the wood of the table. Her nails – her *claws* – left deep gouges in the surface. "You know what book I refer to. It is ours by right. We want it."

"You are not the only ones," Alessandra said, softly.

"We are the ones here. We are the ones close to you." Bera leaned in, her jaw jutting slightly. Her nostrils flared, and Alessandra had the uncomfortable realization that the other woman was taking in her scent. Memorizing it. "We are the ones at your threshold. Give us the book and we will leave you be."

"And if I refuse?"

A sound emerged from Bera's lips. Not a laugh; a snarl. Deep and rough. The hairs on the back of Alessandra's neck rose and she gripped the table to keep herself from instinctively leaping to her feet. Bera's glasses slid down her nose, and her eyes blazed with an ugly light. "Then we will eat you, thief."

In any other context, such a statement would have been amusing. But here and now, they were the most terrifying words she'd ever heard. Bera was not threatening her. She was merely stating fact.

Alessandra took a deep, steadying breath and sat back. "I do not have the book you are looking for. But I intend to find it."

"And then you will give it to us?"

"You may certainly make me an offer." Alessandra forced a smile. "As I said, there are others to consider. You want to kill me, well, get in the queue. There are several people ahead of you, and they all want the same book."

"The Comte d'Erlette," Bera growled.

Alessandra paused. "You know him?"

"We do. And we will deal with him in our own time." Bera sat back, languid once more. The tigress at rest. "We will not let him have the book. We will not let you give it to him. You will find it and give it to us, and then you will go away." She raised her glass, as if in salute, and took a gulping swallow. Then she set it back down and looked out the window.

Alessandra sat for several moments, until she realized the audience was at an end. She had been summoned, lectured and dismissed. Like a servant. Anger bubbled away beneath her serene expression, but it was tinged with wariness. Bera was not some pedigreed fool. Alessandra wasn't even sure she was entirely human.

So, rather than arguing, she rose and gave the other woman a polite nod.

"Well," she murmured. "We shall see."

CHAPTER EIGHT
Chateau d'Erlette

Pepper sat back in her chair and tugged at the leather straps that bound her wrists. Her hands were tied together rather than to the chair, meaning she could get up and move around, if she wanted. Whether that had been done as a courtesy, or because they didn't want to damage the chair, she couldn't say. Looking around the place, she had a hunch it was the latter.

The house – the chateau, rather – was big. Bigger than anything she'd ever been inside, including some of the fancier homes in Arkham. It was practically a castle. She figured that the room she was in was the study, full of towering bookshelves and furniture that looked expensive, but uncomfortable. Case in point, the chair she was sitting in. It looked cushy, but it was as hard as a church bench.

The ride from Paris had been equally uncomfortable. She'd been tossed into the back of a motor car, gagged and blindfolded. After a few hours, she'd started to think they'd forgotten her, but eventually they pulled over and let her conduct some business in the undergrowth on the side of the road. She'd kept her eyes on them the entire time, just in case one of them decided to get frisky, but someone had obviously warned them to keep their hands to themselves.

More, they'd seemed… nervous. She didn't think it was on account of her, though – or the kidnapping. It was like they were worried about something or someone. They'd kept looking around, starting at every sound. As if something were on their trail. She felt it too; had ever since she'd been tipped into the drink. She kept catching little flickers of nonexistent motion out of the corner of her eye, like a tattered curtain rippling in the breeze.

She'd lived in Arkham long enough to know when something was in the air. A wrongness that permeated every facet of the day and night alike. It led to people locking their doors and making secret gestures meant to protect them from God alone knew what.

The Comte didn't share his men's nervousness. If he was feeling anything, it was smug satisfaction. He'd been staring out the window for almost an hour, humming softly to himself. She'd been expecting him to try and interrogate her, like in the pulps. Only he didn't seem interested in anything she had to say.

In the hour she'd been sitting in the study, she'd made and discarded half a dozen plans for escape. The big windows looked out over a manicured lawn bigger than the Miskatonic common. Ornamental trees lined the paths that wound away from the front of the chateau. She hadn't seen much of the rest of the place, but there were guards everywhere. All of them armed. All of them with the same look as the guys who'd bundled her out here from Paris, wherever here was. Including the one who stood behind her chair, arms crossed over his barrel chest. He was big and bald, with a handlebar mustache that was so black it looked painted on.

The Comte turned to her. "Forgive me, I am being a bad host," he said, in English. His voice was smooth. He hooked his thumbs into the pockets of his waistcoat. "I cannot recall if I introduced myself earlier. I am Henri-Georges Balfour, the Comte d'Erlette."

"Yeah, I got that," Pepper said, flatly. "You the guy who sent those mooks to try and rub us out?"

The Comte frowned, as if trying to parse this. Then, he nodded. "It was necessary. Something was stolen from me. I want it back."

"A book, right?" Pepper said. "Lot of trouble to go to for a book."

"It is a special book." He went to a sideboard where a decanter and several tumblers were arrayed. He poured himself a drink, and looked at her. "Care for one?"

"What is it?"

"Whiskey. I developed an affection for it during a brief visit to your country."

"Two shots, if you please," Pepper said. She held up her hands. "Cut me loose?"

"I think not."

"Can't blame a gal for trying."

"I have heard similar sentiments expressed before," he said, amused. "By our friend, Alessandra. You have not known her very long at all, have you?" The Comte poured her drink. "A year – pfaugh. What is a year? Nothing. A drop in the bucket, as you Americans say. I've known her for almost a decade." He paused and smiled. "We were quite friendly, once. I even thought… well. That is neither here nor there, I suppose."

He brought her the drink, holding it just out of reach. "She betrayed me, of course. As soon as she had reason and opportunity. Our friendship meant nothing to her, you see, if it got between her and what she desired. I expect it is the same for you." He let her grab the drink. "Drink it slowly. It is good quality and if you gulp it, you will only choke on it."

Pepper followed his advice, sipping the whiskey. She'd had better, but she kept her opinion to herself. Mouthing off wasn't going to get her out of here. And part of her wanted to play along and see what else he had to say about Alessandra. The other woman had always been close-mouthed when it came to certain aspects of her previous life, before Arkham, and Pepper was naturally curious. "If you believe that, why bother taking me?"

He smiled again. "Because it frustrates her. Infuriates her. She will do as I ask not because your life is at risk, but because she cannot allow herself to be bested – not by me. It is something we share, that refusal to admit defeat. She will find the book, if only to burn it in front of me. Your survival is surplus to requirements. I tell you this not to frighten you, but merely to impart a fuller understanding of your place in this affair."

Pepper took another sip of whiskey and said, "And that is?"

"Finished. You live only because I find the thought of murdering you distasteful. Otherwise, I would have dispatched you the moment we had you someplace quiet." He finished his drink and tapped the empty tumbler against the side of his leg. "That does not mean I will not have you shot in the head and dumped in the river, if you inconvenience me in the slightest."

Pepper swallowed. She'd heard a lot of tough talk in her life; she'd been threatened more than once as well. But this was the only time she thought somebody had meant it. Even the gangsters she'd driven for had never threatened her so mildly, or so bluntly. "So, what are you going to do with me? After, I mean?"

The Comte refilled his tumbler. "That is up to you. Go where you wish. I have no interest in your fate, young lady. You are a means to an end. Nothing more."

"Gee, thanks. That makes me feel better about the whole kidnapping thing."

The Comte snorted. "You do not have to enjoy the experience. You merely have to accept it." He turned back to face her. "In any event, it is only two days and some scant hours. Then you may leave."

Pepper paused, and looked down into her tumbler. She gave the whiskey a swirl and said, "What if she doesn't bring you the book?"

The Comte's smile was hard and sharp. "I am a man of my word."

Pepper fought to keep the dismay she felt off her face. She didn't want to give him the satisfaction of seeing her scared. The Comte struck her as the sort of guy who liked seeing people – women, especially – scared. Otherwise he wouldn't have gone through all this rigamarole. He was trying to get on top of her, the way the wiseguys back in Arkham did. She took a deep breath and knocked back her drink.

"Yeah, well, I've heard that before."

He raised an eyebrow. "Yes, I expect you have. You are a most interesting young woman. Adaptable. Clever. Tough. Tell me, how did you find yourself in such bad company?"

"We met in Arkham," Pepper said, carefully. The Comte nodded, as if this were to be expected. "That's in America…" she added.

"I know where it is. She was there to steal something, I expect."

"Maybe. Who can say?" Pepper shrugged as best she was able with her hands tied. "I just drove the cab."

"You are a… chauffeuse, then?" the Comte asked, seeming puzzled by this revelation.

"Cabbie," Pepper corrected.

The Comte gestured dismissively. "And… what? She hired you?"

"She's teaching me."

"About what?"

Pepper fell silent. The Comte studied her for a moment, and then laughed. "Ah. Perhaps I was wrong, then. When I said you were unimportant. You are her apprentice. How unexpected. How… delightful." His teeth flashed as his smile widened. "I had heard that she had turned over a new leaf, as they say, but I had dismissed it as mere hearsay."

"People change," Pepper said, wondering if she'd said too much.

"Nothing ever changes," the Comte said. "That is the problem with this world. Today is the same as yesterday, as tomorrow will be like today." He poured himself another tumblerful of whiskey, but drank it more slowly than the first two. "Time accretes. It does not stretch or grow or change. It just layers over itself. Old things rot and crumble beneath the weight of the new, but nothing is ever different." He paused, staring into his tumbler. "Nothing ever changes," he repeated, softly.

Pepper felt uneasy, listening to him. It was like watching a stray dog growl at nothing. The Comte looked at her. "Or at least it has not. But it may yet. If our friend Alessandra returns my property to me. Then – then things will change." His smile turned ugly and feral. "Oh yes, things will change."

"Yeah? Good luck with that," Pepper said, her tone dismissive.

The Comte blinked, startled. He looked at her for a moment and then turned away. "You will be made comfortable for the duration of your stay. I have had a room prepared. Food will be brought up to you. You will have to use a chamber pot, I fear, but as I said you are an adaptable young woman. I am sure you will make the best of it."

"Oh yeah, I'm looking forward to it," Pepper said.

"Selim, if you please." The Comte gestured and the big man reached down and jerked Pepper to her feet by the back of her coat. She yelped, but didn't resist. Unlike his boss, the big guy didn't look like he'd hesitate to smack her around. He was a goon, and in her experience, goons hit first and worried later.

Selim frogmarched her out of the room and up the stairs. She was fairly certain that he hadn't been with his boss in Paris. At least not that she'd seen. Then again, she hadn't seen much from the back of the car. He seemed a cut above; head mook, maybe. Guys like the Comte always had a hatchet man.

Pepper studied him surreptitiously, the way Alessandra had taught her. She had always thought of herself as a good judge of character. She could tell he was a rough guy; the scars on his hands and face attested to that. There was a puckered hole on the top of one big hand – a bullet wound, healed up into a nasty-looking scar. But he didn't seem scared, like the others. He was more like the Comte. But not too much, she hoped.

"You going to untie my hands, big guy?" she asked, as he maneuvered her down the hallway. Selim reached into his belt and produced a long, cruel-looking knife. He yanked her close and slit the leather thongs holding her hands tied.

Pepper eyed the knife, and then realized he was studying

her. "You would not make it," he said, firmly but not in an unfriendly way. More like he was discussing the weather. He opened a door and indicated that she enter. She did so reluctantly.

"Yeah, but maybe you don't know me so well," she said.

His lips quirked slightly in what might have been a smile. "No. But even so, there is nowhere to go. This chateau is guarded day and night. There are men with guns, dogs and... well. There is no escape."

"Lot of hardware. Your boss scared of something?"

Selim frowned. "Yes," he said, finally, as he closed the door. "And you should be as well."

CHAPTER NINE
Angoulême

The bookseller, Mellin Thevet, resided in that part of Angoulême that was colloquially known as the old town, between the ancient ramparts of the medieval city and the town center. An area of winding streets and small squares; of old buildings and forgotten passages. Alessandra quite liked this part of the city, away from the smell of the paper mills and the noise of the river port.

Ordinarily, Thevet maintained a certain amount of anonymity in his dealings with both buyers and sellers. Oh, they might know he lived in Angoulême, but not which part, or even anything explicit about him as a person. Thevet was a nonentity by choice; isolated from the maddening crowd. An urban hermit, hidden away in his sanctum at the city's heart. According to him the Thevets had long been a part of Angoulême's history, but he refrained from specifics. He was proud, but not foolish.

She knew where he lived, of course, because she'd made certain to learn the location after their first meeting. She knew where all the middlemen of her acquaintance lived – and made certain that they knew that she knew. If they knew she could show up at any time, it made getting properly reimbursed less of an issue.

She liked Thevet, insofar as their relationship went. He was always happy with a new consignment of books – or book-shaped things – and always managed to move them quickly and efficiently, with only a few questions to better judge their authenticity and potential asking price. Most importantly, he took only a small commission.

His house was a narrow building at the far end of a cul-de-sac. Wooden shutters badly in need of a fresh coat of paint overlooked an empty square of cobbles. Getting inside was easy enough. She'd done it before, and Mellin had never bothered to change the locks.

Once inside, she took in the musty gloom that was the natural habitat of the bookish recluse. The air was patterned with floating motes of dust. All the windows were closed, though the day was bright and sunny. Mellin had no servants; not even a cat to keep the mice from his books. He lived alone and seemed to prefer it that way.

She moved through the house like a ghost, checking each room for any untoward surprises. Mellin did not maintain a shop, as such. Rather, he sold things by post. He put together a catalog once a year and sent it out to subscribers. Sometimes subscribers wrote in, looking for specific items. More than one of her escapades had had its origins in such a letter. Mellin's stock occupied every available free space in his home.

Tottering towers of books rose in uneven curves along the walls, or sprawled like Angoulême's medieval ramparts across the width of rooms. There were books on the shelves, on the floor, in the halls, on every available surface. Some had slips of paper sticking out of them, noting prices or the names of interested buyers. It was a labyrinth of literature.

The house smelled of decaying paper, glue and coffee. Rolls of brown parcel paper occupied an umbrella stand, awaiting the gentle slice of scissors and the bite of twine. In a cramped study that doubled as a bedroom, she found a rolodex and a stack of ledgers. Neither provided the answer she sought. Then, she hadn't expected them to. Half of Mellin's business was in his head. There was only way to pick that particular lock. She needed to talk to him.

She took a seat in the study and lit a cigarette. There was an ashtray on the side table, and a stack of crumbling newspapers. Books had been arranged in untidy piles around the chair, for ease of retrieval. She straightened her shirt as she tried to get comfortable. She'd worn her working clothes – men's clothes, tailored to fit her frame – and a shapeless sailor's cap, in order to hide her gender. She pulled the cap off and threw it aside. No need for it in here.

She knew Mellin's schedule. It never varied and wasn't exactly complicated, therefore easy to memorize. He woke before dawn, prepared his accounts for the day, and then went to buy a coffee and a pastry from the café down the street when it opened. Thus fortified, he would make his rounds among the book stalls and shops of the old town. He returned home by midday, to read or nap, before venturing out for food in the later afternoon.

A sedentary, predictable existence. Alessandra thought it would drive her mad in under a week. She enjoyed a good book as much as the next woman, but entombing oneself in the written word seemed a sure plan for a slow death.

She checked her pocket watch. It was almost midday. Mellin

would be returning soon. She heard the rattle of the front shutter echo through the silent house, and smiled. "Speak of the devil," she murmured.

She didn't have long to wait. Mellin made for his study immediately, as she'd known he would. The rest of the house was nothing more than storage space for his collection. She said nothing as he came in, humming tunelessly to himself. He bustled around the edge of the room, a bag full of books held in his arms. He opened the study's lone window, and threw back the shutters. Pale light flooded the room. He sighed in satisfaction.

"Hello, Mellin. How's the trade?"

Mellin yelped and spun. "What! Who…?" He was gawkish and skinny; an elderly adolescent, wearing frayed clothes that were meant for a heavier man. He had on spectacles, and his narrow head was covered in a sparse mop of hair.

"You seem nervous, Mellin. Have I said something to upset you?" Alessandra stubbed out her cigarette in the ashtray, smearing ash over the Thevet coat of arms painted on it. The bookseller clasped his burdens to his chest and stared at her in shock. But shock quickly turned to annoyance and then, just as swiftly, into resignation.

"How did you get into my house?" he sighed.

"I am a thief, Mellin. And this house has had the same locks for almost a century. A better question is why did I break into your house?"

Mellin hesitated, processing this. Then, "Why did you break into my home?"

"Why would anyone break into your home? I need a book."

Mellin straightened. He was on familiar ground, now. He adjusted his spectacles and assumed a stern expression. "You could have called. Or written. I provide an annual catalog for my customers—"

"A specific book," Alessandra clarified.

Mellin paused. "Title? Author? Genre?"

"*Cultes des Goules*. Francois-Honoré Balfour. Nonfiction."

Mellin swallowed. "I'm afraid I am not familiar with that particular volume."

"Oh?" Alessandra fixed the little man with a steady look. "How strange. I could have sworn the book in question was in my last consignment. You were very excited to receive it as I recall. Something about having a buyer already lined up."

Mellin grimaced. "Has anyone ever told you that you have an annoyingly good memory, Countess?" He set his burden down on the occasional table near the door. "You know that I pride myself on maintaining the privacy of my customers."

"I do, and I admire your dedication to ensuring the sanctity of your profession. Nonetheless, I require that book."

Mellin went to a cluttered sideboard to pour himself a drink. The cabinet was mostly empty, save for a few dusty decanters, full of dark liquid. "Be that as it may, I have my reputation to consider."

"And I have a gun." She didn't touch the weapon, or reveal it. It sat in her coat pocket; a reassuring weight.

Mellin paused, drink not yet poured. "Is that a threat?"

"A statement of fact." Alessandra gestured dismissively. "I would never be so crass as to threaten one of my oldest clients. But, if it helps, you may tell whoever you wish that I did so. Now give me a name and an address. Either will do, both is preferable."

"I cannot do that."

Alessandra sighed. "Mellin, be reasonable for once in your

misanthropic life. I would not be here if the need were not great. Lives are at stake."

"Yours?"

"No."

Mellin turned. "He caught you, then. Henri, I mean. He finally caught you." He sighed and ran a hand through his thinning hair. "I suppose I shouldn't be surprised. He is quite dogged, the Comte. One of my best clients, you know."

Alessandra raised an eyebrow in surprise. "I did not, in fact. A dangerous game, Mellin. If he had realized that you were the one who had sold his precious collection…"

"But he didn't, because I take great pains to hide myself. You are the only one who knows where I live, and only because you made a point of finding out – after I had asked you not to, as I recall."

Alessandra chuckled. "I took it as a challenge."

"It was more in the way of a polite request," Mellin said, pointedly. "But that is beside the point. If I tell you the location of the book, whatever foolishness you are up to might well come back on me. Endangering my business – endangering me."

"I would pay, obviously."

"My life is worth more than money."

Alessandra studied him for a moment. "What do you want, Mellin?"

Mellin finished making his drink and took a swallow. He gave her a sly look. "That is an interesting question."

"Ponder it swiftly."

"In a hurry, are we?"

"I told you, lives are at stake. Time is not my ally in this."

"Time is no ally to any man," Mellin said. He paused and

made to continue, but a knock at the door interrupted him. It boomed through the house like thunder. "Who could that be at this time of day?" he asked, looking at her as if she might know the answer. He made to go to the door and Alessandra caught his arm.

"You are not expecting anyone?"

He looked at her. "No. Why?"

"I am not the only one looking for the book. And at least one of the others was on the train down from Paris with me. If she has come here…" Alessandra trailed off and reached for her weapon. "She was a most unpleasant woman. Better we leave her on the other side of the door, if it is her."

The knock came again. Louder this time. Insistent. "And if it isn't?" Mellin asked.

"They will come back at a more convenient time."

Mellin frowned and pulled his arm free of her grip. "This is my home, Countess. I will not hide inside it like a mouse." He adjusted his neck tie and went to the door. He paused before he opened it, and Alessandra joined him. She couldn't fault his courage, whatever else.

As she'd feared, Madam Bera stood on the other side of the door. She was dressed in a long coat, gloves and a wide-brimmed hat, decorated with black roses. She wore a pair of spectacles with smoked lenses, and held her clutch in front of her. "Countess," she murmured. "Is this where the book is?"

"There are many books here," Mellin said, his eyes widening slightly as he studied Bera. "We are just now looking for it. But it might well be some time before we find it. Come back tomorrow." He made to shut the door, but Bera caught it and held it unmoving.

"No. Tonight. We can afford to wait." Bera gave a tiger's grin;

all teeth and promise. "You will bring it out to us. It will not go well for you, if we must come in and get it."

"And so we will," Alessandra said. Bera grunted and released the door. Mellin shut it hastily and looked at her.

"You did not tell me you had dealings with them," he hissed, eyes flat with fear. She felt a momentary surprise that he knew what they were dealing with. Then, given the sort of books he dealt in, it would have perhaps been more surprising had he not known.

"You know what she is?"

"I know enough to know she is not human, and that she is almost certainly not alone." He ran his hands over his pate nervously. "What have you gotten me into, Countess?"

"Whatever it is, I will get you out." Alessandra turned to Mellin. "Is there another way out of here?"

He shook his head. "There's a door on the other side of the house; it was originally used for deliveries and such, but it's been bricked up for years." He rubbed his face. "What do we do now?"

Alessandra looked away. "I do not know," she said. "But I will think of something." She went to the window and peered through the crack in the shutters. Bera stood in the shadow of one of the nearby buildings, watching the door with a steady, yellow gaze.

Like a predator, watching its prey.

CHAPTER TEN
Getaway

"She's still out there," Mellin said, turning from the study window. "She hasn't moved once. She doesn't take her eyes off the door." Outside, the sun was a red line on the horizon, casting long shadows through the crooked streets of the old town.

Alessandra nodded absently. "She is determined." They'd been trapped inside all day. She could feel time slipping away from her. She sat in a chair, staring at nothing, a lit cigarette clutched loosely in her fingers. Motionless, her mind nonetheless hummed with calculation. There were several ways out of the building for an experienced thief, but not for Mellin; and that was the heart of the problem.

Going across the rooftops was the best possibility, but the bookseller lacked the acrobatic skill to follow her. Leaving him to his fate had crossed her mind, but only for less than a moment. They weren't friends, exactly, but Mellin deserved better than to be abandoned to the tender mercies of Madam Bera.

There had to be a way, there was always a way, but so far it eluded her. At this point, she was considering going out the front, gun in hand, and making a run for it. But for that, they needed a distraction.

"Any progress?" she asked, looking up. She'd hoped Mellin might have a volume they could pass off as *Cultes des Goules*, at least long enough to escape.

Mellin shook his head. "No, sadly. Though I do have some editions of the right age. In bad light, they might fool her, but not for long. Perhaps not at all." He took a shaky breath. "As I said before, she is not human."

"I heard you," Alessandra said. "She looks human enough." But she knew better. She'd gotten a good look at Bera on the train. Mellin was right. She wasn't human. Not entirely, at least.

"Then you did not look closely. Her eyes, her teeth – they do not belong to a human. She is clearly one of… those folk." He hesitated. "You know to whom I refer, Alessandra. You have been to Marrakesh and Istanbul. To Cairo and Budapest. The circles you travel in, surely you will have heard the stories of them."

"I hear many stories," she said, softly.

"You would remember these. About those who dwell in churchyards, and make meals of the dead. Some of them can pass for people, but most look like nothing you would ever wish to see." He hesitated and then, clearing his throat, recited, "'They are neither man nor woman; they are neither brute nor human – they are ghouls.'" He smiled thinly at her look of puzzlement. "Edgar Allan Poe."

"Ghouls," she said. Mellin was correct. She had heard the stories; it was impossible not to. Of broken tombs and ravaged gravesites; of strange, loping things fleeing into the wastes, pursued by men and dogs. Of children stolen from their cribs, and something with yellow eyes and milk-fangs left in their place.

She wondered if Bera was one of these changelings, stolen away and raised in the dark by a people not her own – until at last, she became as they were. Or maybe she was what had been left behind. A replacement child, hungry and alien, and only growing more so with every passing year.

Mellin studied her. "When last we spoke, you would have laughed at my suggestion."

Alessandra looked at him. "When last we spoke the world made sense, Mellin. I am sad to say that it no longer does. At least not to me." She considered explaining, but pushed the compulsion aside. There was no time.

He was silent for a moment. Then, "Saint-Bertrand-de-Comminges."

She frowned. "What?"

"Saint-Bertrand-de-Comminges. A city – well, a town. That is where I sent the book. A Monsieur Cinabre bought it. He had been in search of a copy to add to his collection. Paid a pretty sou for it as well."

"Why tell me this, after all your protestations?"

"You said a life was at risk. I believe you now."

"Because of her?"

"Because of them." He paused. "And because you never believed in any of it, but now you do. That means I must as well." He sighed and ran his fingers through his thinning hair. "You know why they want the book, of course."

She took a pull on her cigarette. "I do not. Enlighten me."

Mellin shook his head. "Francois-Honoré Balfour. The writer. The current Comte's ancestor. Supposedly, he learned the secrets of the ghouls and wrote them down in his book. But it is said that the ghouls took a dim view of this betrayal and killed him. They spent years altering those copies which they could find, so as to render them harmless to their kind. Or mostly so. Though as to what that might have entailed, I cannot say."

"Then why is this one so important?"

"Because it is the first edition. Unexpurgated, unaltered – pristine. *Cultes des Goules* as it was meant to be read. That is why I sold it for so much money."

"Yes, it was a surprising amount," Alessandra murmured. She'd hoped that sales of the Comte's collection would effectively finance her retirement from thievery, though she'd already burned through most of it, sadly. "So why does he want it back?" she said, half to herself. Mellin frowned.

"He who? The Comte, you mean? Is that who are working for?"

"Under duress, I assure you."

Mellin rubbed his face. "Henri isn't the sentimental type. He…" They both fell silent as the sound of something sharp scratching against stone echoed through the house. It was a persistent noise and unsettling. Alessandra stubbed out her cigarette and rose from her chair.

"Do you have a cellar?" she asked, softly.

Mellin nodded jerkily. Alessandra gestured and he led her back into the small kitchen. He indicated a heavy wooden door, made in the medieval style, occupying the far wall. As quietly as she could, she crept to it and opened it. Light flooded a set of slabbed stone steps going down. She saw nothing, at first. But the scratching sound continued. Intensified, even. As if whatever was making it was in a hurry.

"Light," she murmured. Mellin retrieved an electric torch from a cupboard. She clicked it on and descended. Prudently, the bookseller waited at the top of the stairs. The cellar was small; tidy, unlike the rest of the house. It was clear Mellin didn't use it, save to store a few cases of inexpensive wine, and some old furniture. She swept the light over the wine shelves and a deconstructed armoire and saw nothing, save blank stone. The sound continued.

Skritch. Skritch. Skritch.

Like someone taking a chisel to mortar. A puff of dust caught her eye and she swung the light toward a section of wall. More dust, slipping out and down, piling on the stone floor. Against her better judgment, she went to the spot and crouched down. There was a hole – just a small one. A chink in the wall. She shone the light into the hole and caught a flash of something reflective. A muted growl echoed from the other side.

Alessandra turned the light off. There was a yellow mote, flickering within the hole. Someone – some*thing* – was watching her and she felt a chill of horror at the sight. She wanted to flee. Instead, she drew her revolver and cocked it next to the hole. The sound echoed through the cellar and the mote vanished. "Let that be a lesson to you," she said, out loud. "No one likes a sneak."

Quickly, she made her way out of the cellar. Mellin stared at her as she returned, his face pale and his expression strained. "They said we had until dark," he hissed, his eyes wide.

"It will be dark by the time they get through." She closed the door to the cellar and thrust a chair beneath the handle. It wouldn't stop them, she knew, but it might buy a few extra moments. "We are rats in a trap here." The time had come to act, plan or no plan. She looked at him. "You said you had something that might pass as the book in dim light?"

"Yes, but one good look at it and she will know."

"Then I will make sure that she does not get a chance to look at it."

"How?"

"By running very fast."

He blinked owlishly. "Are you suggesting we flee?"

"No. I am suggesting that I flee. I will take the book and make a run for it. They will follow me."

Mellin blanched. "That is a terrible plan. You will never make it."

"It will divert their attentions. The address in Saint-Bertrand-de-Comminges – do you have it written down?"

He led her to the study and tore a card from his rolodex. Alessandra studied it for a moment and then said, "The book. Quickly." He fetched an old volume, bound in some dark leather that made her skin crawl when she touched it. "Is this … ?"

"Human skin? Oh yes. It was quite common in earlier centuries to bind books in it."

"And was the original … ?"

He nodded. "Yes. Roughly the same shade and consistency as well."

Alessandra grimaced. "Wonderful. Thank you." She slipped the card into the book, having memorized the address. "I will make certain that they find it, so that they will follow me. They will have no reason to bother you after that."

Mellin darted a glance in the direction of the cellar. "You hope."

"I do. But it is the best we can do. I must get to that book before they do. But as long as they are chasing me, you will be safe." She paused. "I would suggest taking a holiday, however. Somewhere sunny, perhaps. Away from any graveyards."

"And what if they come after me anyway?"

"Then tell them what you told me. Do not lie, or hesitate. Give them what they want."

Mellin blanched. "Alessandra, I–"

She held up a finger, silencing him. "I have spent the better part of my life getting in and out of trouble, Mellin. This will be no different." She checked her revolver and went to the front door. It was almost dark outside, and the scratching had started up again. She looked at Mellin. "Get upstairs and lock yourself in somewhere. Do not come out until morning."

He nodded shakily. "Good luck, Countess."

She gave him a smile and, book in hand, hauled open the front door. Bera was already moving toward the door, and she wasn't alone. A hulking shape, swaddled in an overcoat and a slouch hat, loomed behind her. Yellow eyes gleamed beneath the hat's brim. "Time is up, Countess," Bera called. Her voice was almost a howl.

"And I have your book," Alessandra shouted, holding up the decoy. "But the only way you are getting it is to catch me!" And with that, she sprinted out the door and down the cul-de-sac toward the street. Bera screeched like an enraged cat and her companion bounded in pursuit of Alessandra.

Bera's wailing cry was taken up by other voices in the tangle of streets. The howls of the ghouls echoed from all directions as Alessandra ran. She had no direction in mind; just away from Mellin's house.

As she fled, she caught glimpses of movement around her; prowling shapes that were at once simian and canine. They were all around her, trying to cut her off. She raced down an alleyway, heading for the street on the other side. She slid to a stop as a shadow raced across the mouth of the alleyway. Something clattered behind her.

She whirled as a great, shaggy shape in a billowing overcoat lunged for her. A carrion smell enveloped her as the force of its leap carried them both out onto the street. She landed hard, the cobbles thumping against her spine like fists. The thing atop her snarled, and claws dug into the material of her jacket as she tried to squirm out from beneath its bulk. It had lost its hat during its leap, exposing a broad, piebald skull, and a stiff, greasy mane.

Yellow eyes blazed with hunger. Hyena-like jaws parted above her, and lashings of drool dripped onto her face and neck as it leaned down as if to give her a kiss, or, more likely, bite her face off. A car horn sounded suddenly, the blaring noise of it echoing from the close-set buildings rising around them. Headlamps flashed and her attacker reared, squealing and pawing at its eyes. She clawed her revolver from her jacket, firing as soon as the barrel cleared her pocket.

The ghoul fell away from her, writhing in evident pain. As it fell, its claws snagged the fallen book and it scrambled away, moving like a wounded animal, whimpering and screeching, the book pressed to its chest. She fired again as it fled, but couldn't tell whether she'd hit it or not. Panting, she rose to her feet and turned toward the car – froze.

"You," she said, in surprise.

Trish cocked her semi-automatic pistol and leveled it at Alessandra. "Hello, Countess. Enjoying Angoulême?"

"Trish. How unexpected. If you will forgive me, I am a bit busy..." Alessandra took a step back, but Trish gestured with her weapon.

"I'd prefer not to shoot you, but I will." Trish smiled coldly. "Neat trick, back at the hotel. Nearly had me."

Alessandra forced a confident smile. "Well, I have always been good at thinking on my feet." Her smile vanished as shrill howls echoed on the air. More ghouls were on the way. She looked at Trish. "You seem to have me at a disadvantage."

"I doubt that." Trish lowered her weapon. "Get in. Quick, before they get here."

Alessandra hesitated. Trish sighed, an impatient look on her face. "Look, right now, your only chance of saving your little cabbie friend is to get in this car." Trish leaned out her window.

"Now, are you coming, or not?"

CHAPTER ELEVEN
Escape

Pepper was somewhere else. She knew this because of the smell that permeated everything. At once inexplicably sweet and impossibly foul, as if one odor overlaid the other. She could make out little of her surroundings; something like muslin covered her face, making everything appear blurry and out of focus.

She thought she was walking down a long corridor, lined with great pillars that seemed to stretch to impossible heights. Between the pillars were windows, and from the other side of those windows came moonlight and the sound of something that might have been water. A river, maybe, or a lake.

She was walking slowly, in no hurry. Or maybe afraid. She couldn't tell. Her head was muddled, her thoughts hers but... not hers. It was as if she were riding in the back of her own cab while someone else drove. And if that wasn't bad enough, she knew what – who – was waiting for her at the end of the corridor. Not their name, but their face. That colorless oval, with its half-smile and heavy-lidded eyes. She'd thought at first that it looked like Alessandra, but the more she pondered it, the more she realized that it wasn't anyone's face.

Or rather, it was everyone's face.

She could hear the rustle of cloth now. As if someone was shifting impatiently. A murmur of voices – no, just a single voice, but echoing from all directions. She stopped and turned toward a window. Something black passed across the face of the moon. The rustling became almost frenzied. She heard the thunder of approaching footsteps.

A hand fell upon her shoulder. She turned, though she didn't want to. She wanted nothing more than not to see who – what – was standing behind her. Eyes that burned like the Hyades stared down at her. Through her. She felt frozen and burnt all at once. Its grip tightened. *No mask,* it said.

Pepper awoke with a start and sat up on the bed, heart pounding with mingled fear and something else. Anticipation, perhaps. The feeling reminded her a little of a dream she'd once had about owning her own cab stand; at once excited and afraid.

She was still dressed; she hadn't intended to fall asleep but falling off a speedboat and getting kidnapped wore a lady out. She ran her hands through her hair. The dream was already fading, going wherever nightmares went when they'd done their job.

The bed was a big four-poster; old and smelled like it. The sheets were fresh, but that was about it. The room smelled stuffy and the windows were locked, so there was no chance of fresh air. She scooted off and found her hat on the floor. She brushed the dust from it and pulled it on. It was dark outside and the house was quiet. She wasn't going to get a better opportunity.

Pepper went to the windows and studied them the way Alessandra had taught her. They were sturdy and lead-lined, so trying to bash through them wasn't going to work. She ran her hands along the frame, but found no drafts or cracks. Solid, then.

She peered out, toward the forested edge of the wild lawn, trying to ignore the fading hints of her nightmare. There would be time to be scared later. Past the ornamental statuary that dotted the overgrowth, she spied a boundary marker – an old, low stone wall – and beyond it, real wilderness rather than the tame wilds of the lawn. Forests and hills. A good hiding place, even for a city girl. If she could get to it.

She turned away and looked around the room. Her gaze paused at the fireplace. No fire had been laid for her. They probably weren't that concerned about her comfort, the Comte's assurances aside. She went to the fireplace and peered up into the chimney. The flue would be a tight fit, but she was small enough to make it work. Maybe. The chimneys in older houses were often larger than those in newer builds, or so Alessandra had sworn.

A ripple of panic echoed through her. Just for an instant. Pepper closed her eyes, fighting it down. She breathed out slowly, forcing her heart to slow. It was harder to control her fear when she was alone. She wondered where Alessandra was; what she was doing. Looking for the book, hopefully. Or planning to spring her.

A part of her thought it might be wiser to sit and wait, but she didn't think she had that kind of time. The Comte didn't strike her as the sort of guy to hold up his end of the bargain. She'd known enough guys like that in Arkham. The O'Bannions would whack a guy as easily as they might pay him, if it suited them. And the look in his eyes when he talked about Alessandra... No, waiting wasn't a good plan. Better to try her luck and see how far she could push it.

She paused, trying to recall what else Alessandra had taught her about chimneys. No shoes, for one thing. Bare feet were best. Divest yourself of any loose clothing or nonessentials. Moving quickly, she went to the bed, stripped off a pillowcase and threw her shoes, her coat and her hat into it. She also stripped off the top sheet and knotted it at several points, thrusting it into the pillowcase as well. She was going to need a rope.

After a moment's hesitation, she packed the bed to look as if she were asleep. It wouldn't fool anyone coming all the way into the room, but it might buy her a few extra minutes. She then tied the pillowcase to her belt with a curtain cord, letting it dangle several feet behind her. Then, taking a deep breath, she ducked into the fireplace and reached up, feeling for a handhold.

She found one, and then another. A few claustrophobic moments later and she was on her way. It was tricky at first. And tighter than she'd estimated. Her elbows and knees would be raw by the time she got out. A bit of skin was a small price to pay to escape. Not that she had any idea where she was or how to get back to Alessandra, but those were future-Pepper's problems. Present-Pepper was more concerned about getting stuck in the chimney.

She had a moment of panic when she reached the top and found it blocked by a chimney pot. Thankfully, the pot was loose and with a bit of effort, she sent it toppling from its perch. She winced as it struck the roof and then rolled off. She was already squeezing out the mouth of the chimney when it finally struck the ground with a crash.

Lights came on in the house. Shouts. Dogs barking. She ignored all of it, remembering Alessandra's teachings – panic was a thief's enemy. Not dogs or guards, but panic and the rash mistakes that came with it. She hauled her bag out of the chimney and pressed herself against it, out of sight of anyone on the ground. Carefully, she began to pull on her shoes and jacket, giving herself time to find the fallen chimney pot and come up with a suitable explanation. They'd check on her, of course. But that was why she'd packed the bed.

Down below, the voices faded. The guards were moving off, looking for intruders. She counted to ten, and tied the curtain cord to the pillowcase and looped the whole thing around the chimney, before tying it to the knotted sheet.

Grasping the sheet, she started creeping down the incline toward the edge of the roof. It wasn't far to go, luckily. She still had plenty of sheet left. From above, she could make out the glow of flashlights piercing the gloom. Watching them, she realized that they weren't worried about an escape. They weren't looking for her – not yet. They were worried about something else. She thought about what the guy had said when he was locking her into her room. What was the Comte up to?

She pushed the thought aside. She'd figure it out later. Right now, she needed to concentrate on getting to the ground in one piece. The chimney had been a cakewalk in comparison. She looked down, and felt a rush of vertigo. The ground was a dark blotch, riven by pools of light, and for a moment she was back in her dream, listening to an unseen lake lap against an unknown shore.

She closed her eyes and fought down the rising tide of nausea. "Not that far to the ground," she murmured. "Just a little jump. Nothing to worry about, right? Right." She opened her eyes. Closed them again. Forced them open, took hold of the sheet in both hands, turned away from the edge, took a breath, and… stepped off.

Her stomach barreled up into her throat as she plummeted down, only to stop short as her improvised rope caught. She spun through the air, hit the wall, juddered away. It was all she could do to hold on. She hissed obscenities between her teeth as she waited for her stomach to stop heaving. Carefully, she swung her legs up until the soles of her boots touched the wall. Swallowing, she pushed off, and dropped; pushed off, and dropped.

Pepper reached the end of the sheet far too quickly for her liking. She dangled for a moment and spotted a window. She stretched out a hand but it was out of reach. She swung herself toward it, conscious of the sudden give in the sheet. She hadn't heard it rip, but she could tell it was going. Heart thudding, she clawed for the window frame. Her fingers hooked the lead and she cast the sheet away as her feet found purchase on the ledge. Through the window, she spied her room. All was as she'd left it. She looked down. One floor to go.

A sudden spill of light blinded her. She blinked away spots and realized someone had opened her door. She froze, eyes wide, watching as Selim stepped into the room. He dragged the duvet from the bed and looked around. He paused, staring at the window. At her. Without thinking, she gave a little wave and looked down. With the aid of the light, she could just make out one of the motor cars that had brought them to the estate.

She was already jumping as Selim came toward the window. She'd never had a problem with heights. Not really. It was the idea of falling that bothered her. That and the impact. But like Alessandra said, any fall you could walk away from was a good fall.

She hit the roof of the car, tore through it, and landed in a heap in the backseat. She struggled up, got the door open and nearly fell into the courtyard. Someone shouted from the portico, and she could hear Selim yelling. She kicked away from the car, got to her feet and started running. She picked a direction at random, ducked her head and pumped her legs.

Dogs barked to her left, and flashlight beams intercepted her path as she cut across the great lawn. Someone fired a rifle, taking a branch off an ornamental tree to her right. She put on a bit of extra speed. If she could make the boundary wall, she had options. She heard an engine start up behind her. Her heart was hammering against her ribs, her lungs burning – but the wall was right there, just in reach.

She hit it, and went over. Not a smooth leap, like Alessandra might have made, but an awkward bump and roll. It did the job, though. She hit the ground, bounced and came up, her body all aches and pains, but full of adrenaline too. "Keep moving," she hissed to herself. "Keep moving. Don't matter where – just go!"

Lights speared the dark overhead. The sound of dogs was getting louder. Men's voices, shouting back and forth. They'd seen where she'd gone. They'd be at the wall in moments. She headed into the trees, moving as quickly as she could.

In the dark, she hit something and nearly fell. A post, set into the ground. Something white gleamed at the top, and as she stared at it, the world contracted until all she could see was a white oval. She pulled herself to her feet and circled it cautiously, aware of her pursuers drawing ever closer.

She stopped with a startled hiss. The white thing was a skull. A human skull, with some unpleasant mark carved into it. It faced out at the darkness, like a warning. But for whom? She suddenly recalled Selim's words from earlier and shuddered. The bark of a dog startled her, and she stepped back. She already knew the Comte was bad news. What was one more warning?

Pepper turned and fled into the darkness.

CHAPTER TWELVE
Allies

Trish was impressed. Zorzi waited until they'd left Angoulême to ask the obvious question. She even phrased it as a statement. "Your timing was impeccable."

Trish didn't take her eyes off the road. The Peugeot was a loaner; one of the bureau's French assets. A tricked-out roadster, with enough horsepower to get them to where they were going in under the average time. Not that she knew where that was, just yet. Zorzi had intimated that Bordeaux was in the right direction, so that's where they were heading. "I didn't follow you, if that's what you were wondering."

"It was not." Zorzi sounded confident; smooth. The reports she'd read had made Zorzi out to be a cool customer. Everything she'd seen so far had borne that out. She wondered if anything could rattle the other woman.

Trish glanced at her. "Because nobody could follow you, right?"

Zorzi inclined her head. "Not without my knowing," she said. She reached into her jacket. Seeing Trish tense, she added, "Do you mind if I smoke?"

"Only if you give me one."

Zorzi smiled, and Trish felt a flutter. She stamped on it. Now wasn't the time for a distraction. And Zorzi was distracting. Trish cleared her throat and tried to concentrate on the road. They were heading south along the route nationale, in the direction of Bordeaux.

To say her superiors hadn't been pleased was an understatement. But they'd understood. Despite what some governments thought, the Great Game was anything but – games had rules and strategies. Being out in the field, you saw it differently. It wasn't some vast chessboard or even a checkers board. It was mob rule. Chaos. Bloody, boring chaos. The best field agents learned how to ride the waves of entropy, to keep on top of ever-shifting terrain. You had to be able to react to opportunities as they presented themselves.

It was clear from her behavior that Zorzi was on the hunt. That was what they'd wanted. It didn't matter why. But if she was working for someone else, they needed to know who and why, if only to make sure the Silver Twilight Lodge weren't trying to pull a double-cross.

Abner Whitlock had come to her rescue once again; his files had mentioned a rare bookdealer in Angoulême – Mellin Thevet. Whitlock hadn't been certain that he was connected to Zorzi, not directly at least, but it was a place to start. She'd taken the car and arrived at Angoulême in the wee hours of the morning.

She'd spent the day in a nearby café, and let a few locals do her watching for her, courtesy of her bureau field stipend. When they'd reported a strange woman hanging around, she'd almost dismissed it as too obvious.

Trish wasn't sure who this Madam Bera Zorzi had told her about was, but she was pretty sure she knew *what* the woman was. Seeing Zorzi's attacker, if only for a moment, had convinced her that the Comte was the least of their problems. Trish had seen some strange things over the years; more in the last few than she cared to admit.

The world was full of dark corners and those dark corners had things in them. Hungry things. The Black Chamber was doing its best to keep said things from becoming public knowledge, even as it tried to untangle the mysteries around them. If such… individuals were involved in the matter, then it might be that this wasn't a simple case of property retrieval after all, but something deeper and more complex. That would complicate things.

"So," Zorzi said, breaking the silence.

"So."

"How did you manage to be right where I needed you?"

Trish smiled. "We knew about Mellin Thevet. I figured you had to have fenced the Comte's books through Thevet. It made sense he'd be your first port of call, if you were looking for the book."

Zorzi nodded, as if unsurprised by this, and handed Trish a cigarette. "And here I thought I had been clever with my little ruse back in Paris." She lit her own cigarette first, and then Trish's.

"I almost bought it. Then again, my brains were still a bit rattled from the whack your sidekick gave me." Trish studied Zorzi's face in the dim glow of the cigarettes. She looked composed. Not panicked, not worried. She looked as if everything were going according to plan. Trish recalled Chauncey's warning, and resolved to keep one eye on Zorzi at all times. She couldn't afford to underestimate her again.

Zorzi smiled thinly as she rolled down her window. "Who

is we, Trish? Not the Comte, nor Madam Bera, I think. So who do you work for, really?"

"I am not at liberty to divulge that information, but I can say that our offer still stands. Give us the book, and you will be protected."

"And what about Pepper?"

Trish frowned. "What about her?"

"The Comte has her."

Trish's frown deepened. Chauncey hadn't mentioned that, but it explained why Zorzi had suddenly decided to go talk to a bookdealer like Mellin Thevet. Maybe Swann hadn't known, or maybe he hadn't cared enough to share that particular detail. An oversight she'd take up with him the next time she saw him. She tightened her grip on the steering wheel and thrust down the sudden flicker of guilt. She'd never been a fan of collateral damage. "You know him better than me – what are the odds she's still alive, Countess?"

Zorzi turned away, watching the countryside flash by. Finally, she said, "Even so, I must try. I promised her I would try."

"The Comte cannot be allowed to have that book."

"He had it for thirty years and did nothing with it. Why should it matter now?"

"Maybe the time wasn't right," Trish said. She could feel Zorzi's sidelong glance boring into her. "I'm sorry about Miss Kelly, but that's the truth. That book is too dangerous to be in the wrong hands, so it needs to go away."

"With you."

"With me."

Zorzi blew a plume of smoke out through the open window. "And who are you, exactly, Trish? Other than the woman who set the hounds of Hell on my trail and got my friend kidnapped?"

Trish flinched. She couldn't find it in her to be particularly fond of anyone who hit her on the back of the head, but Kelly was just a kid. She didn't deserve whatever the Comte had planned for her. Neither did Zorzi, come to that. "I'm your best chance of getting Miss Kelly back," she said, after a moment.

"And how do you intend to do that?"

"First things first – Thevet told you the location of the book, didn't he?"

Zorzi fell silent. Trish scowled impatiently. "I want to help, but I'm going to need that book. It's a matter of national security."

Zorzi gave a bark of laughter. "I knew it! You are a spy, then."

"I'm not a spy," Trish said, pretending to be annoyed. She'd made the slip intentionally. The more Zorzi thought she knew, the easier she'd be to handle. In theory, at least. The truth was, she had no idea what was going on in the other woman's head. The funny thing was, Zorzi was probably thinking the same about her.

"Then what are you, Trish?"

"Your only friend in the world, at the moment," Trish said, flatly. Zorzi was trying to get a handle on her. Working an angle. Trish knew the signs, because she'd done the same herself on more than one occasion. "You know where we're going; so spill. Tell me."

Zorzi hesitated. Then, "How can I trust you?" Her hand was in her pocket; on her revolver, Trish knew. Trish's own weapon was holstered under her arm. She was fairly certain she could draw it before Zorzi could shoot her. But fairly wasn't a hundred percent. Those were bad odds when it came to guns.

Trish shook her head. "You can't. But like I said, I'm your best chance. You need help, and I'm offering it."

"Without the book, I can't get Pepper back."

"You know as well as I do that the Comte isn't going to let you just walk out of there after you turn it over. Why would he do that?"

Zorzi was silent for a moment. She pulled her hand out of her pocket and rested it on her knee. Trish relaxed. "What do you propose?" Zorzi asked.

"First, tell me where we're going."

"Saint-Bertrand-de-Comminges. Have you heard of it?"

"No," Trish said, but she had. And she felt something curdle inside her as she considered what it might mean. The year previous, on her last visit to Venice, she'd made contact with a certain organization. During her preliminary investigation, she'd learned that one of its members, a Monsieur Cinabre, resided in Saint-Bertrand-de-Comminges.

It couldn't be a coincidence. The organization in question, the so-called Red Coterie, rivaled the Silver Twilight Lodge in influence and capacity for disruption. While the Black Chamber wasn't sure which was more dangerous, the Coterie supposedly had resources that Sanford's bunch couldn't dream of.

The Black Chamber was trying its best to put the two organizations to work on behalf of the United States government, but it was tricky. In her opinion, Sanford was barely on a leash as it was; and the Red Coterie hadn't made a peep since their initial contact. Maybe this was why Chauncey – why Sanford – wanted the book. Were they trying to pick a fight with the Red Coterie? Or worse, maybe trying to make the Black Chamber pick a fight for them?

Maybe Sanford didn't like the idea of sharing his government connections.

"It is a town that calls itself a city, largely because it has a cathedral," Zorzi went on. If she'd noticed Trish's hesitation, she gave no sign. "There is a gentleman there by the name of Cinabre – a curious name, I know, but such fellows are often eccentrics."

"Weirdos who buy creepy books, you mean," Trish said, drolly.

Zorzi sniffed. "I will have you know that those are some of my best clients, and ask that you show them some respect." She paused and grinned. "But yes."

"Have you ever met this… Cinabre?"

"No. I did not even know of his existence until today. Mellin is one of my faces, and he knows the names. I know nothing."

"And you like it that way, I bet," Trish said. Zorzi frowned.
"I did."

Trish paused, wondering if Zorzi was referring to what had happened to her in Arkham. She knew a little about what had gone on, but not much. Enough to know it had been bad. Then, given what she knew about Arkham, it was the sort of place that made everything worse. She turned her attentions to the matter at hand. "Right. Here's what I think, Countess. We get in, we get the book, arrange a meeting with the Comte and then we get your friend – if she's still alive."

"You make it sound so simple, Trish."

Trish grinned. "That's because it is. My people can protect you from the Comte, you get your friend back and I get the book. Everyone's happy." She squinted at the horizon. The sky was lightening, but the sun wasn't on the rise just yet. "How long did the Comte give you?"

Zorzi frowned. "Three days. Well, two days now."

"Not much time," Trish murmured. "That thing that attacked you – they'll be on our trail in no time." There was an official term for such creatures, of course. She'd seen it on a number of mostly redacted after-action reports, though it seemed flat and ill-fitting after having spotted one in the flesh.

Zorzi nodded. "I know. I made certain of it."

Trish looked at her. "You what?"

Zorzi's smile could have sliced glass. "I left them directions. They know where I am going." Her eyes flicked to Trish. "Where we are going." She paused, taking in Trish's expression. "I couldn't very well leave poor Mellin to their mercies, now could I? This way, they have no reason to kill him."

"Unless they're annoyed – or hungry," Trish said. "I've read enough reports to know these… things don't like leaving witnesses. Your pal Mellin might be dead regardless."

Zorzi stared at her for a moment, and then looked away. Trish couldn't tell whether her words had had any impact. Zorzi's expression was one of studied boredom when she finally replied.

"Then we had best hurry, don't you think?"

CHAPTER THIRTEEN
Chapel

A branch cracked. Pepper froze.

She'd always been a city girl. The countryside didn't scare her, but it was unfamiliar terrain in a way that even the most foreign city wasn't. Something about all the trees. You never knew what was hiding behind them. Not muggers, that was for sure.

Another crack. A rustling. Something small, or maybe something big. She didn't know. But she wasn't planning on drawing its attention, whatever it was. So she waited, breathing through her nose, eyes flicking from one shadow to the next.

The trees were old, and big; they reminded her of the trees in Arkham and she wondered what they fed on. She pushed the thought aside. She didn't want to think about Arkham or its trees, not here, out in the dark and the cold. She tried to remember what Alessandra had told her about the woods in France. She remembered something about wild boar. Maybe that was what she'd heard.

It was getting on toward morning. The sky was the color of a ripe plum, and there was a bit of light – not much, just enough. A chill mist was seeping up from the uneven ground. She couldn't hear any birds, though. That made her uneasy. The birds sometimes went quiet in Arkham too. She thought about the skull on its post, and the others she'd seen since. At least a half dozen, scattered at odd intervals throughout the forest. All facing away from the direction of the estate.

A sudden yelping cry brought her around, eyes wide. Dogs. They'd set dogs on her trail. Heart hammering, she took to her heels. She'd read about people being chased by dogs in the pulps, but never expected to be the prey herself. She headed away from the sound, all too aware that she had no idea where she was going and no plans beyond the next ten minutes. Her nerves were jangling, fear all mixed up with adrenaline.

She nearly had a heart attack when she spotted the church. It came out of nowhere, rising up between the trees. When she got closer, she realized how small it was. Not a church then, but a chapel. A ruined one at that. The roof had fallen in, leaving only the steeple rising up out of the boughs of the trees that were growing through the structure. Roots and branches burst through the old stones. The whole thing looked like it was about to fall apart at any moment, but it was better than nothing.

Pepper went to the doors. Both were rotten and hanging off busted hinges. Inside, motes of dust haunted the air. Shafts of light from the rising sun pierced the shattered roof, illuminating a scene of natural devastation. She'd seen overgrown buildings before, but nothing like this. A massive tree rose through the buckled surface of the floor, filling the nave and spreading its branches outward. The chapel was like a shell that the tree was slowly but steadily outgrowing.

There were no pews to be seen, no sign of habitation or use, save for the fallen shape of a large crucifix that lay at a slanted angle on the broken floor. There was moss growing on it, and the Christ had been reduced to a mottled shape of warped proportions. Something about it reminded her of her nightmare and she hastily looked away. She shivered, clutching herself. Her belly rumbled and she realized that she hadn't eaten since Paris.

Dogs barked and she turned back to the doors. She heard the stamp of a horse's hooves and then the doors were falling from their abused hinges and a horse and rider galloped into the chapel, followed by a swirling pack of dogs. The animals headed right for her and she scrambled back, looking for something – anything – to use as a weapon.

Atop his horse, the Comte laughed. "It has been a long night, mademoiselle, but we have reached the end of it I fear." He pulled a silver whistle out of his waistcoat and blew on it soundlessly. The dogs retreated in good order, to be replaced by Selim and several other men. All of them were armed.

The Comte climbed down off his horse, one hand on the sword sheathed at his side. Pepper, no judge of swords, thought it looked like a cavalry saber. "Truly, Alessandra taught you well. Your escape was a thing worthy of the great Rocambole. But it was not to be. Take her."

One of his men – a stocky guy with a nose like a bruised peach – made to grab her. She spied the revolver thrust through his belt and knew she had only one chance. As he caught her arm, she stamped on his foot and was pleased to hear something crunch. He yelped and staggered, and she drove her knee into his groin. His yelps rose an octave and he hunched forward, clutching at himself.

As he did so, she snatched his revolver from his belt and retreated, cocking the weapon as she went. The sound was loud in the confines of the chapel. The Comte and his men froze as she swung the weapon up and took aim at him.

"Not to be, hunh?" she said, loudly. "Well, we'll see about that." Weapons rose to cover her, and she tried her best to ignore them. "Better tell your boys to back off, pal, or this place is going to be looking for a new Comte," she shouted. "Understand?"

The Comte flung out his hands. "Back, back! All of you, back!" Pepper took another step backward, the revolver extended before her. Her eyes darted around, looking for any possible avenue of escape. The Comte licked his lips. "What are you going to do with that, eh?"

Pepper glared at him. "Dunno. Filling you full of holes seems like a good place to start." She hoped they couldn't hear the fear in her voice or see how her hand trembled.

The Comte nodded slowly. "A sensible plan. But a flawed one. Killing me will not preserve your life. The only way you can do that is to surrender." He held out his hand. "Give me the gun, girl. I promise you will not be harmed." He smiled as he said it, and that made it even harder to believe. Like he was joking. Like it was all a game. She was just a piece on the board to him.

Pepper stared down the barrel at the Comte. "Ah bushwa," she said, and pulled the trigger. The gun clicked. Pepper stared at it in disbelief, and the Comte blinked, clearly startled. Then, he threw back his head and laughed uproariously. Selim wrestled the gun out of her hand and shoved her to the ground.

The Comte shook his head and grinned. "You did it. You actually pulled the trigger, mademoiselle! How unexpected. How delightful. Alessandra chose well when she picked you to be her assistant." He looked down at her, a wide smile on his face. "I do not know why I doubted you. Your escape alone proved your character." He looked around. "And to find you here, of all places..." His smile faded and his voice lost its humor. "He died here, you know. My grandfather. It was meant to be his refuge, but the gods of men are as nothing before the true rulers of existence."

He strode past her, to the fallen cross. He looked down at the moldering image of Christ and his face twisted into a grimace. "They left nothing of him behind. Nothing save the stain of his blood and the echo of his screaming. That was the price for his sacrilege. It is a price many have paid down the long black tunnel of years." He turned back to her. "They killed him because he dared expose their secret foulness to the light. Because he dared to learn the truth of things, and dared to share it with others."

He drew his sword, raised it over his head, and brought it down on the rotten wood of the cross, separating the desecrated image's head from its shoulders. "Thus to all gods... starting with theirs." Pepper stared at him in incomprehension. He was clearly a looney, with a chip on his shoulder the size of a boulder.

He turned and extended his sword in her direction. "That is why I need the book, you see. For to destroy a god, one must enter its heaven. And for that, one must have a map. Preferably a guide, as well." He paused, as if something had suddenly occurred to him. He gestured. "Get her up. I've thought of a better use for her."

Selim hauled her to her feet – not gently, but not roughly either. He leaned close as he did so. "Be brave, girl," he muttered. "Whatever else, be brave."

Pepper didn't know what to make of that, so she kept her

mouth shut. The Comte climbed back onto his horse and kicked the animal into motion. Selim and the others followed, Pepper trapped within their phalanx. They moved through the tomb-yard to a high stone mausoleum with an onion dome and bronze doors gone green with age. Gnarled roots crawled up the sides of the mausoleum, and a stunted tree sprouted incongruously from the base of the dome like a second head.

"More than ten generations of my ancestral line are interred in these vaults," the Comte said, as two of his men unfastened the heavy padlock that held the doors closed. Unlike everything else, the padlock was new.

Pepper glanced at him. "Yeah? Swanky joint. Very classy." She had a bad feeling that whatever was coming next was going to be a lot less pleasant than being locked in a room.

The Comte chuckled. "Yes. It is all but forgotten now, much like my grandfather. At least these ones left bones and dust behind." The doors creaked open and he peered into the darkness beyond. Pepper saw a set of steps going down and felt a chill race along her spine. The Comte looked at her. "It has another purpose now."

Pepper swallowed. The Comte gestured. "Throw her in."

Two of his men grabbed her by the arms. She heard Selim protest, but the Comte ignored him. She squawked and struggled, but to no avail. She even managed to kick one in the knee, but they were ready for her this time. The Comte watched as they bundled her toward the open doors, a contented smile on his face. "I have been wondering how best to reach an accord with a guest – an unwilling guest, I must add. I have given him every consideration, but he refuses to accept my hospitality. Perhaps you can convince him otherwise."

With that, they pitched her into the black maw of the

mausoleum. She hit the stairs and rolled down them, cursing loudly the entire way. The doors slammed shut as she hit the flagstones at the bottom, her hat flying from her head.

A stink like nothing she had ever encountered enveloped her and she gagged, her empty stomach heaving. She felt around blindly for her hat, and something smooth and broken rolled beneath her fingers. Skin crawling, she reached into her jacket and fumbled about until she found a book of matches from the hotel.

Hands trembling, she lit one. A flare of light briefly illuminated the darkness. There were bones everywhere, littering the floor. What had the Comte said? Ten generations? It looked like more than that to her.

Somewhere past the feeble edge of the light, bones clattered. The sound of it echoed oddly in the distorted confines of the mausoleum. It seemed to come from all directions at once. Abruptly, it ceased. Then a new sound intruded – a soft, hungry panting. Like a dog.

Pepper snatched up her hat even as the match went out. "Ah futz." She didn't bother to light a new one. The panting got louder. Closer. She felt a thrill of fear course through her. Whatever it was, it wasn't a dog.

Pepper balled her fists. "Why don't you just dry up?" she snarled. Whatever it was snarled back and more bones clattered as it approached. Fear curdled in her belly.

Then, in a rush, it came for her.

CHAPTER FOURTEEN
Saint-Bertrand-de-Comminges

Saint-Bertrand-de-Comminges was not a city. To call it a town was stretching it. It was a village with pretensions of grandeur, thanks to the presence of the cathedral. Alessandra sat on the bonnet of Trish's car, watching the other woman search fruitlessly for a telephone kiosk. They'd parked beneath a tree on the main street, and the branches rustled in the morning breeze.

"I told you," Alessandra called out, as Trish made her way back to the motor car.

"We passed phone lines coming in," Trish protested.

"We also passed sheep. What is your point?"

"If there are lines, there are phones. So where are they?"

"Private residences, most likely."

"In a place this size?" Trish scoffed.

Alessandra had to admit that she had a point, but felt no urgency to say so. Instead, she hopped off the car and thrust her hands into the pockets of her coat. It had taken them nearly five hours to make the journey from Angoulême. The sun was up and the day was cool. She could hear the sound of sheep in the distance, and the quiet murmur of the town as it made ready for the day. "What does it matter?" she asked.

"It matters because I need to contact my superiors."

"Why?"

"To let them know things have changed."

"To let them know where we are, you mean." Alessandra looked around. The village still held to its medieval origins, with prominent arches and vaults. The influence of Rome was evident as well, in the pattern of the streets. Her gaze found the distinctive shape of the cathedral, rising above the village. "Did you know that there is a crocodile in there?"

"A what?"

"Crocodile. Stuffed, of course."

Trish pulled out a pack of cigarettes and selected one. She didn't offer the pack to Alessandra. "Yeah, I figured. Why does it matter if I let them know where we are? You got something against the United States government?" She lit her cigarette, eyeing Alessandra as she did so.

"Well, there are several warrants for my arrest in your fine country." Alessandra reached for her own cigarettes. "But more generally, I do not trust any government to have knowledge of my doings. Especially one prone to tapping its own lines of communication."

Trish frowned. "And where did you hear that?"

"Do you think you are the first spy I have met?" Alessandra said. She lit her own cigarette and watched the other woman's face. "I know who you work for, though you have not mentioned their name. Or, I have a good guess at least."

"Do you now?" Trish murmured. "And does that change anything?"

"Not if you can help me, as you promised."

"I can."

"Then we have no problem." Alessandra paused, blew

a smoke ring and watched it diminish. "Earlier, when I mentioned where we were going, you hesitated. A small thing, but noticeable. Why?"

"I was trying to recall if I'd ever heard of the place," Trish said.

"But you hadn't."

"No."

Alessandra studied her. Trish was lying, though she wasn't sure about what exactly. If she had heard of this village – of Cinabre – why not say something? Unless there was a good reason not to. Perhaps Trish was hoping to use such information as a bargaining chip. Alessandra sighed, tapped some ash onto the street and said, "I am hungry. There should be a café somewhere. Breakfast, and then we pay a visit to Monsieur Cinabre."

"Think we really got time for that?" Trish said, taking a last pull on her cigarette before flicking it into the gutter. "Only two days left, remember?"

"A lot can happen in two days, and I would prefer to deal with it on a full stomach." Alessandra finished her own cigarette and dropped it to the ground. She snuffed it with her heel. "Besides, it may be that Monsieur Cinabre contacts us first."

Trish paused. "You think Thevet called him."

"I have seen enough in the past year to know that men like this Cinabre have ways of knowing things before they might otherwise be expected to do so. It is always best to wait for an invitation before attempting to pick the locks."

"What's that, like a bit of professional wisdom?"

"It is something an old teacher of mine used to tell me. Come."

They found a café easily enough. If there was one compliment she could pay the French, it was that they made food and drink incredibly easy to locate. They got some looks, of course. Two strange women – foreigners at that – were bound to attract attention. Alessandra paid them no mind.

Trish sat back in her chair and wiped pastry crumbs from her hands. "Tell me something… did you really leave them the address just to protect Thevet?"

Alessandra took a sip of coffee and looked out at the street. They'd taken a table near the door. "Is that so hard to believe?"

"A bit. Given what I've read about you."

"And what have you read about me?"

Trish's smile was cold. "Enough to know that I should take anything you say with a grain of salt. You're a third-generation criminal. Your parents were grifters and thieves, and so were your grandparents."

"The family business," Alessandra murmured.

"Not quite. You have sisters, all of whom are married. Good marriages, by continental standards – older men, with considerable estates. You have a two year-old niece in Milan, and a pair of nephews in… Genoa, I think. Have you met them?"

"No." Alessandra paused, in some consternation. She had not realized that Isabetta had had her baby. Then, she had been busy of late. Still, a card was in order, if nothing else. "You know all that?"

"I like to be thorough," Trish said, in a mild tone. "Have you ever worried that someone like our friend the Comte might go looking for them, for payback?"

"No."

"Really?"

Alessandra was silent for a moment. "My sisters can look after themselves. Our grandfather saw to that." She forced a smile. "If you think I am the dangerous one in the family, you are not as thorough as you claim. My sister Pelegrina, for instance, has already killed two men that I am aware of."

Trish frowned. "Two…?"

"It might be three now. Is she still married to that Genoese fellow? If not, then it is definitely three." Alessandra's smile widened and she finished her coffee. "She does use them roughly, poor dears. Always has."

Trish grimaced. "She sounds like a wonderful woman."

"I am quite fond of her. Though absence might be the reason for that." Alessandra set her cup down. "To answer your question, no, saving Mellin was not my only thought. Simply, I would rather have hounds on my trail than lurking someplace unexpected. If they are following me, then I know where they are."

Trish nodded. "I figured it was something like that." She paused, her eyes on the door. "Looks like you were right about Cinabre."

Alessandra followed her gaze and saw a short, thin man standing in the doorway to the café. He was dressed better than his surroundings, in a suit and tie. The tie was a vibrant red, and it drew the eye like a wound. He spotted them immediately and made his way over to the table, where he took a seat without waiting for an invitation.

"This is most discourteous, Miss Scarborough," he said, in English. He was young and handsome, if you liked the type, and had a guttural accent, not French. Something from around the Black Forest, Alessandra thought. She felt only the barest flicker of surprise that the newcomer had addressed her companion first. Clearly Trish knew more about this Cinabre than she was saying.

Even so, Trish seemed somewhat taken aback to be addressed so. "That wasn't my intent, I assure you, Mister…?"

"Lapp. I am Monsieur Cinabre's representative. He wishes me to inquire as to why an agent of the Black Chamber is sitting in his café, in his village, with no prior warning. The Coterie takes a dim view of such things, mademoiselle."

Alessandra looked back and forth between them. The Coterie – something about that name sounded familiar, though she couldn't place it just now. Instead, she smiled and touched Lapp's balled fist, where it rested on the table. "Would you care for a drink, monsieur?" she purred. He looked at her, as if startled that she had spoken.

"Be silent," he snapped.

Annoyed, Alessandra drew her pistol from her coat and thrust the barrel into his groin beneath the table. Lapp paused in shock. "What…?" he began.

"You are a fine one to speak on discourtesy, monsieur. I can only imagine you were poorly raised. It is the only explanation. Apologize, please."

"I–" Lapp began, face flushing.

Alessandra cocked the revolver and smiled sweetly. "Apologize. Please."

Lapp swallowed. "My master will hear of this," he hissed.

"I expect he will. I hope he disciplines you properly for your impertinence after you tell him how rude you were to us. Now apologize or I will ensure you sing castrato from here on out."

"You will not shoot me!"

Alessandra shrugged. "Why not?"

Lapp looked at Trish. "Tell her to put her gun away."

Trish raised her hands as if in surrender. "Sorry, pally. She ain't one of mine. Free agent, you might say. Annoyingly so."

But she was smiling as she said it. She was clearly enjoying the performance.

Alessandra leaned forward. "Last chance. Apologize."

Lapp looked mad enough to spit, but he said, "Fine. I apologize. Now take that gun out of my basket."

Alessandra lowered the hammer on the revolver and slipped it back into her coat. "Apology accepted. Now, what were you saying about Monsieur Cinabre?"

Lapp sat back and adjusted his tie. He stared at Alessandra for a moment, and then turned his attentions back to Trish. "He is perturbed by your presence here. Explain yourself."

Trish's amused expression had faded, replaced by a professional mask. "I will. To him. Not you."

"That is impossible. Monsieur Cinabre is a recluse. He likes his privacy."

Trish nodded, as if she had expected this. "Then he must linger in ignorance, I'm afraid." She looked away and gestured so disdainfully that Alessandra was impressed despite herself. It would have done an Italian noblewoman proud.

Lapp looked as if he'd been slapped. He glared at them both in silent fury for long moments. Then, he gave a cruel smile and stood. "Fine. He told me that if you would not be reasonable to extend you an invitation. You may come to see him… if you dare." Message delivered, he retreated, leaving them alone.

Alessandra glanced around the café. If anyone had noticed the confrontation, they were studiously pretending otherwise. Maybe they had experience with such encounters. Or maybe just with Lapp. "It was a setup," Trish said, softly. "He baited us."

"Oh?" Alessandra murmured. She didn't find it curious that Trish already knew where Cinabre lived. She'd expected a woman as efficient as the American to already have that detail squirreled away.

"It's what they do. They choose the game, but make you think it was your idea. So when you lose, you have no one but yourself to blame." She hesitated. "He wanted us to come see him. Something's going on. He knows something."

"Are you speaking from experience?" Alessandra asked. She'd been right to be suspicious of the other woman, but it was somewhat gratifying to see that Trish was equally in the dark. She wondered just what Trish knew about Cinabre. Was he a spy, like her? Or something worse?

Trish paused. "Look, what I said before…"

"Applesauce."

Trish looked at her. "What?"

"That is what Pepper calls it. Applesauce. Feather-horses."

"Horsefeathers?"

"Whatever it is, it is a lie. You lied."

"And you're telling me you didn't know that?" Trish asked.

Alessandra smiled. "I knew. I wanted to see if you would at least try a bit of honesty. But it is of no importance. I know where we stand now, and we can move forward."

"Is that your way of telling me that you don't trust me?" Trish asked. She didn't sound particularly upset. She was probably used to it, given her line of work.

"I never trusted you," Alessandra said, as she rose from her chair. "But now I know I was right not to do so. We should go. Monsieur Cinabre is expecting us."

CHAPTER FIFTEEN
Oubliette

It was fast. Big too. Pepper flung herself aside as it barreled toward her. It crashed into the wall and scrabbled awkwardly around to face her – or so she assumed. She could just make out the glint of its eyes, reflecting the little light that slithered in around the edges of the doors at the top of the steps.

Something long and hard rolled beneath her foot, and she stooped to snatch it up. It was a bone, or at least she thought it was a bone. It had the same heft as a baseball bat, which was good enough for her. She took a two-handed grip on it and tapped it against the floor.

"Batter up," she muttered. The thing growled softly and she could hear the click of nails against the stone floors. She was afraid, but her adrenaline was up and she told herself she'd been in worse situations.

"Come on, then. Come on," she said, casting the words before her like arrows. The challenge was more for her benefit than the creature's. "I won't duck this time. Promise." She raised the bone and set herself. "What are you waiting for, pally? An engraved invitation? I'm getting bored over here."

The thing scrambled toward her, panting and growling. Her heart sped up as everything else seemed to slow. She felt as if she were moving through molasses as she swung the bone out toward the gleaming eyes. It connected with bruising force, and she felt the impact radiating up through her arms and into her shoulders. The bone broke, and the thing fell with a yelp.

But its momentum carried it into her regardless, and she was knocked sprawling by its ungainly weight. It flailed at her, tearing her jacket and the arm beneath. Pain flashed behind her eyes and she stabbed blindly at her attacker with the broken remnants of the bone. It yelped again and rolled away from her, scattering more loose bones in its haste.

Arm going numb, Pepper lurched upright and started running. She kept hold of the broken bone. It wasn't much, but it was better than nothing. Her arm was all but a dead weight, but she could feel her fingers starting to tingle. It was going to hurt in a moment, but pain was better than numbness. She took corners at random, trying to get as far from where she had been as possible.

She stumbled along a wall, listening for any sound of pursuit. But there was nothing. Maybe she'd hurt it. She took an experimental sniff of the broken bone and gagged. It smelled like she'd stabbed a pile of compost – or maybe a corpse. She slowed and leaned against a wall, trying to catch her breath. Clutching the bone under her arm, she probed her injury. The cut was shallow, thankfully.

Bones clattered, and she paused, listening. She hadn't seen much of the place before she'd been interrupted, but she knew a maze when she saw one. It reminded her of the old typhoid tunnels under Arkham. Halls of empty brick, carved out for the express purpose of transporting diseased bodies to Christchurch Cemetery. Only this place wasn't for transportation so much as storage.

A distant scuffling drew her around, but the noise faded. Was it following her? Or was it trying to get ahead of her? Worse, what if there were more of them? She muttered a few unladylike phrases as she tore a strip from her shirt and wrapped her wound. "I knew I should have stayed in Arkham," she murmured. Her heartrate was slowing now, adrenaline giving way once again to the cold clutch of fear.

She squashed the feeling as best she could. What was it Alessandra said? Fear was good. It gave you an edge. But you had to keep it under control. You couldn't let it dictate your actions. She closed her eyes and tried to concentrate on slowing her breathing.

She needed to find a way out. But first, she needed to deal with whatever it was. She was fairly certain that there was only one. If there were more of them, they'd have come out of the woodwork by now. That was good. She could handle one of them. She'd dealt with worse driving a cab. At least that was what she told herself.

Pepper tried to come up with a plan. What would Alessandra do? Something smart, probably. But smart was for people who had time to think. She needed something workable. She paused again, listening. She could hear a faint snuffling, like a dog sniffing a fire hydrant. It was trying to catch her scent.

The first inkling of an idea came to her. She slid off her jacket and began to drag it behind her. There was blood on the sleeve. It might be enough to create a trail. But she needed somewhere to lure her pursuer to. She lit a match and took a quick look around. Nothing useful stood out, so she started moving.

She was down to her last three matches when she saw the

pallid face staring at her out of the dark. She was so startled she dropped her match and fell back against an archway. She thought she heard something in the dark – not her pursuer, but something else. Like the rustle of a shroud, or the soft rasp of bones rubbing together. Hand shaking, she lit another match.

There was no face. Only a skull, impaled on a broken bit of stone. The remnants of a burial shroud twisted in a thin breeze. Was it supposed to be some grisly joke? The skull was yellowed and cracked, missing most of its teeth. The shroud was a dirty mustard hue, from age and decay. The match flame danced in the breeze.

She followed the breeze into a chamber, decorated with skulls. They rested on stone shelves, all facing the center of the chamber where a trio of sarcophagi rested. The sarcophagi were stone, and rested on raised plinths. Each was decorated with a carving likely meant to represent an ancestral member of the Comte's family. All three of the sarcophagi had been broken into.

Cupping the match to protect it from the draft, she made her way around the chamber, looking for the source of the breeze. She found it a few moments later, as the match guttered and went out. A part of the wall had been dismantled and repaired, but badly. There was a large crack in it, like something had forced its way through the wall at some point. She could make out little beyond the crack; there was another chamber, she thought. Similar to this one, but smaller. The breeze was coming from there, though. Maybe there was a door or a grate or something that she could use to escape.

But that was for later. For right now, she needed a trap. She looked at the sarcophagi and nodded to herself, as her idea crystalized. She went to the sarcophagi and circled them, looking for the one in the best shape – the one on the far end, as it turned out.

By the light of her third and final match, she could just make out the delicate stonework, and something written in Latin along the side. The lid had been forced aside. There were claw marks on the stone, and something had clearly been at the contents. She tossed her jacket in, shoving it as far out of sight as she could with her length of bone. Then she reached under her bandage, dipped a finger in her wound and spread a smear of red on the edge of the lid. It hurt, but she kept her mouth shut.

Then, she snuffed the match, tossed it into the sarcophagus, and retreated to the far side of the chamber, near where the wall had partially collapsed. She quickly made a blind for herself, beneath the fallen bones and tattered shrouds pulled from the other sarcophagi. It was disgusting, and her stomach threatened to revolt, but she knew it was her only chance.

Whatever it was, it was probably starving. There was no telling how long it had been locked up down here, with only the dead for company. If it was hunting her, it wouldn't be able to resist the smell of her blood. That was what she hoped, anyway.

As she waited there, shivering in the dark, she recalled the stories she'd heard back in Arkham. Most of them from a guy who worked in the South Church burying ground. Shakespearean type, prone to giving drunken soliloquies in the back of her cab. Father Mike watched out for him – Father Mike watched out for a lot of people – and had told her not to pay the guy any mind. But she was thinking about those stories now. About coffins broken into from below, and cadavers covered in bite-marks.

She closed her eyes and tried to think of something else. Anything else. She wondered where Alessandra was; hopefully she was coming to the rescue.

All thought of the other woman was driven from her mind by the sound of something approaching the chamber. She huddled down as the thing prowled inside, sniffing the air. It was a blotch of black against black, but her eyes were used to the darkness now and she could sort of make out its shape. Something about the way it moved reminded her of a dog, but no dog could stand on its hind legs to better sniff the air.

It gave a gurgling snort and she knew that it had detected the odor of her blood. It crept toward the far sarcophagus, moving stealthily but eagerly. Its panting grew in volume, and the reek of it reached her where she crouched. Silently, she urged it on. It laid a paw on the lid and paused. For a moment, she thought it had figured out it was a trap.

Then, with a wild cry it flung itself into the sarcophagus, burrowing beneath the lid with desperate urgency. Quickly, Pepper erupted from her hiding place and charged toward the sarcophagus, bone gripped in both hands. The creature gave a frustrated wail and rose out from beneath the lid, yellow gaze sweeping the chamber. Its eyes widened almost comically as it caught sight of Pepper, and it hesitated.

That hesitation was her salvation. She bounded up onto the plinth and cracked it across the head with her bone. The blow was a good one this time, and the thing slumped back into the sarcophagus with a stifled grunt.

Pepper tossed the now-thoroughly shattered bone aside and threw her shoulder against the lid of the sarcophagus. It creaked, but didn't move. She hissed obscenities as she flung herself at it again and again, until finally it started to move. The creature began to stir as the lid began to slide back into place. A clawed paw – hand? – erupted from the shrinking gap and slashed wildly at her, knocking her hat from her head.

The claw was jerked back, out of sight, as the lid crashed into place at last. The echo of it filled the chamber. Pepper stumbled back, panting. Her shoulder ached, her arm hurt and she was hungry. But she'd done it.

"How do you like them apples, you dirty rat?" she bawled, kicking the side of the sarcophagus and immediately regretting it.

She hopped back, clutching her foot. The thing inside the sarcophagus began to shriek and hammer at the lid. It trembled and shifted, but not enough. It looked like it was trapped, at least for the moment.

Its shrieks took on a particular timbre – not just animal noise, but sounds that might have been words, in a dozen different languages. She knew only a bit of French, but she'd heard sailors swearing on the docks in Arkham, and recognized Portuguese and Italian when she heard it. Mind whirling, she reached down for another length of bone but froze as the noises became horribly familiar.

"Let me out, let me out, *let me out!*" the creature howled, in what was unmistakably, if somewhat guttural, English.

CHAPTER SIXTEEN
Red House

Alessandra watched the house the way a cat might study a bird. A cigarette hung limply from her lips, all but forgotten. A thin drizzle of smoke emerged from her mouth every so often. Finally, she plucked at her trousers and said, "Curious."

Trish gave her an impatient look. "Yeah? That all you got to say? We've been cooling our heels out here for twenty minutes. Are we going to knock or what?" They stood across the street from Cinabre's residence, in the lee of the local post office.

Alessandra glanced at her lazily. "You tell me. What do you know about Monsieur Cinabre that you did not share with me earlier?"

Trish looked away, as if checking the narrow street for observers. There were none, of course. Saint-Bertrand-de-Comminges was quiet, even this close to midday. They'd seen few locals, and always at a distance. No one had noticed them yet. Alessandra wondered whether Monsieur Cinabre had made his wishes known, somehow. Or perhaps it was simply that they were on the farthest outskirts of the village, in the foothills of the mountains.

Cinabre's home was not what she had expected. It was an

unusual 'L' shape, with a stone courtyard wall completing the square. The wall was not particularly high, or in particularly good shape. In fact, it looked as if a strong breeze might blow it over, save for the arched gateway. The house was in better condition, but at least two centuries old. The upper story was a new addition, probably within the last century. There was a wide expanse of lawn to the rear, blanketed in fruit trees. Beyond them, a mountain view fit to take one's breath away. All in all, a more humble abode than she'd pictured.

After a few moments, Trish said, "Have you ever heard of the Red Coterie?"

Alessandra shook her head. "No. Enlighten me."

"When you were in Arkham, you tangled with a guy named Sanford, right?" Trish looked at her. "The Coterie is like Sanford and his bunch, only they're spread across the world rather than the just the US of A. A global network of occultists, with their fingers in every pie you can imagine."

"And you are working with them?"

Trish gave a slight smile. "In a manner of speaking. Look, we both know the world is a lot stranger than the average citizen would believe. A strange world calls for strange alliances. Sometime back, I made contact with the Coterie – better to have them in the tent than out, you know?"

Alessandra didn't answer. Trish fell silent. Her revelation was calculated, Alessandra suspected. Trish wasn't a fool. She would tell Alessandra only the bare minimum – enough to string her along, not enough to cause any trouble. After a moment, Trish said, "Cinabre is a member. I've never spoken to him. His name came up once."

"And that is all you know?" Alessandra doubted that.

Trish nodded, then paused. "I don't suppose I have to tell

you that we need to be careful here. These Coterie types aren't generous sorts. Once they've got their hands on something, they don't give it up."

"Which is why I have no intention of asking," Alessandra said. The Coterie was familiar enough, though she'd never heard of them. Secret societies were a ducat a dozen these days, especially in Europe. It was no surprise to find one involved in this matter. She finished her cigarette and stubbed it out on the wall. "You take the front, I'll take the back."

"What?"

"Did I stutter? I intend to retrieve the book. To do so, I need you to distract this Cinabre, as well as Monsieur Lapp, should he be there."

"And how am I supposed to do that?"

"Improvise. I am certain you two will have much to discuss." Alessandra started down the street without waiting for a reply. To her credit, Trish didn't argue.

Alessandra followed a circuitous route through the streets until she thought she was far enough away from the house. Then she made her way to the back lawn and the fruit trees. There were enough trees that she could use them as cover. If good fortune was with her, she could also use one to get to a second story window. As old Nuth had often said, trees were a burglar's best friend.

As she navigated the orchard, she noted that it seemed as if no one was tending it. The husks of rotted fruit decorated the ground, and the faint hum of insects was audible. She reached the back of the house with no incident, and quickly kicked off her shoes and shimmied up a tree close to the rear wall of the building.

The trees were old and sturdy, and the branch she selected

had no trouble bearing her weight long enough for her to reach the second story window ledge and step off. It was a narrow perch, but she had some experience with that.

The shutters had been painted red; not recently, but it had only just begun to fade. She gave them a tentative tug, and found them locked. The shutter would have a latch on the inside, but there was only a slim gap to reach it. She reached into her coat and extracted a thin, flat strip of metal. She had a number of tools stashed about her person for just such an occasion. Most were small and easy to conceal. This was the largest, and could be passed off as a nail file at a pinch.

She slid the strip into the gap and blindly maneuvered the end of the tool beneath the latch. When she was certain she'd hooked it, she popped the free end hard enough to chip paint off the shutter. The latch rattled loose and she hurriedly swung it outward, exposing the windows. Often, the windows would be left unsecured if the shutters were latched. That proved to be the case here, thankfully. She wasn't particularly worried about being heard. Despite what popular fiction insisted, strange noises were rarely investigated on the rare occasions they were heard.

She flipped the strip flat and slid it between the window and the frame. Then, slowly, she began to turn it. The metal was stiff enough to force the window open a crack, enough for her to get her fingers through. She caught the window and dragged it upward. A rush of cold, almost damp air buffeted her as she did so.

The interior of the house was far cooler than she thought it ought to have been, even given the time of year. Perhaps Monsieur Cinabre did not care for the heat. She'd heard there was a Barcelonian physician of some note – now living in New

York – who espoused the theory that cold conditions were the key to physical longevity.

Once inside, she slid the metal strip back into her coat and took a look around. She was in a well-appointed bedroom – thick carpet, and a bed made of handcrafted oak. Empty shelves sat along one wall, and the roof beams sloped at an angle on the other. The only thing out of the ordinary was the wallpaper – no, rather the walls themselves.

What she had first assumed was wallpaper was, in actuality, paint. Someone had decorated the walls to resemble a thick jungle, like something Rosseau might have painted – save that all the foliage was in varying shades of red. There were even hints of animals – there, a flash of emerald feathers; and there, the twitching tip of what might have been a monkey's tail.

In fact, the longer she studied it, the more real it seemed. The cool air became damp and heavy with a subtle heat. She could smell growing things and wondered if Cinabre was a gardener. That might explain the mural. Almost against her better judgment, she reached out to touch one of the painted trees and felt something rough beneath her fingers. She jerked her hand back and heard the cry of something that might have been a tropical bird as it rose into the air, wings whirring.

The musky, sweet smell of flowers enveloped her, and she heard grass rustle beneath her feet as she stepped back. Red grass, red trees. Red sun overhead. Red heat beating down. She was sweating beneath her jacket; it was hard to breathe. It reminded her of Malaysia. Only in Malaysia the trees weren't the color of blood, and the air didn't smell of – what was that? Something sweet, but sickly as well.

She shook her head, trying to banish the vision. "Not real," she murmured. It wasn't real – couldn't be real. Something arose from the bushes to her left. It looked like a bird but it wasn't. Not any sort of bird she was familiar with. She turned, but could not find the bed or the window, and felt the first flicker of fear.

She started walking, trying to find the walls, but she could find nothing but trees and grass. It was as if the room had evaporated – or had never been. She searched for long minutes, until, from behind her came a low, throaty growl.

She turned, reaching for her revolver as she did so. There was something in the trees, moving between them. Something big; she thought of Rousseau's tiger, with its wide, staring eyes and red jaws, and the flicker of fear became a flame. It wasn't real, couldn't be, and yet she could smell the raw, animal stink of whatever was stalking her – like an abattoir on a hot summer's day.

Rubbery leaves that stung her skin like nettles brushed against her as she turned. It was as if the impossible jungle was closing in on her. The growling persisted, growing louder before fading away, as if whatever it was were pacing about the room.

She backed away from it even as she tried to watch all directions at once. When it lunged, she ducked. The smell of it – rancid and perfumed – washed over her as it vanished into the trees with a flick of a strangely segmented tail. She drew her revolver, but didn't fire. There was no telling whether bullets would even hurt such a creature, whatever it was.

But following it with her eyes, she spotted something incongruous; a doorknob, jutting from the trunk of a tree. Could that be the way out? There was only one way to find out. She scrambled toward it, through the red grass and stinging leaves.

The animal pursued her in a leisurely fashion, as if catching her were not the point. She caught a glimpse of a face that might have been a man's, but stretched across a great skull. Worse was its familiarity. Whatever it was, it resembled Lapp. It was Lapp's smile that curled across those distorted features and Lapp's eyes that blazed impossibly yellow. But those were not Lapp's teeth – not those serrated fangs.

It circled her, forcing her back toward the doorknob, until she felt it dig into her back. She fumbled for it, waiting for the creature to make a leap. But it didn't. A door opened in the substance of the jungle, swinging outward. She backed through it gratefully and slammed it shut in the grinning face of her pursuer.

Behind her, someone coughed politely. She spun, pistol raised. Lapp stepped back, hands at his sides, a cruel smile on his face. "Monsieur Cinabre sent me to check on your progress – and to ask if you would like some refreshment." He checked his pocket watch.

She stared at him, her finger on the trigger. "What was that?" she asked. She could see a window in the hall beyond him. Orange light filtered through. It was later in the day than it had been. Afternoon now, rather than morning. How long had she been in there?

He cocked his head. "What was what?"

"That!" she snapped, yanking the door open. Lapp peered past her.

"The guest room, I believe."

She risked a glance and saw that the room was as she'd first seen it. The trees were back on the walls and safely two-dimensional. The only difference was the wide moon-face of the creature, barely visible between two trees. Its smug expression mimicked that of Lapp. She turned back to him and something in her gaze made his smile falter.

He swallowed and stepped back as she let the door swing shut. "Yes, well. They're waiting downstairs. If you'll follow me." He turned, but paused. "I would advise against wandering off. This house is deceptively large and it is very easy for one unfamiliar with it to become disorientated." He laughed sourly.

"We would hate to lose you, at this late stage."

CHAPTER SEVENTEEN
Monsieur Cinabre

Trish tossed aside her cigarette and headed for the front of Cinabre's house. She figured she'd given Zorzi enough time to break, if not enter. The plan rankled. It wasn't bad, but it lacked a certain panache. It was all too brute force for Trish's liking. She preferred her plans to have as few moving parts as possible. There was less chance of something going wrong, that way.

Not that Zorzi's plan was particularly complex. But it relied on an assumption of unpredictability. Zorzi assumed that Cinabre wasn't expecting someone to break in. Or maybe she just assumed that she could avoid or outwit whatever defenses he had in place. Either way, it was an assumption and Trish didn't like assumptions.

She crossed the street to the gate and found it open. It had appeared closed before, but maybe she'd simply been mistaken. The courtyard was empty, save for some outdoor furniture and a few odds and ends that might have interested an antique dealer. The heavy flagstones had the appearance of being regularly swept, and she wondered whether Lapp attended to it personally. The thought made her smile.

No dogs barked, no one called out. She paused in front of

the door – and knocked. A brisk knock. She liked to think of it as her official knock. The knock of someone on important business. There was no immediate answer. She didn't knock again. No point. They were expected, and no doubt she was being left to cool her heels. Petty, but standard with these old world types. The American upper crust prized the Protestant work ethic; even the Catholics. They liked to hustle you in and out according to a strict schedule, just to emphasize how little free time they had. But the Continentals – French, Spanish, whoever – made you wait, just to show you who was in charge.

Trish had gotten good at playing that game. She knew from experience that they wanted you to get impatient; to cede the advantage by getting upset before a single word had been spoken. So, she didn't. She just waited. Sometimes, depending on the importance of the conversation in question, she even left. That usually rustled their jimmies some.

She suspected that wouldn't work on Cinabre, though. He'd probably dealt with worse than her in his lifetime. She didn't know much about him; information on the known members of the Coterie was sparse at best – mostly just photos, a few intercepted letters and the like. There was the old knight, in Alexandria; the woman in Shanghai; the cavalier, in Venice. And here, Cinabre.

An assumed name, of course. What else could "Mister Cinnabar" be? A taunting reference to his membership in the Coterie. Some of them were like that; flamboyant. Or maybe arrogant was a better word. She'd found that was a common trait shared by most of these secret society types. A bit of hidden wisdom and they suddenly thought they were the elite. It was one of the reasons she didn't like being in bed with these sorts. There was no telling which way they'd jump when it came down to it.

She heard footsteps on the other side of the door, and put a smile on her face. The door opened and Lapp glared at her. "You are late," he said.

"I wasn't aware I was on a timetable," she said, blithely, stepping past him and into the foyer. Lapp closed the door behind her and wordlessly showed her into the sitting room, where it turned out that Monsieur Cinabre awaited her.

He was much as the pictures had depicted; an older man, but how old was impossible to determine. He wore a red dressing gown over his thin frame, and his long, colorless hair was bound in a single serpentine plait. He wore red slippers on his feet, and was reclining on a claret-colored divan, reading a small book. A cup of coffee sat by his elbow on a side table, alongside an ash tray and a large, brass lighter.

The room was crowded; claustrophobic. Shelves of various styles and materials lined the walls. They were stuffed with books and bric-a-brac. Grotesque statuary crouched in the corners, or lurked atop the highest shelves like covert gargoyles. Decorative palm fronds, dyed red, covered the walls and a similarly hued Turkish rug had been unrolled across the floor beneath the divan. The plaster walls had been painted with scenes that looked as if they had been drawn from the planetary romances of Burroughs; great swooping towers and alien vistas that filled Trish with the faintest apprehension.

"Nice place," she said, as Cinabre set his book aside and looked at her.

"Aren't you dally?" he said. "Clobber's a bit naff, mind, but that's to be expected from a sharpy polone such as yourself. Care for a puff?" He offered her a cigarette case, but she declined with a polite wave. His greeting threw her for a moment. Circus lingo, she thought. Was it a joke, or a test? Maybe both.

"I'll smoke my own, thank you."

Cinabre gave her a comically sad look as he waved her to a seat opposite. "You wound me, dona. As if I would poison a representative of the United States government in my own home."

"Stranger things have happened."

Cinabre lit a cigarillo and nodded. "Mais oui, ducky." He snapped his lighter shut and thrust it into his dressing gown. "So what's the cackle?"

Trish paused, translating the slang. "We need to talk."

"I was under the impression that is what we were doing." He paused, head cocked, as if listening for something. A slow smile spread across his face and he chuckled. He gestured to Lapp. "Upstairs," he said. Lapp nodded and left the room. Cinabre saw her quizzical expression and said, "Someone's disturbed the kitty."

Trish nodded as if she understood. "It has come to our attention that you recently came into possession of a certain proscribed text. We would like to acquire it from you – for a fair price, of course."

"Of course," Cinabre said, reclining in his seat. "And which text might that be? I am a collector, as you know. Books are constantly coming in and out of this house."

"*Cultes des Goules*," Trish said. Despite his professed ignorance, she was certain he already knew what she was after.

"I am not certain I have a copy of that," he said.

"I think you do."

"No flies, I've nanti a volume by that title in the latty."

Trish wasn't sure what some of those words meant, but she got the gist. She sighed and pulled out her pack of cigarettes and made a show of selecting one. It gave her a moment to think. "I don't suppose mentioning that it's a matter of national security would change your mind about that?"

"Your nation or mine?" he asked, with a crooked smile.

Trish paused. "I don't think it's too much to ask that you stick to the terms of the deal we have in place, Monsieur Cinabre." It was a risk to bring that up, but a calculated one.

Cinabre was silent for a moment. Then, "Our… alliance with your organization is a great disappointment to me, personally. I spoke against it, but was outvoted."

"Times change," Trish said, smoothly. "The shadows aren't as deep as they used to be. Not as easy to stay hidden, these days."

"No, sadly, it is not." Cinabre puffed on his cigarillo and studied her through heavy-lidded eyes. "Once, my privacy would have been inviolate. Now, unexpected and unwelcome guests are the norm."

"Guests plural," Trish said. "Someone making a nuisance of themselves, monsieur?" Not the Comte, she thought. Bera, then? Or was there yet another player in the game? One she hadn't managed to identify yet.

"Besides yourself, you mean?"

Trish gave him a sultry smile. "Obviously."

Cinabre snorted. "You're aiming that gun at the wrong target, my dear. I like a bit of fruit, me. Never been one for willets and thews, even in my youth."

Before Trish could parse that enough to reply, Lapp stumbled back into the room, rubbing the back of his head. He straightened and turned, mouth open as if to say something, but instead backed away. Hands raised, he said, "I found her in the jungle room. She is… somewhat perturbed, I believe."

"That is putting it mildly," Zorzi said, as she stepped into the room, her revolver trained on Lapp. "Something tried to eat me upstairs. One of your pets, I assume."

"I am not a pet sort of person," Cinabre said. If he was startled by the sight of her weapon, he gave no sign. Instead, he expelled a cloud of cigarette smoke and added, "I am not a gun person, either. Never been one for a bit of rough trade, me."

"You should try it before you dismiss it – or maybe Lapp here takes care of all of your needs, eh?" Zorzi said. Lapp flushed angrily, but said nothing. Zorzi grinned savagely. "A bit of a dolly dish, if you like the type."

Cinabre guffawed. "I happen to, yes."

Zorzi lowered her weapon. "I make no judgments, auntie." She began to prowl about the room with a sort of insouciant carelessness. It was an act, Trish knew. Zorzi was rattled, but trying to take control of the situation in the only way she knew how. It was an admirable attempt, but Trish didn't think Cinabre was buying it. He didn't seem the type to be easily impressed by a bit of swagger.

Cinabre puffed on his cigarillo and watched Zorzi. "So, you would be the young woman who so upset Sanford in Arkham." He pulled his cigarillo out of his mouth and examined it. "Not that he doesn't deserve it, that boy."

Zorzi snorted. "Bonaroo."

Trish sighed. "Would you two stop with the funny talk, please? I'm unfamiliar with the dialect and I find it off-putting."

Cinabre laughed and looked at her. "My apologies. I picked up the local lingo while working a Punch and Judy show in the

West End. Once one starts, it is quite hard to stop. Isn't that so, Countess Zorzi?"

"Quite. Though you do not look like a Punch and Judy man to me."

Cinabre chuckled good naturedly and made a dismissive gesture. "It was an idle pleasure. One seeks them out, when one gets as old as I. Though maybe you know something about that, hmmm?"

Zorzi smiled. "It was not exactly a pleasure in my case. I was pretending to be a young man, in order to… well. That is neither here nor there."

Cinabre returned her smile, and Trish found herself vaguely discomfited that they were getting along so chummily. A glance at Lapp showed he shared her sentiments, even if he wasn't as good at hiding them.

"A story I simply must hear the rest of, one day," Cinabre said. "If you are looking for the book, it is not here. As I told your friend earlier."

"Then where is it?" Zorzi asked, turning to face the old man. "Be a dear and give me a hint, would you?"

Cinabre rose slowly to his feet and gave a desultory puff on his cigarillo. "Do you know how many unsavory sorts wish to acquire that volume? Frankly, I am doing the world a favor by keeping it safely under lock and key." He pointed the cigarillo at Zorzi. "Something you know a bit about these days, I think."

Trish looked at Zorzi, and saw that the other woman was somewhat taken aback by this statement. Cinabre continued. "I was surprised to learn of your new raison d'etre. A bit disappointed as well, I must say. You were the best thief I have ever known, Countess. Such talent, such élan, like the great thieves of the previous century. And now you do the little work of little men in little rooms. Academics – pfaugh. What do they know about the true value of anything?"

Zorzi paused and glanced at Trish. "The Americans call it a 'come-to-Jesus-moment', I believe." She raised her revolver and aimed it at Cinabre. Lapp tensed and made a strangled sound. Trish was on her feet a moment later.

"What's the play here, Zorzi?" she hissed.

Zorzi ignored her, her attentions fixed on Cinabre. "And whatever your opinion of me, I am still the greatest thief in Europe, whatever the reasons for my thievery. I want that book, monsieur, and I will have it one way or another."

CHAPTER EIGHTEEN
Jules

Pepper stared at the shuddering sarcophagus in shock. "You can talk?"

Silence fell. Then, "Of course I can talk. Why wouldn't I be able to talk?" The creature's voice was a bestial rasp, with the hint of an accent – not French or English, but something she'd never heard before. The sound of it made her slightly queasy.

Pepper blinked. "I mean, I just assumed … y'know, monsters can't talk."

"Monster?" it growled, in an offended tone of voice.

Unsettled by the incongruous tone, Pepper thumped on the lid of the sarcophagus with her bone club. "You did try to eat me, pally. Seems like a monster sort of thing to me."

A yellow eye appeared in the gap between the lid and the edge. "If I apologize, will you let me out?"

Pepper snorted. "Do I look like an idiot?"

There followed a moment's hesitation from the sarcophagus' captive. "… No?"

Pepper frowned. "What are you?"

"Jules."

"Jules?"

"My name is Jules."

"You have a name?" Pepper asked, bewildered by the turn the conversation had taken. It could talk – and now it had a name?

"Don't you have a name?"

"Yeah, but…" Pepper trailed off and shook her head. "Jules?"

"He was the first corpse I dug up. Jules Dupont, of Petit-Bersac. So… Jules." The eye narrowed. "What is your name, then?"

Pepper hesitated. "Pepper."

"Like the spice?" it asked, in evident confusion.

"Yeah. What about it?"

"It's funny." The thing – Jules – made an odd, coughing sound that she realized was supposed to be laughter. "You named yourself after food, just like we do. I didn't think your people did that sort of thing." A thin claw emerged from the hole and scratched at the stone. "I am very hungry, Pepper."

"Yeah?" she replied, at a loss as to how best to answer.

"Yes," Jules said, retracting his claw. "May I eat one of your fingers?"

Pepper took a quick step back from the sarcophagus. "Hell no!"

"Why?"

"Because it's my finger!"

"You are being rude."

"You're the one asking to eat my finger," Pepper shouted. Her voice echoed eerily back to her. "I don't know about where you come from, but in Arkham we don't ask to eat each other's fingers." She paused. "Not most of us, at any rate."

"Ah. Forgive me." Jules was silent for a moment. "In that case, how about a toe?" Then, slyly, "Surely you would not miss a toe?"

"No," Pepper snapped, faintly nauseated by the idea of it. "Forget it. You ain't eating any part of me, pal. I need all my bits. I got plans for them."

"But I am very hungry, Pepper. I have been trapped here for weeks, with only moldering bones to gnaw on. And while I am ordinarily very fond of chewing on bones, I could do with something a bit more… filling."

"I bet. No dice, wiseguy. You stay right there, until I can figure a way out of here." Pepper went back to the broken wall and peered into the gloom. It was definitely a cellar – but whose? She heard Jules' raspy laugh again and turned back. "I say something funny?"

"There is no way out. I looked."

Pepper hiked a thumb in the direction of the broken wall, though she was certain the creature couldn't see her, or it. "There's a door over there that says different."

Jules growled. "You do not want to go that way. It leads to his lair."

"Yeah, and who's that?"

"The one who put me here."

Pepper paused. "You mean the Comte?"

Jules grunted and fell silent. Pepper paused, considering her next words carefully. "He's the one who threw me in here. I guess he figured you'd eat me. Kill two birds with one stone, or something like that." She pushed her cap brim up and scratched her head. "Why'd he put you in here?"

"What does it matter? We are both trapped here. And when I get out of this sarcophagus, I will eat you. I will not be able to help myself." A low, slobbery sound emerged from the sarcophagus, and Pepper shivered. Jules continued. "Perhaps I will rename myself Pepper, as an apology."

"That a compliment, where you come from?"

"Yes. It is how we show honor to those without whom we would starve." The lid of the sarcophagus shuddered slightly. It stilled, and she heard the creature pant in frustration. If what he was saying was true, he probably didn't have the strength to get out. Not yet, at least. "If you are going to run, I would do so now."

She turned back to the broken wall. "I'm through running. You want me, you can try your luck." The crack was bigger than she'd first thought. Not big enough for her to squeeze through, unfortunately. Not unless she were a lot skinnier and a lot more desperate. She gave the wall a tentative shove, and was rewarded by a soft grinding sound and a nose-full of dust. She sneezed and stepped back, flapping her hat in the direction of the wall.

"What are you doing?" Jules called out. He gave the sarcophagus lid another heave, and Pepper heard stone scrape stone. He'd managed to move it, if only a little bit. She needed to buy some time. It might help if she could get him talking.

"Nothing. Hey, so, what do you know about the Comte?" She started working at the edges of the crack with her hands, hoping she could loosen enough bricks to allow her to slip through. "Besides the obvious, I mean."

Jules gave a rattling snarl. "He is a heretic. A blasphemer."

"Really? That don't sound like him." Pepper pulled a brick loose and set it down as quietly as she could. No sense alerting Jules to what she was trying to do. He might find it in him to heave the lid off the sarcophagus if he thought she was about to escape. "You guys share a church or something?"

"He lied to us," Jules said. Then, hesitantly, "To me."

Pepper paused and glanced back at the sarcophagus. "Oh yeah? How so?"

"I do not wish to speak of it. What are you doing? I hear bricks moving."

"Just a bit of redecorating. Keep talking. Why does he have you in here? You do something to upset him?"

"I refused to help him. He did not take it well."

Pepper paused again. "Help him do what?"

"Let me out and I'll tell you."

Pepper snorted. "You just said you'd eat me."

"But I'll tell you what you want to know first. Won't that be satisfying?"

"Not so much." Pepper pried loose another brick. "So, you refused to help him and he shut you up down here – why?"

"He hopes to starve me into submission," Jules said. The sarcophagus lid bumped against the rim. "Almost got it that time. Are you certain you do not wish to run?"

"Will that work?"

Jules laughed. "Running? No."

Pepper tossed a brick at the sarcophagus, eliciting a yelp from Jules. "Not that. Starving you … will it work?"

"No. Better death than what the fool has planned. Only… I am so very hungry. If I could taste just a bit of meat, a slathering of marrow, I could resist him all the better." Jules paused. "Really, when you think about it, it's in your best interests to feed me. With enough food in my belly, I might even be strong enough to kill him, when next he comes down here."

Pepper turned back to the crack and redoubled her efforts. She'd widened the gap some, but not enough. She flung her shoulder against it, hoping to loosen a bunch of them at once. "I'll think about it. He come down here often?"

"More often of late," Jules said, panting slightly. He sounded worked up, like he was excited about something. "It's almost time, you see. Almost time." He paused. "I can smell you. Your sweat – your fear. I am sorry you are afraid."

"Who said I'm afraid?" she barked. But he was right. Her heart was pounding, and her arm was starting to hurt again, and her head ached from lack of water and sleep. She wanted to drop what she was doing and run away, maybe find someplace to hide. But she kept at it. "And almost time for what? He planning a shindig?"

Jules was panting louder now, and she could hear his claws scraping the stonework. "The walls between this world and the other grow thin this time of year, and soon they will grow porous enough for your kind to travel between them, the way we do."

Pepper bit back a cry of triumph as a small section of brickwork gave way, enlarging the crack a suitable amount for her to squeeze through. She glanced back at the sarcophagus. "Yeah, so? He planning a trip?"

Jules gave a hoarse laugh. "He wants me to lead him to the sacred places of my people. But I will not. *I will not!*" He gave a convulsive heave against the lid. It cracked in half, and he erupted upward.

Thinking quickly, Pepper snatched up a brick and chucked it toward the dim, pale shape of the creature as it leapt down out of the sarcophagus and bounded toward her. Then, without waiting to see whether her missile struck home, she dove through the crack and into the room beyond.

She scrambled hastily to her feet as Jules struck the wall from the opposite side. Bricks fell, bouncing off her raised arm and legs, knocking her sprawling. Jules clambered upright, snarling wordlessly, his yellow eyes fixed on her. She snatched up a brick and flung it at those awful eyes, but the creature ducked aside and caught at her leg.

Pepper screamed as ragged claws scratched her skin, and she lashed out with her other foot. Her wild kick connected with something and her attacker fell away with a grunt. She rolled over and flung herself at the steps she'd glimpsed earlier. If she could just get up them – what? It wasn't like they were going to let her out. But a chance was better than nothing. She half-ran, half-crawled up the steps to the door and slammed her fists against it, calling out hoarsely. "Someone, anyone! Get me out of here!"

Jules raced up the steps behind her, eyes blazing with a wild hunger. Pepper spun, ready to make her final moments count – when there came the sound of a lock being opened. The door was dragged backward, and she toppled into the well-lit room beyond with a startled squawk. She hadn't actually expected that to work.

Jules froze as the light struck him, and he raised a thin claw to protect his eyes. Pepper stared at him. She thought she'd been prepared for whatever he might look like, but she'd been wrong. The creature was short and hunched, but thickly muscled. It looked as if it had been cobbled together from all the worst elements of a hyena, an ape and a corpse. It fell back from the light, tumbling down the steps with an eerie wail.

Selim caught the back of her shirt and dragged her aside, before stepping into the breach and firing his revolver down into the tomb below. She heard the wail trail into silence as Jules fled back into the darkness, and she felt an impractical stab of pity for the creature. "What was he?" she asked, as Selim slammed the door and relocked it.

"A *ghul* – a tomb-thing. An eater of the dead. Are you injured?"

"Scratched up, but I'll live," she said, climbing to her feet.

She looked around and found that she was in what looked to be a wine cellar. "Let me guess… we're in the chateau?" She wondered why he'd opened the door. Why had he even been down here? Was he coming to find her? His face gave no answers.

Selim nodded. "It broke through the old wall, into the new crypt below," he said. "Originally, we hoped to keep it confined to the ancestral vaults, but it was too hungry – too persistent. Like you, it was looking for a way to escape." He held up the pistol in his hand, as if weighing it. "Like you, it failed."

"Yeah, so I see. Now what?" Pepper asked, looking up at him. Selim grunted and gestured with his weapon before holstering it.

"Come. The Comte will wish to speak with you."

CHAPTER NINETEEN
Hospitality

Cinabre laughed. "You will not shoot me, I think." He raised a hand, interrupting Alessandra's reply. "Not because you lack the fortitude, obviously. But because you know that if you do, your chances of getting what you have come for lessen substantially. And you know that I know this, thus I can say with some confidence that this is not a threat – merely an affirmation of the seriousness of the situation."

Alessandra paused, then smiled and lifted the revolver and rested the barrel on her shoulder. She found herself oddly pleased by his reaction. She liked Cinabre, despite herself. "How astute of you, monsieur. But surely now you see my predicament. I must have the book, and I am driven to extremes to acquire it."

Cinabre glanced at Trish. "So I see. Allying with the Black Chamber is proof of that, if nothing else." Trish grimaced and looked away from the man's amused smile. Cinabre gestured to Lapp. "Coffee for our guests, please," he said.

Lapp frowned. "I do not think I should leave you here alone."

Cinabre sniffed. "I am perfectly capable of protecting

myself, boy. Now go do as I asked – please. Merci." Lapp's frown deepened, but he departed. Alessandra watched him go. She didn't trust Cinabre's associate. There was something unsettling about the man; or perhaps it was just the lingering unease from her experience upstairs.

Since her time in Arkham, she'd come to understand that the world was a far stranger place than she'd previously admitted. But she was not so hardboiled as to shake such encounters off with a laugh and a smile. Her skin crawled at the thought of that alien jungle and the unseen beast that stalked it. Had that been a trap, or something else?

As if reading her thoughts, Cinabre said, "I have resided here for a considerable amount of time; and in those years, I have made the place my own. The only traps here are for those who mean me harm." He smiled. "Be glad I sent Lapp to look for you. More than one would-be assassin is still wandering in the red jungle and far worse places besides." He looked at Trish again. "I do believe you might even know one of them, my dear. A Russian fellow – Muscovite, rather. Following the same trail you did, though a good deal less efficiently I must say."

Trish snorted. "That's Bolsheviks for you. Couldn't follow a paper trail if it was marked in crayon."

"Not something your lot have a problem with," Cinabre said. "Very good at sniffing out breadcrumbs, aren't you? Too good, I would say. That is why I argued against our alliance, if you were wondering. But others were convinced that your resources might prove useful to our agendas. As ours will no doubt prove useful to your own."

Trish spoke up. "And as I mentioned earlier, that's why we're here, monsieur. You have a resource that we need."

"So this is Black Chamber business, then?" Cinabre asked.

Trish shrugged. "Call it what you like. So long as you give us what we came for."

"Or else what? I know she won't shoot me."

"She might not. But I sure as hell will." Trish drew her own weapon from under her coat and pointed it at the old man. Cinabre seemed momentarily taken aback. Alessandra knew how he felt. She didn't particularly want to see the old man dead.

"I thought you were the one who wanted to talk to him," she said, staring at Trish.

"We are talking. Think of this as a tried and true colonial conversational gambit." Trish sat back down and gestured for Cinabre to do the same. He did so, somewhat reluctantly. Alessandra wondered if he regretted sending Lapp out of the room.

"I thought better of you, Miss Scarborough," he said.

"You'd be surprised at how many people say that to me." Trish settled back in her seat. "If I limited myself to the expectations of others, I'd never get a damn thing done. So… talk, monsieur."

"Your superiors will hear of this," Cinabre began.

"No they won't." Trish glanced at Alessandra. "Take a load off, Countess. Monsieur Cinabre was just about to tell us where the book is."

Alessandra sat down in a nearby chair. Though Trish had not yet spelled out who her masters were, Alessandra had made the educated guess. The Black Chamber was America's spy apparatus – diligent, if somewhat inexperienced in her opinion, compared to similar European networks. But obviously Trish had more experience than she'd let on, even if her methodology was somewhat clumsy.

"It is not here," Cinabre protested.

Trish smiled. "No? Well then, tell us what you know about all this."

"Who says I know anything?"

"Your bunch pride themselves on knowing everything. So spill."

Cinabre glanced at Alessandra. "Is this who you have chosen to work with, then?"

She looked at him. "Desperate times call for desperate measures."

Cinabre nodded, though whether in agreement or merely acknowledgment, she couldn't say. It was hard to read him. He was extraordinarily composed for a collector of old books – especially one with a gun in his face. Again, his gaze strayed to Trish. He sighed. "There has been a certain… murmuration of late. A ripple in the water, so to speak. A little fish, aiming to bite off more than he can chew."

"The Comte d'Erlette," Trish said.

Cinabre puffed on his cigarillo and nodded again. "The very same. My associates and I have been keeping a weather eye on that young man. Too much knowledge can be as bad as too little when it comes to these sorts of matters."

Alessandra frowned. "Your associates… would that be the Coterie?"

Cinabre smiled. "You are more well informed than I thought." His eyes flicked to Trish. "Or perhaps someone decided to fill you in, eh?"

"Forewarned is forearmed," Trish said, with a shrug. "Besides, what's a few spilled secrets between friends?" She smiled and lowered her pistol. But she didn't put it away. "And we are all friends, aren't we? Because it sounds to me like we want the same thing."

"And what might that be?" Cinabre asked.

"To stop Henri," Alessandra said. Cinabre paused.

"Ah. I had heard that you and he had once – but, who is not a fool in their youth?" He waved a hand in a gesture of dismissal. Alessandra frowned.

"I only wanted to get close to his library, I assure you." She slid her revolver back into her jacket. "And it is something from that library he wants back."

"*Cultes des Goules*, yes, so Miss Scarborough said. But I cannot in good conscience let you have it back. Especially not if you are going to give it to him."

"Why especially? What is he up to?" Trish broke in. "You said the Coterie have been watching him – why?"

Cinabre took a pull on his cigarillo. "Why do we watch anyone, madam? Because they have something we want, or because they are planning something we cannot allow. Since the former has already been taken care of, it stands to reason it would be the latter, no?"

Alessandra felt a flicker of impatience. She wasn't above a bit of banter under the right circumstances, but she was keenly aware of time's passing. Every moment wasted in cryptic conversation was another moment Pepper drew closer to death. "What is he planning? Why does he need the book?"

Cinabre paused and studied her. "Why are you helping him?" he asked, after a moment's silence. "After all the trouble you went to, to steal that book in the first place… why help him now?"

"He is holding a friend of mine hostage. I return the book, he returns them."

"He won't, you know."

Alessandra closed her eyes. "I admit the probability is high.

But I must do something. I cannot simply leave her to her fate – even if she is already dead. Whatever else, I must try."

Cinabre grunted. "Why not simply rescue her?"

Alessandra looked at him. "I know Henri well enough to know that he has already thought of that. He will be waiting for me to try something. And he probably has people following me even now, with orders to take the book once I find it." She sank back into her chair, suddenly very tired. "I am in a bind, monsieur. I cannot get close to Henri without the book, and I cannot rescue my friend unless I get close to Henri."

"Add to that, we don't even know where he's taken Miss Kelly," Trish said.

"His estates," Alessandra said, absently. Trish looked at her. Alessandra met her questioning gaze with a crooked smile. "Henri took her back to his estates. He did not mention a location – only a deadline. Thus, he intended that I should bring the book to him at a place known to both of us. Ergo, his estates."

Cinabre clapped politely. "Clever. Then, as I said, I have long admired your cunning." He stubbed out his cigarillo and stood. "Very well. We cannot let an innocent suffer for our sins, can we? Rude, if nothing else."

Alessandra shot to her feet. "You mean you will give us the book?" she asked in disbelief. She'd thought Cinabre a harder nut to crack than that.

"I will."

"Why the change of heart?" Trish asked, suspiciously.

Cinabre looked at her. "I have a soft heart."

Trish laughed and stood. "I wouldn't buy that with a wooden nickel."

Cinabre shrugged. "What you believe or do not believe is

of no concern to me. Come. The book is in my library. I… ah! Lapp. We will not need the coffee after all." He directed the last at Lapp, as the man came in bearing a tray. Lapp paused.

"The library?" he said, in a tone of horror. "B- but… why?"

Cinabre smiled benignly. "Because that is where my books are."

"I thought you said the book was not here," Alessandra said.

Cinabre nodded. "It is not. It is in my library. Come, this way." He left the room, crooking a finger for them to follow. Alessandra looked at Trish, and the other woman gestured for her to go first.

"After you. I insist."

Alessandra followed Cinabre through the house, to a small door set at the back. At first, she thought it must lead to an extension, or perhaps the back lawn. But as he reached it, Cinabre murmured something she didn't quite catch and gestured. There was a flare of violet light, and something that might have been a sigil blazed on the surface of the door for an instant and then was gone. It happened so quickly that she found herself uncertain as to whether it had occurred at all. Cinabre opened the door and let it swing inward. The smell of old stone and something else – like rotting vegetation – wafted out.

"Please, enter," Cinabre said. Alessandra stepped past him, and found herself in a stone room of impossible proportions. She turned and saw Cinabre whispering to Trish. The other woman looked shaken – disturbed. Then Cinabre stepped into the room, hands clasped behind his back. As he did so, dozens of wall sconces erupted with light. Electrics, she assumed, but could see no wires.

In the sudden rush of light, dozens of heavy oaken

bookshelves were revealed. More than any room in the house should have been able to contain. Alessandra stared at them in bewilderment. She turned, taking in the rest of the room – the width of the walls, the height of the ceiling, the expanse of flagstones...

"You look perturbed," Cinabre murmured, at her elbow.

"It is too big," Alessandra whispered. She looked at him. "The room, it is too big." She felt her heart rate speed up, and a seed of ache bloomed at the base of her skull. It was the same feeling she'd had in the jungle room. A sense of wrongness, of being somewhere she should not be. She looked around, trying to calm herself.

"What do you...? Wait," Trish began. Alessandra knew that the other woman had seen it now as well. The room was simply too large to be contained in the house that it was ostensibly a part of. And the smell – it wasn't the smell of an old farmhouse, or indeed anywhere she was familiar with – it was more like the stink of jungle. As if in stepping through the door, they had put themselves across the world rather than a threshold. "What the hell is this?" Trish continued, glaring at Cinabre. "What are you trying to pull, Cinabre? Where are we?"

"My library, as I said." Cinabre ambled toward the shelves.

"Now let us find your book, eh?"

CHAPTER TWENTY
The Library

Alessandra traced the curve of the library wall with her fingers, trying to calculate the chamber's dimensions. But it resisted her efforts. Twice she circled the chamber, and twice she came up with a different result. The walls were stone – warm to the touch, which implied that outside was unpleasantly hot. "We're not in France anymore, are we?"

"Far from it, my dear," Cinabre called out, as he perused his shelves. He tapped at the spines of the books as he went. "I told you the book was safe in my hands. Every title in this library possesses a malign potency. That is why I seek them out and place them here, where no one can make use of their secrets."

"Except you," Trish said. "You and your pals in the Coterie." She was watching Cinabre like a hawk, sticking close to the man even after Alessandra had wandered off. If she was unsettled by their surroundings, she was doing a good job of hiding it. Alessandra wondered how often Trish had been… somewhere else.

Cinabre laughed. "But of course. How else are we to wage this long war of ours?"

"War?" Alessandra asked. "What war?"

"A figure of speech," Cinabre said, blithely. "There is always a war being waged, is there not? That is the story of humanity. At least in my experience." He paused. "I do not suppose we could switch out a Danish copy of the *Liber Ivonis* instead? I have always thought it a rather shoddy translation."

"I am afraid not," Alessandra said. She paused. "Just how many of these books did I acquire for you?"

Cinabre chuckled. "More than a few, I will admit. And not just books; and not just for me. Individuals of your perspicacity are rare indeed, Countess. When we find one, the Coterie makes certain to put their skills to good use."

"How often have I worked for this Coterie of yours?"

Cinabre looked at her. "More often than you might believe, but less than you are probably imagining. We have our own people to acquire things that catch our fancy. When they will not do, for whatever reason, we turn to outsiders such as yourself."

"Is Mellin Thevet a member of your... organization?"

Cinabre shook his head. "Goodness no. Thevet, like yourself, is simply a talented professional, whose services I employ when it suits me to do so." He turned his attentions back to his books. Alessandra turned hers back to the stone wall, and touched it again. The heat was still there, and the faint odor of rot.

She spoke up again. "There are no windows in your library."

"There are not." Cinabre looked at her again. "Does that matter?"

"I am curious about what is on the other side of the wall."

"You know what they say about curiosity," Trish muttered.

Alessandra didn't look at her. "No, I do not. Where are we?"

"I told you," Cinabre said. "My library."

"Yes, but where is your library located, monsieur?"

He smiled. "Are you sure you wish to know?"

"It would make me feel better."

"I do not think so. But, if you insist – I believe we are somewhere south of Hlanith, in the red jungles that ride the southernmost coast of the Cerenerian Sea." He gestured as he spoke. He reminded her of a tour guide. "This place has been here a long time. Or perhaps not long at all. It is hard to tell."

"I have never heard of any of those places," Alessandra said, but something about them sounded familiar nonetheless. Almost as if she had heard them before, but in a dream. Her skin prickled and she felt as if she should not be here. She shook her head. "None of this makes sense." She looked at Trish. "Do you understand any of this?"

Trish swallowed and shook her head. "More than I want to. Not enough to be helpful." She took a deep breath and looked around. "All that matters is we get the book and get out of here."

"That is not all that matters, but then, you know that," Cinabre said, coming toward them with a book in his hands. "Books are worthless, save for what they contain. And what this one contains is very interesting indeed." He tapped the cover with two fingers. "Each of the volumes in this library contains certain formulae. These rites can be used to unlock the doors of perception – time – reality itself."

Alessandra wanted to laugh, but given what she'd experienced of late she feared he was speaking the truth. "That is why he wants it back. Because he wishes to... enact one of these rites?"

Cinabre nodded. "I believe so."

"Which one?" Trish asked, glancing at Alessandra.

"How many days did he give you to find the book?" Cinabre asked. He looked at Alessandra. "Was it three?"

Slowly, she nodded. "Yes. Is that significant?"

"In two days' time, it will be the autumnal equinox. Such periods are often the best times for these rituals. They are when the walls between worlds are at their thinnest."

"Do you know which rite it is?" Trish asked, softly.

"No. And I would hesitate to even hazard a guess." Cinabre flipped the book open and carefully turned the thin, yellowing pages. "Do you know who wrote this book?"

"His grandfather," Alessandra said. They both looked at her. "So he claimed," she added. "I did not check the provenance of the book myself, you understand."

"No, I don't suppose you would have," Trish said. She reached for the book, but Cinabre stepped back. "What?"

"I am not giving the book to you, Miss Scarborough," he said. He snapped the book shut and extended it to Alessandra. "I am giving it to the person who needs it."

Alessandra hesitated, but only for an instant. She took the book and looked at it. It was a humble thing, to hold so much weight. A plain black cover, with a heavy spine and faded lettering. Hardly the moldering, maggoty tome one might expect. Henri had told her that he'd had it rebound, when the original cover had started to crumble. He'd been quite proud of his library; of the work he'd done to preserve it. But it had been as nothing compared to Cinabre's.

Cinabre tapped the book with a finger. "The original manuscript was composed by one Antoine-Marie Augustin de Montmorency-les-Roches, the Comte d'Erlette – an ill-starred ancestor of the current holder of the title. I am told he was involved in some way in the Affair of the Poisons, though that could be hearsay. His notes, taken during his unfortunate association with a Parisian ghoul-cult of some infamy, were later compiled and organized by his descendant, Francois-Honoré Balfour, who expanded it with his own... researches and published it at his own expense."

"A family affair," Alessandra said.

Cinabre nodded. "Oh, very much so. The d'Erlette line is one plagued by tales of vampirism, lycanthropy and other assorted horrors. They are polluted by shadows, in the way of only the best families of Europe."

"I am aware," Alessandra said. During her brief time with Henri, she had attended more than one so-called black mass – though at the time, she'd thought them nothing more than a dalliance of the idle rich. Now, she could not help but wonder what exactly she had unwittingly participated in. The thought sent a shiver through her. "What does it matter?"

"It means the Comte knows what he's doing," Trish supplied. "It means, if he wants the book back, it's because he's got something big planned. And whatever it is, it'll probably come with collateral damage."

"Like Pepper," Alessandra said.

"Like Paris," Trish corrected. She paused and ran a hand through her hair. "I should call this in. I haven't reported to my superiors since Angoulême. If he is planning something, we might need backup – or at least more bodies to throw at the problem."

Cinabre grunted. "Bodies are not the issue. The d'Erlette line is rooted in grave earth. They have long made common cause with the charnel hounds."

"Charnel..." Alessandra snapped alert. "You said ghoul-cult.

As in, eaters of the dead?" She had encountered something similar in Arkham – a society of aristocratic necrophages. Cinabre glanced at her.

"If you are thinking of the late Mr Orne and his debauched group, I am afraid that they were but dilettante pretenders to a legacy that outstrips our species itself. The creatures I am referring to are not human. Some of them may have once been as we are, but now they are something far worse."

"Madam Bera," Trish said, glancing at Alessandra. "Does that name mean anything to you, monsieur?"

Cinabre frowned and for the first time Alessandra thought he was truly startled. "Perhaps. Why do you ask?"

"She wants the book," Alessandra said. Cinabre raised an eyebrow.

"And you know this how?"

"She told me."

"When?"

"Angoulême," Alessandra said. She paused. "And she might know that you have it."

Cinabre paled. "That is… unfortunate. I…" He trailed off, head cocked to the side. Like a dog hearing a whistle. "Do you hear that?"

Alessandra was about to ask what he meant, when she did – a familiar, faint scratching. Like a chisel on mortar. Her skin crawled as the sound permeated the room.

Skritch. Skritch. Skritch.

"How could they have found this place?" Trish asked, reaching for her pistol. "That's impossible, right? You said it was impossible, Cinabre."

Skritch. Skritch. Skritch.

"Not for them," Cinabre said, grimly. "They can travel

through these lands more easily than I." He turned toward the door. "We must go. Hurry!"

Skritch. Skritch. Skritch.

Alessandra and Trish hurried after him as he headed for the door. But even as Cinabre reached it, it was smashed from its hinges. Alessandra jerked Cinabre back as the door crashed to the floor. Madam Bera stepped inside, dragging Lapp after her by his collar. The man was alive, but dazed, his temple bruised by a forceful blow.

Bera grinned at them, the edges of her smile stretching too far, too wide. "Hello again," she purred. "Is that the book?"

Alessandra shifted the book out of easy reach. "You can have it when I am finished with it. How does that sound?"

Bera cocked her head. "Give me the book." She held out her free hand. "Give me the book, and we will feast on your marrow."

"Surely you mean or," Alessandra said.

Bera gave a guttural chuckle. "No. My cousins and I have journeyed far, and we are hungry. You have led us a fine chase, Countess. But it is done. We will not let the traitor d'Erlette use what he has stolen." She lifted Lapp to his feet with no sign of strain, and shoved him into Cinabre's arms. "Now give me the book," she howled, all pretense of civility vanished in an instant.

"Absolutely not," Trish said, her pistol swinging up. She fired, and Bera ducked aside, quick as a cat. But as she did so, a heavy, bestial shape barreled through the doorway and launched itself at Trish, claws wide. It crashed into her, and they rolled across the floor. Alessandra turned to help, but felt a bone-cracking grip on her arm and found herself face-to-face with Bera. The other woman caught her by the throat and flung her backward with a single, convulsive heave.

Alessandra crashed into a bookshelf, and felt it sway with a groan. Books rained down on her and as she fought her way free, she shoved the *Cultes des Goules* into the pile. Bera swooped down on her, teeth bared. Still on the floor, Alessandra kicked the ghoul-woman in the gut. Bera doubled over, and Alessandra hit her in the head with a copy of the *Book of Eibon*. Bera sprawled beside her, and Alessandra raised the book and drove the spine into the other woman's throat – or tried to, at least.

Bera caught the book and ripped it from her hand. "I will gut you," she hissed. Her eyes were wild – yellow. Beast-eyes. Alessandra almost froze at the sight of them. But instead, she snatched up another book and flung it full in Bera's face, momentarily distracting her. Alessandra scrambled to her feet, and went for her revolver.

Even as she fumbled the weapon from her jacket pocket, Bera crouched – and sprang.

CHAPTER TWENTY-ONE
Intruder

Pepper sat hunched in her chair in the Comte's study, trying to ignore the hunger pangs gnawing at her insides. It had been nearly a day since she'd eaten, and everything was starting to go blurry at the edges. Just as she'd started to worry that they were planning on letting her starve to death, Selim came in, carrying a covered platter. He set it beside her on the desk and removed the cover, revealing an assortment of fruit, cheeses and pastry.

"Eat, girl," he said. "You will need your strength."

"For what? Your boss got something special planned?"

"You might say that," the Comte said, as he closed the door to the study behind him. He went to the sideboard and poured himself a drink. He looked... worn down, somehow. Like he'd been up all night. While he sipped his drink, she reached for a pastry. It was good. Then, she figured a rotten apple would have tasted good right about then.

"So, you survived," the Comte said, as he watched her eat. "I honestly was not expecting that. Perhaps Alessandra chose more wisely than I appreciated." He set his glass down and gave her a glance. He was as tight as an owl, Pepper realized –

or at least part of the way there. Maybe that was what he'd been up to all night. She wasn't sure whether that was a good thing or not. She had the Comte pegged as a mean drunk. "Would you care for a drink, Miss Kelly?" he asked, after a moment.

She glanced at the window. "Bit early, ain't it?"

"Hair of the dog, as you Americans say."

"Then yeah, I could go for a snootful," Pepper said, carefully.

The Comte smiled. "Wine or coffee? I would offer a pastis, but – well. You may dress like a man, but we both know better, don't we?"

Pepper sank back into her chair and forced a smile. "I thought we were talking about drinks, not pastries." Despite her comment, she knew what a pastis was; Alessandra had let her taste it, just the once. But once had been enough; it had been like drinking licorice.

The Comte frowned. "Coffee, then?"

"Depends. You got any whisky?"

Selim snorted, and the Comte rang for a servant. When the latter arrived, he said, in English, "Bring a coffee for Miss Kelly, please." He turned back to Pepper. "I would not want you to get the idea I am planning on poisoning you, no?"

Pepper leaned forward. "You already locked me up in a tomb with a monster. Poison is way down on my list of concerns."

The Comte chuckled. "Yes, well, you handled yourself with aplomb, from what Selim tells me. Trapped the brute in a box – ha! I am mortified I did not think of such a thing."

"Yeah, well, not everyone is as smart as me," Pepper said. She was hoping to get under his skin, but he either wasn't paying attention or he just plain didn't care. The Comte laughed and nodded.

"You are clever, yes, I must admit. The way you escaped

taught me that, if nothing else." His smile faded. "But there is clever and then there is clever, no?" He tapped the side of his head. "Myself, I am the latter. I always have been."

Pepper gave him a smile. "So, is that why you got a monster locked up in your basement? Because that doesn't sound very clever to me."

The Comte gestured at her, as if she'd made a good point. "Ah, but you lack all of the facts in the case, eh?" He turned back to the sideboard and poured himself a new glass of wine. "You do not see the – what do you people call it – yes, the big picture." He took a sip of wine and paused, staring at the wall for several moments. "You do not see what I see." He shook his head and looked at her. "No one does. No one understands. I thought there was someone, once, but... ah." He made a helpless gesture.

Pepper, in a sudden fit of intuition, said, "Alessandra."

The Comte did not look at her. "The very same."

"You and she were... ah. You know?" She gestured and the Comte raised an eyebrow.

"Does that surprise you?"

"You don't seem her type is all." She was a bit surprised by this admission. She'd never thought much about such things when it came to Alessandra, but she couldn't see her playing the aristocrat's moll.

The Comte sneered. "And what would a child such as yourself know about love, eh? Or hate, for that matter. As much as I loved her then, I hate her now."

Pepper reached for another pastry. "Seems a bit harsh. She only stole a few books."

"Only a few books – pfaugh!" He swept his hand through the air like a blade. "She stole more than books, girl. She stole my birthright!" He went to the window and looked out. "She set back my life's work by a year… it might as well be an eternity." He shook his head. "A year, wasted." He glanced at her. "Then, perhaps I should be thankful. I had intended to share with her the wonder and glories to come. I shudder to think what she might have done with what I planned to bestow upon her."

"And what was that?" Pepper asked, around a mouthful of pastry.

The Comte gestured without looking at her. "Nothing you would understand. What are you, after all, but a simple peasant? An alley cat Alessandra has decided to adopt. You are nothing more than a convenient lever by which to motivate Alessandra to retrieve my property." He turned and selected a piece of cheese from the tray. He opened a drawer on the desk and pulled out a knife, with which he proceeded to expertly cube the cheese as he continued. "In all honesty, I had intended to dispose of you within the day."

Pepper nearly choked on her pastry. "So why didn't you, hunh?" she wheezed.

The Comte stabbed his knife into the desk and ate a cube of cheese. "I am a believer in fate. That you nearly escaped, and survived my subsequent fit of pique, means there is more to you than surface appearances suggest. I am not one to ignore such omens, and it may well be that you can be of some use to me in the trials to come. That is why you are still alive."

Pepper could contain herself no longer. "What trials? What the hell do you even want the book for? And why the hell did you lock up a monster – named Jules, no less – in your own family crypt?"

The Comte looked bemused. "It… told you its name?" he asked. "That is surprising. How did this happen? Why?"

"I asked," Pepper said, bluntly. "What's the matter, you never bothered to ask him?"

The Comte was about to reply when there came the sound of a bell ringing from somewhere on the grounds outside. "Perimeter alarm," Selim said, as he started for the door. "Lock the doors, m'sieu. Stay here."

"I will do no such thing," the Comte said, sharply. He motioned to Pepper. "Bring her. She might find this edifying." He went to the fireplace in the far corner and reached for the sword mounted there. He pulled it down and drew it from its sheath with an expansive sweeping motion. "An ancestor of mine was gifted this blade by Napoleon himself, for... certain services of an occult nature." He peered down the weapon's curved length. "Damascus steel, and blessed besides."

"Fancy. I prefer shotguns. You can shoot people and then hit 'em, like it's a club." Pepper mimed the action. The Comte stared at her for a moment, and then sheathed the sword and looked at Selim.

"Get her up and follow me."

Selim helped Pepper to her feet. She snagged another pastry on the way, and considered going for the knife stuck in the desktop, but decided against it. The Comte had a sword and Selim had a pistol; a knife wasn't much against that.

They went out into the courtyard, where a servant was already bringing the Comte's horse out. A full hunting party had assembled – rough looking men with shotguns and clubs. Dogs on leashes barked and howled in eagerness. "Where?" the Comte demanded, as he climbed into his saddle.

"Northeast perimeter, m'sieu," one of the men said. "One of the patrols... heard it scream." There was a general muttering at this, and a lot of side-eye. Pepper found it familiar. There was a lot of that in Arkham, especially on nights when people swore they'd seen lights down near the river, or heard something on the docks.

"The wards must have caught it," the Comte said, in evident satisfaction. "Come! To the hunt!" He kicked his horse into motion, and the animal raced from the courtyard. Selim and the others followed at a trot, Pepper trapped among them.

They reached the boundary line – the same patch of fence she'd gone over, in fact – and the Comte jumped his horse over without hesitation. She was hustled over the stone wall by Selim, who had his hand on his pistol. He leaned close. "Do not try to run," he murmured. "There may be more of them, and they will tear you apart as surely as they would any of us."

"Who?" she hissed back. He didn't reply, but she figured she knew the answer. She thought about Jules, in his crypt, and shivered. She didn't think it was him, but he wasn't the only corpse-eater, and the others might well be inclined to rescue him.

They went into the trees, following the Comte, and stopped near the strange, skull-topped marker she'd seen. At least she thought it was the same one. Something lay twitching in the undergrowth near it, and she could smell burnt meat.

The Comte, still astride his horse, had drawn his sword and used it to indicate the fallen body. "Here! Look. They grow bolder, but thankfully no brighter!" He tapped the skull marker with the flat of his sword and glanced at Pepper. "These markers keep them out. I have lined the edge of my property with them. So long as they remain standing, so long as the marks remain on them, my enemies cannot enter my lands. A trick I learned from an ancestor of mine. Would that my grandfather had put it to use. It might have spared him the no-doubt awful fate he suffered."

"This happen a lot?" Pepper asked. She craned her neck and saw something that looked like Jules, only bigger. She put her hand to her mouth and stepped back, bumping into Selim, who steadied her.

"Oh, off and on for nearly a year," the Comte said. He leaned over in his saddle and spat on the fallen creature. "Sometimes they come in force. Sometimes only one or two. They never get any closer than this." His smile had a brittle sharpness to it, and Pepper wondered if some of them had ventured closer than the Comte liked to admit.

"What should we do with it?" Selim asked. He moved past her and crouched beside the beast, grabbing a handful of the creature's scalp and lifting its head up. She turned away. Even stunned, it was awful looking and almost more than her stomach could bear. "Throw it in with the other?"

The Comte snorted. "Are you mad, Selim? No." He turned away with a flippant gesture. "Kill it and harvest the remains. It will be more useful dead than alive."

Selim grunted and drew his pistol. But the creature still had a bit of fight left in it. It suddenly flailed at him, claws slicing through his shirt and knocking him backward. The thing shrieked weakly, and tried to rise. The Comte bellowed orders as his horse reared in sudden panic, and his men surged to obey. Rifle butts and clubs served to keep the ghoul on the ground, but it was snarling and screeching fit to deafen those closest to it.

Pepper realized that all eyes were on the confrontation. They'd forgotten about her, if only for the moment. She didn't try to run. No point in that, now. But there had to be something… There! Quickly, she stepped back, close to the grisly boundary marker and scuffed her sleeve across the skull, smearing the sigil. Then, just as speedily, she stepped away from it as a gunshot sounded and the creature fell silent.

She wasn't sure why she'd done it. A bit of defiance, maybe. Or maybe she was just taking Alessandra's lessons about taking advantage of opportunities to heart.

The Comte calmed his horse and looked down at Pepper. "You did not flee," he said, in what might have been approval. Pepper lifted her chin.

"I know when I'm licked."

"An admirable sentiment. Hubris is unbecoming in a young woman."

"So guys keep telling me." Pepper's gaze strayed to the ghoul. "They trying to rescue their pal, or kill you?"

The Comte reined his horse in and turned it back toward the estate. "It does not matter. What I have set in motion will not be stopped by the worms that crawl through the earth. They may have fired the first shot – but I will fire the last." With that, he kicked his horse into a gallop and left her there.

Selim grasped her shoulder. "You will go back to your room now," he rumbled.

Pepper glanced at him. "Yeah. I could use a snooze."

Time alone meant time to think. She had a feeling she was going to need it.

CHAPTER TWENTY-TWO
Attack

Alessandra's revolver thundered and Bera yowled as the bullet creased her side. She crashed into Alessandra, the shot doing nothing to interrupt her momentum. They rolled across the scattered books, Bera's nails digging into Alessandra's throat. Desperate to break the ghoul-woman's hold, Alessandra struck her attacker in the temple with her pistol, wielding the weapon like a club.

Bera reeled, clutching at her head. Alessandra kicked the other woman in the chest and scrambled to her feet. Moving quickly, she grabbed the side of the nearest shelf and gave it a shove, hoping to tip it over onto Bera. It barely moved and she was forced to throw everything she had into it.

The shelf creaked, wobbled and began to topple and then – impossibly – stopped. Alessandra looked and saw Lapp standing on the other side, his hands braced against a shelf and a look of sheer rage on his features. "Are you mad, woman? This is a library, not a schoolyard!"

Bera rose up behind him, teeth bared. Lapp glanced at her, but did not seem unduly concerned, despite how she'd manhandled him earlier. Bera, on the other hand, reacted as if she'd spotted something foul and retreated away from the young man.

Seizing the moment, Alessandra stepped past him, revolver swinging up. She fired again, and again Bera darted aside with preternatural quickness. "*Abasta!* Stand still," Alessandra snapped, in frustration. Bera scuttled sideways across the floor on all fours, her dress flapping about her in an unsettling fashion.

Alessandra fired again and again, her shots pockmarking the floor. Bera leapt over them like a highly strung cat. She'd lost her hat and glasses, and glossy, coarse hair flared about her narrow head like an animal's mane and her yellow eyes bulged with rage. But for the moment, she was keeping her distance. Alessandra risked a quick glance toward Trish, to check on the other woman.

Trish had managed to extricate herself from her opponent's clutches, but not without spilling some blood. Her hat was missing, and her lip was split. But she was backing away, pistol extended before her. The creature that had tackled her was down on all fours, clutching its snout and whining. There were three others, all of them circling Cinabre. The old man eyed them with concern, but had his hands behind his back.

Bera lunged suddenly, and Alessandra was forced to forget about the others and backpedal. "You should know better than to let your attention wander, Countess…" she began, clawed fingers flexing. Alessandra snapped her revolver up, quicker than the other woman could react, and Bera paused.

"You should know better than to lead with your mouth," Alessandra said.

Bera snapped at the air like an angry cur. "But that is where my teeth are."

"And what big teeth they are."

Bera circled her, moving slowly. "The better to crack your bones with," she purred. "I look forward to licking the marrow out of them."

"Not the most pleasant proposition I have ever received," Alessandra said.

Bera tittered and licked her lips. "It did not have to be this way. You could have just given me the book."

"Why do you want it?" Alessandra asked, stalling for time. She was all too aware that even if she put down Bera there were four more of the beasts to deal with, and she doubted that they'd allow to her to reload. She needed to think of a plan, and quickly.

Bera paused, then twitched the question aside. "It does not matter." She tensed, ready to leap, when suddenly Lapp was there, sliding smoothly between them. Bera stepped back, eyes narrowed. Alessandra looked at him in surprise.

"What are you…?" she began. Then, past him, she saw Cinabre, apparently in earnest conversation with one of the larger creatures. Bera, following her gaze, turned and squalled like an angry cat. The large creature flinched and grunted something at her. She stalked toward them, the hair on her head standing almost erect.

Cinabre turned toward her, smiling as if they were at a cocktail party. "Ah, Madam Bera, a pleasure to at last make your acquaintance – awk!" He yelped in alarm as she leapt toward him. But the ever-loyal Lapp was there, one hand snapping out to grab her ankle faster than Alessandra could follow. In a show of surprising strength, Lapp slammed Bera against the floor, winding her.

Her followers snarled at this, but did not intervene. Clearly some accord had been reached while Bera was otherwise occupied. Alessandra glanced back to where she'd last seen Trish, and felt some relief to see that the other woman was still on her feet and in one piece. The creature she'd been tangling with had joined the others, still holding its snout in almost comical fashion.

"Lightweight," Trish muttered, as she joined Alessandra. "Like popping a mutt with a rolled-up newspaper."

Despite her bravado, the other woman was clearly rattled by her scuffle. Her hands were shaking as she made to light a cigarette. "What the hell is going on?" she asked, as Alessandra lit it for her.

"Apparently Cinabre can talk to them."

"Man of many talents," Trish said.

Alessandra nodded. "He is a tricky one."

"Wish he'd mentioned that particular trick earlier." Trish offered Alessandra the pack of cigarettes, and Alessandra took one. It was some awful British blend, but she sucked in a lungful of smoke gratefully. It helped calm her pumping pulse. Twice now, these creatures had almost been her death. She was determined that there would be no third time.

Lapp had allowed Bera to her feet, and she was glaring sullenly at her followers, who all resolutely avoided her yellow gaze. "Ah, ladies," Cinabre said, looking in Alessandra and Trish's direction. "I am just having a chat with our guests here."

"You know these creatures, then? Know their language?"

"Ghouls, you mean? Yes. Picked it up in my youth, during a sweaty winter in Tunisia. A most curious language, and difficult to learn – but rewarding, nonetheless. Be but a moment." Cinabre turned back to the ghouls and spoke quickly, in a series of meepings and guttural whistles that sounded like no language Alessandra had ever heard.

Bera replied in kind, gesturing sharply as she did so. Alessandra couldn't follow what they were saying, but she thought she got the gist. Cinabre was trying to calm things down and Bera wasn't in the mood for calm. "This is going to go sideways," Trish muttered, dabbing at her split lip. "You can't trust these things."

Bera's ears were sharp and her gaze snapped around to pin Trish in place. "It is humans who cannot be trusted," she snarled. "It is you who break our most sacred laws and take what you are not entitled to!"

"Says the woman who eats corpses," Trish fired back.

"If you did not want them eaten, you should not have put them in the earth," Bera hissed as she took a threatening step toward Trish. "That was the compact our peoples made in the ancient days. You offered us the dead so that we would not harm the living, and we have abided by that agreement – despite all of your provocation!"

"You tried to kill us just now," Trish protested.

"If we had wanted you dead, you would be dead," Bera growled, but Alessandra could tell it was simply bravado. The truth was, the ghouls had tried and failed. More, she suspected that their attack had been motivated by desperation.

Cinabre spoke up. "Regardless, it is time to turn swords into plowshares, I think." He looked at Trish and then at Bera. "Bygones, as you Americans say, Miss Scarborough."

"What are you suggesting, monsieur?" Alessandra asked.

"That you come to some arrangement. Violence solves nothing."

An arrangement. Alessandra looked at Bera. The ghoul-woman had her head tilted quizzically, in an almost canine way. It would have been funny, had it not been so inhuman. "Upon consideration, it seems to me that we are after the same thing."

Bera grunted. "What do you mean?"

"You want the book. So do I. You do not wish the Comte to have it – neither do I."

Bera's eyes narrowed. "Explain."

"The Comte has a hostage – a friend of mine. I cannot rescue her without the book."

Bera's eyes widened slightly, and Alessandra wondered why. The ghoul-woman glanced at the largest of her followers and uttered a shrill meep. The hulking creature replied in kind, and nodded its shaggy head. Bera looked back at Alessandra. "What do you propose?" she asked, softly.

"An alliance – a temporary one, if that is more convenient for you. You let me take the book so that I might rescue my friend. Then I will return it to you when I have done so." Alessandra could feel Trish tense slightly as she spoke, but thankfully the other woman said nothing at all about the familiarity of the proposition.

Bera exposed her teeth. "Why should we trust you?" she demanded. "You are a thief. Thieves cannot be trusted."

"I am not a thief at the moment. I am merely someone trying to save their friend." Alessandra paused, wondering what else she could say to convince Bera of her intentions. Finally, she settled on the simplest method. "Please," she asked.

Bera sniffed and glanced at her followers. "Very well." She looked back at Alessandra. "But we will accompany you. To make certain there are no tricks."

Alessandra nodded, somewhat surprised that they had agreed so quickly. Maybe they were more desperate than she'd suspected. "I welcome your help."

Bera made a strangled noise that might have been a laugh

and turned back to her followers. Cinabre joined Alessandra and Trish. "Well done," he murmured. "In truth, they are a soft-hearted folk, whatever their appearance might suggest. And they hold fast to their promises."

"You sound as if you admire them," Alessandra replied.

"Oh, I do. The ghouls are our closest neighbors and could well become our staunchest allies at some distant point and time. Like us, they are children of this world. It is in their best interests to defend it, as it is in ours."

"Why does she look human?" Alessandra asked, watching Bera. "The others… don't. But I thought she was a human at first glance."

Cinabre smiled slyly. "Have you ever read Kipling? Or Burroughs? God smiles on babes in the wood – or burying ground, as it were. Sometimes our corpse-eating friends take it into their heads to adopt a human child, while leaving one of their own in the infant's place. I am informed that such… cultural exchanges are often happy ones, one way or the other. The ghouls are a kindly folk, in their way."

"Why would they do such a thing?" Alessandra asked, feeling slightly sick at the thought. "What profit is in it for them?"

Cinabre grinned. "Such changelings can walk safely where few ghouls dare tread, and achieve such aims as are required by the leaders of their kind. In time, they might even become as their adoptive parents – true ghouls at last. Bera is likely one such, though farther along than most. She is not long for civilized society, I should think. Or, rather, human society, I should say."

"She is not the only one, then?" Alessandra asked, feeling a vague sense of nausea at the thought. Cinabre shook his head, but before he could reply, Trish spoke up.

"Hardly. I know of a few in the States, including a certain artist in Boston who vanished a year or two back. They've burrowed into our society like maggots."

Cinabre shook his head. "They are not invaders, Miss Scarborough. Bera has more in common with you than you might think. Her kind watch and warn, nothing more. It is rare that they are tasked to do anything else – a sign of her people's desperation in this matter; or perhaps merely her own."

"What do you mean?" Alessandra asked.

Cinabre tapped the side of his nose. "Now, now… some secrets you will have to uncover yourself, Countess. Now, if you'll excuse me… I must put my library in order."

Alessandra watched him as he and Lapp began to reshelve the books. Trish took a long drag on her cigarette and said, "So."

"So."

"I hope you aren't planning to go back on your word to me, Countess."

Alessandra took a pull on her own cigarette and eyed Trish. "I want Pepper back. After that, I do not care who gets the damn book." She blew smoke into the air.

"You, or them, it makes no damn difference to me."

CHAPTER TWENTY-THREE
Preparations

Henri-Georges Balfour, the Comte d'Erlette, squeezed a bit of bile from the lump of ghoul-flesh in his gloved hand into the bubbling alembic atop his work table. The stink of the bile was ungodly despite the gas mask he wore, easily filling the cavernous attic space, and the yellowish liquid hissed as it hit the specially treated glass. It was necessary, however. Or would be, when the moment came.

He paused, absently wringing out the final few drops. He'd heard something, or thought he had. A faint hum, as of a trapped insect. He glanced about to make sure his defensive wards were still correctly positioned. One errant breeze could ruin an entire morning's work if he wasn't careful. But no – the hundreds of strips of paper, with their ritual markings, were all still in place on the walls and ceiling beams.

Satisfied, he turned back to his work. But the hum continued, growing louder and fainter by turns. He looked around, trying to pinpoint the source of the sound. The attic was a combination laboratory and ritual space, and had been such for nearly four generations.

Henri had others, of course. No ritualist worth his essential salts kept only one work space. There were those in Toulouse and outside of Marseille. But this space was the first – the oldest – and thus, the most potent. There was a saying among the Western Apache: "wisdom sits in places". It accreted, and made certain places more appropriate for what he had planned than others. The estate, site of so much bloodshed and black magic, was the perfect gateway. Here, the barriers between worlds were frayed to such an extent that one could often simply reach out and take hold of what waited on the other side.

Henri hesitated – and then lunged. His gloved hand, still steaming with bile, closed about something invisible. Something about the size of a house cat, that squirmed and shrieked like a frightened infant. But what infant had so many legs, or a flailing proboscis tipped with a serrated stinger? Splattered with bile, it had lost its concealing glamor and become horribly, hideously visible.

Without hesitation, Henri dashed its skull to pieces against the edge of the work table. He studied its twitching carcass with an inquisitive eye. It reminded him of a corpse-fly. Perhaps it was, in some sense of the definition. Vermin of the outer dark, feasting on God alone knew what, in spaces beyond human perception.

He carefully deposited the corpse in one of the steel boxes that lined the far edge of the work bench. The others held pieces culled from the recently slain ghoul, including its tongue, liver and brain. All would eventually be rendered down into their base elements, for use elsewhere. With the body safely disposed of, he dunked his stained glove into a pot of sterilizing agent and gave it a swish. More vapor filled the air.

Selim, standing a safe distance away, watching it all, coughed politely. Henri turned, glove dripping, and raised his gas mask with his free hand. "What?"

"Is this necessary? The odors are most noisome. The servants are complaining." Selim had his hand on his pistol, but had known better than to draw it, much less fire it. He had seen Henri deal with far worse nuisances than an overgrown housefly in his years of service and uttered not a word of complaint. Yet of late, his concerns had been many.

"They can complain all they like, so long as they do as I say." Henri glanced back at the bubbling alembic and sighed. "But I am done for the moment. I need a cigarette anyway." He pulled off his mask and tossed it to Selim, who caught it one-handed. Henri stripped off his gloves and tucked them into the pocket of his industrial smock, and stepped carefully over the curve of the protective circle painted on the attic floor.

The circle took up most of the floor space. Strange sigils in several languages, some of which he was not familiar with, decorated its circumference. It had been drawn by his ancestor, the first to bear the title of the Comte d'Erlette, and subsequent generations had added to it; though not always to great effect, it must be said.

Over the centuries, the estate had been fortified both within and without. Its bones had been reinforced, as had its spirit. It was a redoubt, in which a man might ride out the apocalypse – or cause one. Henri was still uncertain as to which he was, in this instance. The more time passed, the deeper his misgivings became. But he was determined to see it through nonetheless. He had pledged himself to a cause, and no d'Erlette had ever gone back on his word – even if that promise meant his doom.

He led Selim out onto the widow's walk. It had stout doors of oak, with a reinforced frame and an extendable ladder leading down to the slope of the roof overlooking the courtyard. The balcony was a relatively new addition to the attic, built by Henri's father after a failed experiment. As a certain regular correspondent of Henri's put it, "never call up that which you cannot put down." Henri's father had been able to put the thing in question down, eventually, but it had required some effort and the use of a small ship's cannon, normally kept in the stables.

"How is the mood among the men?" he asked. Selim grunted.

"They are eager. Nervous, but not fearful."

"Good." Henri had chosen his army carefully, selecting men with experiences similar to Selim's and his own. The reverberations of the recent war had loosed many a scurrying horror on the battlefields of Europe. Many a soldier, from both sides of the conflict, had encountered something their training had not prepared them for. Now Henri intended to give them a small measure of satisfaction. Under his leadership, they would strike a blow against the nightmarish shadows that blotted the edges of the map.

Henri lit his cigarette, his back to the breeze. He did not offer the pack to Selim, who preferred his own Turkish blend. "You have that look on your face again, my friend," Henri said. "I do not like it. It makes me think that you doubt me."

"Not you, m'sieu."

"Ah. The situation then? You think it a bucking horse, and myself in the saddle?"

"Tiger, not horse," Selim corrected. "A man who rides a tiger cannot afford to get off, lest the tiger turn on him."

Henri nodded. It wasn't the first time that Selim had made his doubts plain. Nor would it be the last. He did not doubt

Selim's loyalty, and thus allowed it. In any event, the other man was careful not to express his opinion where others could hear. But that he was worried was cause for some concern. "And what wisdom do you have for me, then?"

Selim smiled, but the expression was brittle and mirthless. "Do not get on the tiger in the first place."

Henri laughed out loud. "Well said. Good advice, if a bit late."

Selim looked out over the courtyard. "What you mean to do here… it cannot be done. Even the sorcerers of old could not do such things."

"Ah, but I have an advantage over them." Henri indicated the gas mask in Selim's hand. "Modern technology. We are not limited to fire and shot, my friend. We have more efficient means of disposal these days."

Selim glanced at him and frowned. "Gas, you mean."

"Gas, yes. Explosives. Flame-throwers. Machine-guns. All sufficient to the task at hand. And if not… well. There are other methods." Henri flexed a hand, and a soft, violet light shimmered between his clenched fingers, just for an instant. Selim flinched and looked away. Henri smiled. "You have nothing to fear. What power I have is meant for a single target." His smile faded, as he thought of his enemy – and it was his enemy.

It was the enemy of all men, in fact. But Henri was one of the few wise enough to recognize it. It had many names – the King of Maggots, the Devourer Below… but one name above all others resonated in the whispers of the dead: Umôrdhoth. The primogenitor of the filthy curs that desecrated mankind's graves and polluted its blood with their own foul tomb-ichor. The master of all ghouls; the creator of them, and leader.

It was the ghouls who had first corrupted the d'Erlette lineage; had first taught Henri's ancestors of the hidden world. And when that ancestor had sought to share that knowledge, to reveal to humanity the true horror of what lurked beneath their feet, the ghouls had killed him. Down through the years since, they had taken many of the d'Erlette line.

It was past time, Henri thought, that a d'Erlette take them.

Selim hesitated. "Even so, perhaps caution is warranted."

"We are past the time for caution," Henri snapped.

The sound of an engine backfiring caught his attention. He looked down into the courtyard as a trio of trucks rolled through the gates. Inside the back of each truck were numerous packing crates. Henri felt his pulse quicken and he took a last pull on his cigarette. "Come, Selim. It seems Sanford was as good as his word."

Henri kicked the latch and let the ladder descend from the bottom of the balcony. He and Selim climbed down to the window below and made their way through the house to the courtyard, where a familiar face was climbing down from the passenger side of one of the trucks. Chauncey Swann smiled broadly and tipped his hat in greeting as he caught sight of Henri and Selim making their way toward him.

"Monsieur Swann, you have arrived," Henri called out.

"Of course. And with crates of goodies, courtesy of Mr Sanford and the Silver Twilight Lodge," Swann said, tapping a cigarette on his case. "Just like you ordered." He lit it with a flourish and grinned. "I got bombs, guns, gas... even a few sharp sticks, if you're into that kind of thing."

Henri bent and retrieved a cannister-grenade from one of the packing crates. He weighed it in his palm and looked at Swann. "You had no difficulties with my order, then?"

Swann shrugged. "Mr Sanford has many friends in the military."

"American – or French?"

Swann smiled. "Yes." He lit his cigarette and took a long drag. "So, you're really going into Pnath then, hunh? Have a bit of a look around?"

Henri tossed the grenade to Swann, who nearly lost his cigarette in his haste to catch it. "Unless Alessandra fails me, which I cannot imagine. In which case, I will simply have to cache it until the next equinox." Swann thought this was all about plunder – an other-dimensional raid; as if Henri would ever be a party to such a foolish endeavor. Sanford, however, had financed many such trips into distant realms, often to the detriment of those who dared to go.

Swann carefully put the grenade back in its crate. "Yeah, I heard you got yourself a hostage. That little friend of hers, the cabbie. Clever."

Henri looked at him. "And where did you hear that?"

"Oh, around. I keep my ear to the ground, you know." Swann puffed on his cigarette and added, "Mr Sanford would like to, once again, caution you against what might be considered a somewhat rash action." He grinned. "Ain't every day a guy tries to steal from a god in its own holy fane, you know?"

Henri blew smoke into the air and sniffed. "Is he concerned that I will fail – or that I will succeed? And if it is either, why procure these weapons for me?"

Swann gave an elegant shrug. "What can I say? He's a people-pleaser."

"You did not answer my question."

Swann looked away. "Ain't for me to say, Comte. Mr Sanford is a man of far-reaching vision, but it is a vision I am not privy to.

And between you and me, I'm happy to wallow in ignorance." He paused. "You know she's going to try something, right? The countess, I mean. She don't roll over for the likes of us, Comte."

Henri fixed him with a cold stare. "Do not make the mistake of considering us equals, monsieur. For we are not. And I am well aware of Alessandra's proclivity for treachery." And of Sanford's, though he didn't say as much. Sanford had aided him because he thought there was profit to be had. And there was – just not the sort Sanford or Swann had in mind.

Swann held up his hands in mock surrender. "Hey, no water off my back, Comte. Just a friendly observation. Free advice, you might say."

"Swann, everything you do comes with a price. And until I know what it is, I insist that you remain here as my guest." Henri gestured, and Selim drew his revolver and cocked it. Swann looked at Selim, and then at Henri. He licked his lips.

"I wouldn't want to be a bother…"

"It is no bother," Henri said. "In fact, you might well come in handy." He smiled widely and Swann paled.

"As bait, if nothing else."

CHAPTER TWENTY-FOUR
Negotiations

"You sure about this, Countess?" Trish asked, watching as Lapp brought out Cinabre's telephone. It was an old-fashioned device, housed in a bell jar; as if it were an evil spirit, in need of containment. Given who she was about to talk to, Alessandra thought perhaps that was not far off the mark.

She reclined in a chair in Cinabre's sitting room, a cup of coffee balanced perfectly on her knee. A lit cigarette smoldered on the saucer. She alternated between sips and puffs, trying to sand off the rough edges of the day. Trish sat across from her, her own cup clutched in both hands. Every so often, the other woman would glance at Bera, who studied the walls with the air of one trying to recall where they had seen such images before.

Cinabre reclined on his divan, puffing gently on a bubbling hookah, looking for all the world like Carroll's caterpillar. Every so often, Lapp would come in and whisper something to him in a language Alessandra didn't recognize. When she asked, Cinabre laughed and told her it was a dialect of Sarnath – a place that she had never heard of, but nonetheless seemed familiar. She flicked the thought aside in irritation and looked at Trish.

"Time is our enemy. I intend to make it our friend." She

paused. Contacting Henri directly was dangerous. He might well have ways of tracing such calls, either natural or otherwise. But she needed to make his schedule work for her. "Yes, I am certain."

"It just seems a bit … fiddly, for my tastes," Trish said. "Too many moving parts."

Alessandra smiled. "But one of those parts is me, so success is all but assured."

Bera snorted. "You are confident, Countess. Let us hope it is not misplaced."

Lapp set the telephone down on the side-table near Alessandra, before she could reply to Bera. "You know how to use one of these?" he asked, curtly. She glanced at him. There was more to the young man than she had first thought – much more. She suspected that, like Bera, Lapp was not entirely human. Perhaps Cinabre had conjured him up, like a sorcerer's familiar. She smiled prettily.

"I am a modern woman. Telephones and motor cars hold no mystery for me."

Lapp grunted and removed the bell jar. Cinabre chuckled. "Forgive him. He has an old soul, this one. But it is hidden behind a pretty face, so we must be tolerant."

"And what about your soul, monsieur?" Alessandra asked, as she picked up the receiver. "Is it that of an ancient – or a child?"

Cinabre laughed. "Who can say, my dear? I have not had cause to examine the state of it in many years."

Bera turned from her examination of the wall. "Is that because you put it somewhere and forgot it? You sorcerers often do that sort of thing, I am told." Her eyes glinted with amusement as she spoke, and Alessandra could not restrain a smile at the look of sudden discomfiture on Cinabre's face.

"I am hardly a sorcerer, child. At least not in the professional sense. Strictly amateur, at best. A humble scholar and academic. That is what I am. A dull little man, leading a dull little existence." Cinabre set his hookah aside and sat upright. "At best, I know a few tricks. Nothing more."

"In my experience, anyone who says that knows more than a few," Trish said, as she took a sip of coffee. Her gaze flicked to Alessandra. "Get on with it. We're burning daylight."

Alessandra nodded and quickly connected with the operator. A few minutes later, she rattled off the number to Henri's chateau. She knew it by heart. Her capacity for retaining such information was little more than a party trick, but a necessary one. The smallest detail could mean the difference between getting away with the loot, or being pinched by the rozzers.

It took some time for a connection to be established. When it was, a voice she didn't recognize answered. A servant, she thought. She asked to speak to Henri, and waited for the servant to run and tell their master. In the meantime, she looked at the others. Bera twitched like an anxious cat, clearly unhappy, but doing her best to hide it. Alessandra didn't entirely trust the ghoul-woman, and she was certain Bera felt the same about them. But there was nothing for it. They needed one another; at least for the moment.

Trish was the same; calmer than Bera, if not as blasé as Cinabre. She was obviously considering all the angles to the new arrangement, looking for a way to spin it to her advantage. The only thing they all had in common was a need to prevent Henri from going through with his plan – whatever it was.

"Hello?" a male voice asked, suddenly, in her ear.

"Henri. How are you?" she responded, in French.

"That depends on what you have to tell me," he answered.

"Oh, it is good news, I assure you."

A sudden intake of breath, hastily stifled. "You have it, then? The book?"

"I am looking at it now."

"That is not the same thing, Alessandra."

"It is in my possession, Henri." She heard him sigh in what might have been pleasure, or perhaps relief. She knew then that Cinabre was right – Henri was on a schedule. She smiled. That was good. It gave her an advantage, if she could play it right.

"Where are you?"

"That does not matter."

"I think it does," Henri snapped. "You only have a day remaining to you…"

"No. You have a day remaining. At least until the next equinox." He fell into a startled silence, and her smile widened. She continued. "That is why you gave me three days, is it not? Because after that, there is a decided lack of urgency. What are you up to, Henri?"

"You would not understand," he said, hoarsely. "And you overestimate my patience. I have your friend, remember?"

"Yes. Which is why I decided to call, Henri. I want to speak to her."

"If I say no?"

"Then you will never see the book again."

"I could kill her…"

"As far as I know, you might have already done so. Let me speak with her, Henri."

He fell silent again, and she could tell he was considering the matter. Henri had a strong streak of spite in him; one that was constantly at war with his pragmatism. She suspected that it was what motivated him. The question was – how much did he hate her? And how much did he want the book?

"Very well," he said, finally. "You may speak with her. One moment." She heard him set the receiver down, and call out to someone. She signaled to Trish and the others, letting them know that he'd agreed to her conditions.

A minute later, she heard Pepper's familiar Boston accent on the line. "Countess?" she asked, hesitantly. "That you?"

"Pepper," Alessandra said, in quiet relief. "You are alive."

"Course I am!" Pepper said, as if offended.

Alessandra choked back a laugh and said, "Are you well? Has he… are you well?"

"I'm in one piece, if that's what you're asking." Pepper lowered her voice. "Countess, I- I saw something. He's got something – someone – trapped."

"He has another prisoner?" As she spoke, Alessandra saw Bera tense. The ghoul-woman's expression became intent. So that was what Cinabre had been hinting at. Bera apparently had a hostage of her own to rescue. And from the speculative look on her face, Trish had noticed this as well.

"You could say that. I think he's up to something hinky. I– Hey!" Pepper shouted as someone took the telephone away from her. A moment later, Henri was back.

"There. Satisfactory proof of life, I trust."

"Good enough," Alessandra said.

"You will bring the book to me. You have one day."

"No."

"What?"

"We will meet at a neutral location." She glanced at Trish, who mouthed "Toulouse". She nodded and added, "Toulouse. Somewhere public."

"Very well. Name a place." Henri sounded amused. The

thought made her itch, but she gritted her teeth and continued with the plan.

"The Basilica of Saint-Sernin."

"A surprising choice. You were never one for religion."

"Things change," she said. He laughed.

"No, they do not. But they will. Fine. I will meet you there tomorrow. Noon. I trust you can make it there by that time. Or, perhaps you are already in Toulouse, eh?"

"A good guess, but no."

"It would be simpler if you told me."

"But not as much fun. Tomorrow. Noon. Bring Pepper with you."

"A trade, then?" he asked, his amusement palpable. Now that he thought the book was in his grasp, he was allowing himself to gloat, if only slightly.

She forced herself to keep a civil tone. "Yes. One hostage for another. Come alone, and I will do the same. No tricks."

"Excellent." Henri paused. "I look forward to seeing you again." There was something in his voice that set her hackles bristling. A hint of menace, but also... longing? She was no stranger to desire, and knew that Henri was the sort of man for whom theft and attempted murder were little more than foreplay. Their courtship had been little more than a dalliance for her; enjoyable, but temporary. But for Henri, it seemed as if it had been something greater. The thought made her uncomfortable.

"And I, you," Alessandra said, and hung up. She looked at the others. "He will not keep his word, obviously."

"Never known an aristocrat to do so," Trish said. "With that in mind, I ask again – are you sure about this?" She sat up. "He might just put one in your skull the minute you show up, rather than trying something fancy."

"He will not," Alessandra said. "Henri has always enjoyed an audience, and who better to act as one than myself? He will want to preen. To gloat. So he will take me prisoner, and I will let him, because the closer I am to him, the more distracted he will be."

"And then we will strike," Bera said, biting off the end of the last word with an audible snap of her teeth. Trish glanced speculatively at the ghoul-woman and nodded.

"Yeah. Okay. But where and when?"

"The chateau," Alessandra said. "A man is never more vulnerable than when ensconced in his castle."

Bera grunted. "We cannot get to him there. He is ... protected."

"Protections can be broken," Cinabre said. "Especially when one has someone already inside keeping the guards distracted, eh?" He looked at Alessandra. "A cunning stratagem." Cinabre gestured, and Lapp retrieved the telephone. "But there is still one matter to be discussed."

"And that is?" Alessandra asked, but she already knew the answer. Cinabre smiled and spread his hands.

"The book is still technically my property. We have not yet spoken of what you will offer me in return for it."

Bera growled, but Cinabre paid her no mind. Alessandra folded her hands in her lap. "A favor," she said, primly. "One favor, at my discretion. That should be sufficient, I think."

Cinabre studied her. "Three favors," he countered. "Three favors, to be dealt at a time and place of my choosing."

"One," Alessandra said, simply. "I will allow you to choose the time and place, if you insist, with the codicil that it must not place me – or any associates – in undue jeopardy."

"What do you consider undue?"

"Red jungles and alien landscapes," Alessandra said, softly.

"I will not travel anywhere I cannot get a good coffee to invigorate my mind, or a strong drink to steady my nerves. Nor will I go anywhere that I do not speak the language."

Cinabre frowned. "Hardly generous of you. Two, then. I'll grant you the coffee, but the linguistic hurdles are yours to overcome – as is any danger that might come your way."

"One, and I will deal with what comes." Alessandra tapped her lips with a forefinger. Entering into such a bargain had more than its share of risks. There was no doubt in her mind that it would involve a theft of some kind. But she had precious few options. "One favor, for one book."

Cinabre was silent for several moments. Then, "Done. But, in order to ensure you survive to keep up your end, Lapp will accompany you."

Lapp blinked. "What?"

Cinabre ignored him. "Utilize him as you see fit. He has many talents, some of which even I am unaware of."

"No. No, I will not help them." Lapp glared at his employer. "Aiding them is not my purpose–" he began. Cinabre cut him off with a sharp gesture.

"I am the one who gives you purpose, boy. And I say you will. So… you will." He looked at Lapp, and something seemed to pass between them. Lapp's glare did not fade, but he nodded and finally looked away.

"As you say, monsieur."

"Yes. It is." Cinabre turned his attentions back to Alessandra and rubbed his hands together in obvious excitement. "Now then, let us discuss this plan of yours in more detail…"

CHAPTER TWENTY-FIVE
Protection

Pepper watched as the Comte put the receiver down with a click. He finished his wine, turned and sent the glass hurtling into the fireplace. "Infuriating woman," he said, in English. Pepper figured it was for her benefit. He turned to her. "She always has been, you know. Since we first met, in fact. I caught her stealing my pocket-watch." He gestured to the gold chain looped beneath his waistcoat pocket. "In retrospect, I know now that she let me catch her. She played the ingenue for me, and I could not help but be swept away."

"My heart bleeds," Pepper said, sinking back into her chair. Selim stood nearby, arms crossed, studiously paying no attention to either of them. Even though he was one of her captors, the big man's presence somehow made her feel better. He was a mook, sure – but mooks she knew how to deal with.

"It might, if you do not check your tone," he said. His smile did little to ameliorate the threat. He raised his hand, as if to take a sip from the glass he'd just broken, paused and grunted. He went to the sideboard for a new glass. "In any event, you should consider yourself lucky. She has the book and thus you might yet survive this matter."

Pepper watched him warily. He'd been up and down all day, and the chateau was getting crowded. He'd doubled the guards, and the courtyard was full of trucks. It reminded her of one particular night on the Arkham waterfront, when she'd gotten an eyeful of the O'Bannions bringing in a shipment of hardware. Naomi O'Bannion herself had slipped Pepper a sawbuck to keep her trap shut. But somehow, she didn't think the Comte was planning a raid on a rival bootlegging firm.

"Sounds good to me," Pepper said. "Consider me silenced."

The Comte snorted. "I doubt that. I heard you tell her about my other guest."

"Jules."

The Comte inclined his head, acknowledging the name. "Even so. Though I doubt that information will be of any use to her. Alessandra has never been one for the subtle world."

"Things change," Pepper said. She hoped Alessandra might be able to do something with the knowledge of the ghoul's presence. She wasn't sure what, but if there was one thing Alessandra was good at, it was turning things like that to her advantage. "If you'd seen what we'd seen…"

"Yes, so I am told." The Comte turned from the sideboard. "It does not matter. Things come to a head now, and there is no one who can divert me from my path."

"So you won't mind me asking what you're planning to do with our pal in the crypt," Pepper said. It was risky, asking questions. But she figured the more she knew, the more she might be able to help Alessandra when the time came. If the time came. She shied away from the thought. "Going to off him, the way you did the other one?"

The Comte eyed her over the rim of his glass. "No. I have another use in mind for Jules. Afterwards, of course, I will have to kill it – him. But he might well consider it a mercy, given what I intend to do."

"Which is?"

He laughed. "You wouldn't understand."

"You said that before."

"And I stand by it. You cannot conceive of the task ahead. But I will give you a hint as to your part in it, if you like." He set his glass down and went to his desk. He selected a book from the pile there and opened it. "Do you read Latin? No, a silly question. Forgive me. I intend to open a door, but for the door I need a key." He turned the book around, displaying a faded diagram that Pepper could make neither head nor tail of. In fact, just looking at it made her feel vaguely sick, as if she'd taken a curve too quickly in her cab.

It reminded her of a painting she'd once seen in a book. It was like a knot of stairs and doors, all going in different directions but somehow still connected. She swallowed a sudden rush of acidic bile as the diagram seemed to undulate slowly on its page before her eyes. "What… what is that?"

"The Seven Hundred Steps of Deeper Slumber," the Comte said, and his voice sounded as if it were coming from very far away. She shook her head, trying to clear it, but everything felt heavy and foggy. "Some say there is only one gate, but those with the wit to see know better," he continued. "There is a gate for every step, and a door for every gate."

"Gate? Gate to where?"

"The American occultist de Marigny postulated that it is a state of mind as opposed to a tangible place – a vast, communal hallucination, existent only in the minds of humanity. And perhaps that is true, to some extent. Perhaps it grew out of us; a memetic sargassum, colonizing our unconscious." The

Comte traced a line of steps with his finger, following it around and around, through the gates. Every circuit made Pepper feel worse, though she was careful not to let it show on her face.

She wanted to look away from the diagram, but couldn't. The undulations became faster; more organic. As if the image were alive, somehow. Alive and aware of her observation. There was no color to it, just black ink on paper, but even so, she caught a flash of canary yellow behind one of the gates. Just a flicker, as if something fluttered behind the ever-shifting stonework. A sound teased the edge of her hearing; like distant bells or maybe footsteps. At first far away, then impossibly close – then far away once more.

"But I am a simple man," the Comte continued. "And I think it is nothing more or less than what it appears – another world, next to ours, separated only by the sheerest membrane of accepted reality. To pierce that membrane, one needs only to find the right key and the right gate." Pepper was barely listening, her eyes on the yellow mote that flickered within the diagram. She knew without understanding how that whatever it was, it was looking for her. Not urgently, or desperately. But relentlessly. Tirelessly.

Eventually, it would find her. Perhaps sooner, rather than later. She blinked, trying to banish it. What was it? Why was it looking for her? She thought of a pallid face in the Parisian sewers, and a swirl of rotten yellow cloth in the Seine. Of dead eyes, seeing nothing and everything. The Comte was still talking, but she could hear nothing now but the clangor of her pursuer's inexorable approach.

The Comte snapped the book closed, startling her back to full awareness. "What?" she asked, blinking away the specks that danced in front of her eyes. She felt the fear recede – fade.

Until she could barely recall what it was she'd seen, or why it had frightened her.

"I asked if you were listening. I see that you were not." He tossed the book back onto his desk and frowned at her in obvious exasperation. "But you will see, in time. You might even understand. In any event, it is time to go."

Still dazed, she tried to catch up. "Go? Where?"

The Comte gave her a look. "Why, to Toulouse, obviously. Alessandra wants you there, so you will be there." He gestured in Selim's direction. "Get her up, please. I will see to our transport."

"Then you are doing as she asked?" Selim said.

The Comte sneered. "Do not be a fool, Selim. Of course not. I intend to have my book and the thief both." He paused. "Monsieur Swann will accompany us as well. I would rather keep him where I can see him, no?"

Selim nodded. "Of course, monsieur." He looked unhappy, but the Comte didn't appear to notice, as he headed for the door, whistling softly. Selim motioned for Pepper to stand, which she did, if somewhat woozily. Her head was still swimming from looking at the diagram. "You heard him. On your feet, girl." His tone wasn't particularly gentle, but neither was it unkind. She was starting to realize that he wasn't as much in the Comte's pocket as she'd thought. She wasn't sure that'd be any help to her, though.

"Yeah, yeah. Can I just ask – why do you work for that guy?" Pepper looked at him. "You don't seem like a bad guy. Not his kind of bad, leastways."

Selim frowned. "What would you know of bad men?"

Pepper almost laughed. "Pal, I once drove an O'Bannion gunsel to the emergency room and then went back to pick up the guy she shot. I know bad guys. So why?"

Selim looked down at her for a moment and then said, "I owe him."

Pepper snapped her fingers. "Now it makes sense."

Selim grunted. "Perhaps you can explain it to me, then." He shook his head. "He saved my life, during… a hunt. Those other folk were creeping out of their holes and eating the dead of a village in Anatolia struck by the Flu. I was one of several tasked with seeing them off. We were not aware that the beasts had decided to do to us, before we could do to them." He grimaced and ran a hand over his scalp.

"So he saved you. Big deal."

"I knew you would not understand," he growled and gave her a gentle shove toward the door. "Hurry up. He will want to depart immediately."

"Yeah, he's in a real big hurry. Any idea why?"

Selim didn't answer. Instead, he just manhandled her out the door and into the hall. She went without much protest. She wasn't the only one being frogmarched to the front door either. A lanky, sallow man, dressed in a white suit, was just ahead of her. His face was vaguely familiar, but she couldn't quite place him. As she fell into step with him, she said, "I know you, buddy?"

He looked at her. "I don't think I've had the pleasure, no."

"You sure? You got one of those faces."

He smirked. "Some people say I look like I should be in pictures."

"No, that ain't it." She got it as soon as she said it. "Arkham, right?"

He looked away. "Yeah, maybe."

"No, no, I'm pretty sure. You were running away from Alessandra, weren't you?" She grinned at him, enjoying how uncomfortable he looked. "Yeah, that's it. You're Chauncey Swann!" She recognized him now. Alessandra had told her about the other acquisitionist – the bum worked for the Silver Twilight Lodge.

He muttered something as they stepped out into the courtyard, but she didn't hear it. The space was busy; trucks and pallets everywhere. She paid attention to none of it, though. Instead, her eyes were drawn to a wooden post near the far wall, where the body of the dead ghoul hung. Two men worked expertly to flense its mottled hide from its bones. Its chest and stomach had already been hollowed out.

She stopped and stared as one of them sawed the dead creature's head from its neck. She clutched her stomach and mouth, ready to be sick. The sallow man lit a cigarette and made a revolted face. "Jesus Christ. Can't you do that inside like civilized lunatics?"

"Have you ever smelled a dead ghoul, Swann?" the Comte asked, following them outside. He pulled on a heavy coat as he did so. "If you had, you would know better than to ask such a simple-minded question."

A black motor car was waiting at the gate, and Selim guided Pepper toward it. Swann followed, striding alongside the Comte. "Toulouse, hunh?" he said. "That's not far away at all."

"No. A fine evening's drive," the Comte murmured.

"She's got it, then?"

"Obviously."

Swann snorted. "I'm surprised you haven't already taken it from her. You got guys following her, right?"

The Comte laughed. "Of course not! There is no way to follow that woman, if she doesn't wish to be followed. She expects it, and will act accordingly. Patience is the word of the day when it comes to Alessandra – patience and timing."

"Sounds to me like you're scared of her," Pepper said, swallowing bile. The Comte glared at her, and Swann laughed.

"If he knows what's good for him, he is."

CHAPTER TWENTY-SIX
Basilica Saint-Sernin

In Alessandra's opinion, Toulouse was quiet. Not sleepy, like Saint-Bertrand-de-Comminges; but neither did it possess the vivacity of Paris. It was more like Bordeaux, save that it was larger and earlier in the day. The streets were not full, but neither were they empty. Carriages jostled with streetcars for space, and she could hear Italian and Spanish on the streets, as well as French. A true city of the Middle Sea.

Henri had always had a fascination for Toulouse. His familial roots were in this region. He'd told her that himself, often enough. She wondered if that was why Trish had suggested it.

They'd driven overnight to reach it, or rather, Lapp had driven. Alessandra had dozed, seeking relief from the fatigue that gnawed at the edges of her mind. She'd dreamt of lightless caverns and twisting shadows. Old dreams, those. Ones she hadn't had since Arkham. Ones she'd hoped never to have again, but here they were, as strong as ever.

Pale lights, spinning in the terminal darkness. Shadows bunched inside her like a bad meal, heavy on her stomach, heavier on her mind. Words like a torrent, filling her, even after she'd awoken, heart hammering and temples pounding.

Tsathoggua en y'n an ya phtaggn N'kai.

N'kai.

N'kai.

"Never mind," she murmured, as she stepped into the Basilica Saint-Sernin. She'd left Lapp and Trish behind. And Bera had made herself scarce. She had a feeling the ghoul-woman was close, but wise enough to stay out of sight, until she was needed. Henri needed to believe Alessandra had come alone, or else he might grow suspicious.

She ran a hand through her hair, and adjusted her cap. At any other time, the inside of the basilica might have made her pause in awe. It was vast for a Romanesque church; barrel vaulted and its four aisles were supported by massive buttresses. A marble altar loomed at the far end, near a great Cavaille-Coll organ. Twin rows of narrow, uncomfortable looking pews stretched before her, all the way to the altar.

The basilica was lit, as if for visitors. But she saw no one, save a man in a white suit, sitting in the middle of the rightmost row of pews. He was humming softly to himself, looking away from her. She headed for him, her footsteps loud in the silence.

She held the book in one hand, wrapped in her jacket. Her revolver was still in one of the jacket pockets and she kept her hand on it, for ease of access. As she made her way down the aisle, she kept an eye out for uninvited guests.

Drawing closer to the man, she felt a start of recognition. She sat down behind him and drew her pistol. "Chauncey Swann. You do turn up in the oddest places." The last time she'd seen Chauncey had been in Arkham. She hadn't expected to see him here, but somehow it didn't surprise her. Was Carl

Sanford involved in this? If so, Cinabre was right. Whatever Henri was up to, it was undoubtedly bad for everyone.

"Supposedly, the bones of Saint Saturnin are buried under here somewhere." Swann waved his hat in front of his face, but didn't turn around. "Don't know if that's true or not, but they'd be worth a mint if you could find them."

"I am not here for bones, Chauncey. And neither are you, I expect." Alessandra pressed her pistol to the back of his skull. Swann tensed. "Why are you here?" she asked. Swann set his hat down on his knee.

"It's under protest, I assure you."

"Talk quickly, Chauncey. I am growing bored."

Swann licked his lips. "The Comte … asked me to come. He wanted me to make sure the book is the real deal."

Alessandra paused. "And how do you know Henri?"

"Mutual friends," Henri said, from behind her. She paused, and then lowered her weapon. She turned slowly to see Henri sitting in the pew, a smug expression on his face. "Hello, Alessandra."

"Henri." She turned, presenting herself as if completely at ease. But her eyes swept the interior of the basilica, searching for any sign that he'd brought help with him. She saw no one, however. Perhaps he was simply that sure of himself. "Where is Pepper?"

"Where is my book?"

"Here." She patted her coat.

Henri tapped the floor with his cane. A door opened somewhere, and she heard the sound of footsteps – two sets. Then, at the far end of the basilica, Pepper appeared. A large, bald man stood behind her, one big hand on the back of her neck. He was armed, a pistol holstered under his coat. Henri extended his hand. "There she is. Safe and sound."

"Pepper," Alessandra began, half-rising to her feet. Henri thrust out his cane, tapping her on the shoulder and causing her to stop.

"The book, if you please."

She turned and something in her face made him sit back. "I want to talk to her first."

Henri made as if to disagree, but then shrugged. "Fine, fine. Selim, let her go."

Pepper darted forward as soon as she was able. Alessandra stepped to meet her and caught her by the shoulder. "Pepper, I am sorry about this," she murmured. "About all of it."

"Nuts to that. Most excitement I've had in a while." Pepper paused and looked Alessandra up and down. She smiled. "Borrowing my clothes again, hunh, Countess?"

"Clothes for all occasions, that is me," Alessandra said. "Are you unhurt?"

"Selim takes good care of me. Can't say the same about his boss though."

Alessandra glanced at the bald man and frowned. "What happened?"

"He tried to feed me to a ghoul."

Alessandra blinked. "And...?"

"Well, I'm standing here, ain't I?" Pepper glanced past her at Henri. "I don't think your old beau is playing with a full deck, Countess."

"Enough," Henri called out. "I trust you are satisfied now? All fingers and toes accounted for, yes?"

Alessandra turned. "Yes."

"Then give me my damn book," Henri said, with the hint of a snarl.

Alessandra pulled the book out of her coat and tossed it

to Swann, who fumbled hastily to catch it. Henri frowned. "Childish," he said. "You always were petulant."

"That makes two of us."

"Where did you find it?"

"What does it matter?"

"It matters because I say it matters."

She paused, and then glanced at Swann. "Are you asking for your own benefit, or that of your new friends?"

"I like to know the pedigree of my merchandise before I pay for it."

"A man in Bordeaux had it," she said, blithely. "Sadly deceased now."

Henri raised an eyebrow. "I did not know you had it in you."

"Not my doing, I assure you." She paused again, wondering how much to tell him. She decided to err on the side of paranoia. "His killers were not human."

Henri paused. "What do you mean?"

"They were not human." She emphasized each word, as if for a child, and was pleased to see a vein in his temple throb faintly.

He was silent for a moment. "Once, you would not have said it so baldly." He looked at her with new eyes, as if she were a stranger.

"I saw things. Experienced things." She took a breath. Maybe she was a stranger. The Alessandra Zorzi of a year ago was gone. In her place was someone unfamiliar; wiser, perhaps. But certainly not happier. Ignorance truly was bliss. "They were not human, Henri. But they were very hungry and very determined."

"You saw them?"

"I was almost killed by them," she said, wondering what his reaction would be. As she'd expected, he laughed.

"I would have liked to have seen that."

"I expect you will. They want the book, after all. And now you have it."

His smile faded. "Yes. Yes, I do. I knew I could count on you, Alessandra." He twitched, as if to reach for her, but stopped himself. "It is not too late, you know. The offer I made you then, before you stole my books… it still stands. Now that you have seen; now that you know… I could show you such wonders…" His voice was a whisper, and his gaze soft. But she knew it was a lie. Henri wasn't the sharing kind. It was part of what had attracted her, once upon a time. She'd always found a bit of selfishness to be an attractive quality in a paramour.

"I have seen wonders enough for one lifetime," she said, softly. "And if I must see more, I certainly do not wish to see them with you, Henri."

Henri frowned at her, but said nothing. Alessandra smiled thinly. It seemed she could still get under his skin. His gaze strayed to Swann. "Well?" he asked, in a harsh tone.

Swann flipped gently through the book, using a handkerchief to turn the pages. "You'd know better than me, but it looks like the real deal." He looked at Alessandra. "You actually found it. I can't believe it."

She sniffed. "I am a professional, Chauncey. I always get what I want." She looked at Henri. "You have your precious book. We will be leaving now. I look forward to never seeing you again."

Henri tapped the back of the pew with his cane. "Tell me, did you honestly think it would be that simple?"

She gave him a crooked smile. "No. But I did hope." She fired without raising the pistol. The sound and the ricochet made Henri flinch. She spun as he scrambled back, swinging her weapon around toward Pepper. "Duck!"

Pepper dove to the floor and Alessandra fired at Selim, forcing him to dodge for cover. She reached out and caught Pepper's hand and made for the doors as fast as she could. She heard Henri shout something behind her, but ignored him.

"Hope you got a plan, Countess," Pepper yelped. Alessandra shook her head.

"Just do what I do!"

They hit the doors at a run, scattering a flock of pigeons. Alessandra slid to a halt, Pepper nearly colliding with her. Outside, a dozen police officers waited. All dressed in the dark uniforms of the French police, all armed with truncheons. For a moment, the thought of being confined to a prison cell nearly overwhelmed her. But she pushed past it. She knew that they were here at Henri's behest before he walked out to confirm it.

"I told you it was not going to be that easy," he said, from behind her. He stood in the doorway, leaning on his cane, his book nestled in the crook of his arm. The very picture of the insouciant nobleman. "As you can see, there is nowhere to go," he said. "I have told them you are a wanted criminal, and they are only too happy to take you into custody. Things will go poorly for you from there, I think."

Alessandra gave Pepper's hand a squeeze and murmured, "Remember what I said." Then, without a word of warning, she raised her weapon and aimed it at Henri. He stopped and shook his head.

"Murdering me in front of witnesses will certainly not help your case."

"But it might make me feel better," she said.

Henri sighed and smiled. "Perhaps. But it would be a shame, I think. For both of us." He lifted his cane and tapped the head of it against his chin. "I made my second offer to you in good faith, but I understand why you might have decided against it. Our history is fraught – I do not deny this. But you have changed; enough, perhaps, to be of some true use to me." He glanced at Pepper. "This young woman has told me something of what you encountered in Arkham. That sort of thing is why I needed this book." The head of the cane bounced against the book's cover.

"So you say," she replied.

"I am many things, Alessandra, but only rarely a liar." He sighed and laid his cane against his shoulder. "I will give you a choice: come with me, or go to prison. Either suits me, but I think you might well find one preferable to the other."

Alessandra looked at him, and then at the police. Pepper stood tense and still beside her, not frightened, but ready to follow her example. "What do we do now?" she asked.

Alessandra glanced at her and laughed softly. Things were playing out as she'd hoped, but it was early days yet. Nonetheless, she felt some satisfaction.

"I expect we will be going for a ride."

CHAPTER TWENTY-SEVEN
Toulouse

It had taken them the better part of the evening to reach Toulouse by motor car. Lapp drove. Alessandra sat beside him. Trish sat in the back and dozed. She didn't need much sleep. Didn't want to sleep. But inevitably she did, and found herself back in Moscow, reading a dead man's papers. It was always Moscow in her dreams. She'd been to more dangerous places, but something about that cramped but empty apartment overlooking the Moskva River kept drawing her back.

It had belonged to a dead man – one of the bureau's ghosts. A name without a corpus. A set of records and a photo, but lacking in any substance. A safehouse for agents like Trish, when they were on the hunt. The local spy-hunters kept a watch on it, of course. They'd tapped everything that could be tapped, and read the mail. But otherwise, they kept to themselves. Like the Cipher Bureau, the Bolsheviks were still finding their feet when it came to their national intelligence apparatus. But that didn't mean they weren't dangerous.

But the Russians weren't why she'd been in Moscow. She'd been following a trail of hints and whispers, and it had led her across Europe west to east, all the way from the States. A cult, with its roots in antiquity – Mesopotamian, maybe. It had seemed impossible at the time. But the more she learned, the more possible it became.

It was like an infection of the mind; of the soul. A sickness that she couldn't shake. She began to see patterns where there were none – could be none. Links between incidents, letters sent from Carpathian castles to innocuous New England academics, the bizarre catalepsy that had afflicted a certain professor of economics at Miskatonic University… all of it proof that the shadows of the world were deeper than she'd ever imagined.

Director Yardley had said it best: there was a war on, and they needed to pick a side – before they were drafted. That was why she'd made quiet contact with the Silver Twilight Lodge, the Scarlet Coterie, and others, all on orders from on high, despite her reservations.

The Black Chamber was dealing itself into the game, and it needed allies. The stranger – and stronger – the better. But alliances went both ways. Tit for tat. The Black Chamber fed on information, and the groups that had it were willing to share, for a price.

Moscow had been the beginning, though. The first step. Pages in a scholarly scrawl, detailing the rites of the ancient cult. Descriptions that had led to a man's death, and the disappearance of another. And the smell – God, the smell. Like standing water and rotten fish. Marks on the walls; gouges and slashes.

Something had been waiting for her, in the bathroom. Something that had crawled out of the frozen river, with scales coated in frost and claws and teeth and–

Trish snapped awake.

The motor car was stopped on a side street. Alessandra was

nowhere in sight. Lapp stood outside, hands clasped behind his back. Trish groaned and got out, feeling stiff. She looked around. Toulouse looked much as she recalled. Red rooftops and pale walls. The ding of nearby streetcars. The steeple of Saint-Sernin rose in the distance.

"Where is she?" Trish asked.

"Already gone to deliver the book," Lapp said.

Trish rubbed her eyes. She still wasn't certain it was a good plan. Giving the Comte what he wanted was the opposite of what she was supposed to be doing. But between them, Cinabre and Zorzi had convinced her it was the only way. They needed to keep Bera sweet, stop the Comte, and get the book. "You didn't go with her?"

"She assured me that she would be fine." He checked his pocket-watch. "They should be attempting the handover now. If we hear shooting, we will know she is dead."

She peered up at him. "You don't like her much, do you?"

"I do not like either of you."

Trish snorted. "The feeling is mutual."

He looked at her. "You fell asleep."

"People do that."

"So did she."

Trish hesitated. It was to be expected, she supposed. They'd both been awake for too long, running on coffee and adrenaline. "Like I said, people do that." She paused. "Except maybe you. Do you sleep, Lapp?"

He looked away. "On occasion."

"What do you dream about, when you do?" She wasn't sure why she asked the question. Plain old curiosity, maybe. The same instinct to know that had driven her to accept the Cipher Bureau's offer of employment after the war. Maybe it was just because Lapp felt like a puzzle, and there was nothing she enjoyed more than solving one.

He was silent for a moment. Then, "I sometimes think I am dreaming now, and that other place is my reality. I am a prince there, in turquoise-towered Larkar, where ginkgo trees rise wild on the slopes below." His voice grew soft and his gaze, absent. "Other times, I am a beast, and I prowl through a red forest. Still other times, I think the prince and the beast are one and the same, and that my story is stranger than I can imagine." He looked down at his hands, as if not recognizing them, and then at her. "I tire of this. Let us change the subject."

Trish studied him for a moment and then shook her head. "Where the hell did Cinabre dig you up, Lapp?"

"What?"

"Never mind. Just wondering how you came to work for the eccentric Monsieur Cinabre. He take out a want ad in the local rag?"

"We all must serve someone," Lapp murmured, a sly smile on his face.

"Even Cinabre?"

Lapp snorted and glanced at her. "You will have to ask him that. Though I doubt he will give you an answer." He stiffened and turned. "Do you hear that?"

She did. Police sirens. She turned toward the Basilica, wondering if they ought to go see, perhaps even intervene. But before she could make a decision, Lapp murmured, "Do you know him?"

Trish followed his gaze and saw the familiar, pale features of Chauncey Swann bobbing toward them, coming from the direction of the Basilica. Swann looked nervous; disheveled. That wasn't good. She pushed herself away from the motor car and slid her hand into her jacket. Swann reached them a moment later.

"Jesus Christ, I've been looking everywhere for you," he hissed. "I knew if she had the book, you'd be close by."

"I'm sorry, were we on a schedule?" Trish said, her finger tap-tapping against the holstered shape of her pistol. "You look nervous, Chauncey. Somebody after you?"

"I'm here with the Comte d'Erlette," he said, without preamble.

Trish stared at him for a moment. Then she cursed. "You double-dealing son of a... no. Fine. Hoping to swipe the book?" That had to be it. Maybe Sanford was hedging his bets. Maybe he was hoping to get out of giving the Black Chamber anything of value. Or maybe Chauncey was just looking out for his own best interests, like always.

He glanced around. "Something like that. Look, I ain't got much time. You need to listen to me. I... wait. Who's he?" He hiked a thumb at Lapp, who looked as if he wanted to snap the offending digit off. "Can we trust him?"

"No," Lapp said.

"Definitely not," Trish added. She wondered if Lapp knew who Swann was. She'd have bet money on it if they were in Atlantic City. Cinabre was the sort of guy who probably knew all the players in the game, whether they knew him or not. "But he's in it whether we like it or not. So talk."

"Look, it's worse than we thought, okay?" Swann said. "What he's planning... I didn't think it was this bad." He took off his hat and swallowed. He was genuinely afraid, Trish realized. And that made her heart beat a little faster. If Chauncey was afraid, it must be bad. "Zorzi brought it right to him. I took a chance and slipped away during all the shouting –

he's focused on the countess right now. Wants to make sure she doesn't get away." He paused and dabbed at his face with a handkerchief. "We screwed up. I didn't realize what he was up to. None of us did. I thought it was just a- a sightseeing trip, you know? The sort we do all the time. Only it's not. It's bad mojo, Scarborough."

"I'm getting that impression, yeah." Trish looked at Lapp. "I guess your boss was right. Alessandra's old pal is up to something shifty."

"Yeah, and you just let the key to the whole thing drop into his hands," Swann said. He jabbed at her with a finger. "You were supposed to get the book for us, Scarborough. Not him! And now he's got it and we're all in the hole!"

"Relax, Chauncey. It's part of the plan."

"Plan? This is not a plan! This is the end of the world. He intends to start a war, Scarborough – a war against something we can't beat. We have to stop him. We have to–" He stopped in mid-sentence as a tall, bald man stepped around the rear of the motor car, a revolver in his hand.

"That is enough of that, m'sieu."

Lapp turned toward the newcomer. Trish followed suit, taking him in at a glance. Turkish, she thought. Possibly Persian. Heavy, but with muscle not fat. A wrestler. Maybe a soldier. He was dressed in a suit, but the clothes were down market. Cheap suit, cheap shoes. Muscle, then. "And you are?" she asked.

The bald man ignored her, and addressed Swann instead. "You thought you were so clever, m'sieu. Slipping away like a rodent while we were otherwise occupied. But I saw, and I followed. Now you will come with me, and explain yourself to the Comte."

"I don't think so." Trish drew her weapon and had a bead on

the bald man before he could react. He grimaced, but didn't lower his own weapon.

"You will not shoot me."

"If she does not, I will twist your head from your shoulders," Lapp said, in a mild tone. The bald man flinched. Clearly he'd had some experience with things that looked like people, but probably weren't.

Trish smiled. "Either way, your chances just took a nosedive. So what say we discuss this like civilized people?"

Swann moved to the side, out of the firing line. "She's right, Selim. Only way you're walking away is if you unstop those ears of yours and listen."

Selim glared at him. "The Comte was right. You are up to something."

"Yeah, it's called saving your life, pal."

Selim snorted. "Your own, you mean."

"Mine too," Swann admitted. "Everybody's. Because what your boss has planned, it ain't good for any of us – and I think you damn well know it. You're just as worried about the repercussions as I am."

Selim paused, and Trish seized the opening. "He's right. Much as I hate to admit it. You've probably been with him long enough to see how he does things. Long enough to start to feel some doubts, maybe." She hesitated, choosing her words with care. "You sign up to be a kidnapper, Selim? A murderer?"

He stared at her for a moment. "You know nothing of me. Get over here, Swann," he said, slowly. Swann glanced at Trish, who waved him toward Selim.

"Scarborough…" he began.

"Go, Chauncey. I'm guessing if we start shooting, Selim's pals will come running. How many did he bring?"

Selim grunted. "None, save me."

Trish raised an eyebrow. "He's got the cops," Swann supplied. She frowned. Alessandra had suspected as much. That was probably why she'd left Lapp behind. No sense getting an asset clapped in irons, especially when they'd be needed later.

"The Comte has much influence in this city." Selim paused. "You would do well to depart before someone sees you. He is only interested in the Zorzi woman." He didn't lower his weapon, but something told her he wasn't planning to shoot either of them.

Trish inclined her head. "Good advice." Selim's face was hard to read, but she thought she saw something like consideration in his expression. Was he thinking about what they'd said, or was he just trying to keep from eating a bullet himself?

"Scarborough," Swann said, pleadingly. Selim had him by the collar of his jacket and was dragging him along like an errant schoolboy.

Trish lowered her weapon and called out, "Remember why you're here, Chauncey." She hoped he got the message. If not, it'd be up to Zorzi alone.

"What now?" Lapp asked.

Trish holstered her pistol. "We stick to the plan. Get to the chateau and kick up a ruckus." She glanced at him. "Think you can handle that, Lapp?"

His only response was a smile that was too sharp and too wide. It reminded her of Moscow, and something that stank of river mud, and she repressed a shudder.

"Good enough," she said. "Let's go."

CHAPTER TWENTY-EIGHT
Reunion

"So," Alessandra began.

Pepper looked at her. "That was a terrible plan," she said. Her wrists and ankles were bound with knotted rope, as were Alessandra's, and they sat in the back of a truck, probably heading back to the chateau. They'd left Toulouse in a motor car, but been transferred to the truck after they'd left the city behind. "I hope you don't mind me saying that. But that was awful. I have seen better plans in the Sunday funnies."

Alessandra studied the rope knotted about her wrists. "French prisons are unpleasant. Or so I am told, having never been in one. I thought this was preferable." She began to rotate her wrists in an odd fashion as she looked around the back of the truck. Pepper followed her gaze. It was military surplus, she thought. It had crates stacked in it; so many in fact that she and Alessandra were cramped into a small space at the rear. Alessandra snorted. "Not even a guard to sit with us. How insulting."

"Maybe he figures we ain't going anywhere with our hands and feet tied," Pepper said, jerking her wrists up for emphasis.

The Comte's men hadn't been particularly gentle about it, and she could already feel the bruises.

"Then he does not know me as well as he thinks," Alessandra said. She continued her rotations, moving one fist and then the other, her face tight with concentration. "I will have this off in a matter of moments. Oh, and keep your voice down. No need to alert the driver."

Mouth shut, Pepper settled back against the juddering frame of the truck and eyed her mentor. Her first impression was that Alessandra didn't seem all that worried. Then, she rarely did. Alessandra had a natural poker face. It was hard to tell what she was feeling at any given moment. The other woman looked at her. "Tell me about this ghoul, then."

"What about him?" Pepper stretched her arms as much as she was able, trying to work out the kinks. "Seemed nice enough, when he wasn't trying to eat me." She hesitated. "I think your pal Henri has plans for him – nasty ones. They caught another one yesterday, trying to sneak onto the grounds. Killed it… him. Butchered them, like they were an animal." She swallowed, as the image of the flayed ghoul rose up in her mind. "Only animals don't talk, so why…" She trailed off, unable to process it, and shook her head. "He tried to eat me, but I don't think he deserves that."

Alessandra nodded. "I cannot think of anyone who does. Henri excepted, perhaps."

"Is it true you two used to… you know?"

Alessandra raised an eyebrow. "Is that what he said?"

"He said a lot, usually around a mouthful of booze." Pepper peered at the other woman. "I didn't think he was your type, honestly."

Alessandra paused. "My type?"

"You know." Pepper hesitated, slightly embarrassed. She gestured. "Your type."

Alessandra's eyes narrowed in apparent confusion. "Romantically, you mean."

"Yes!"

"No. Well, perhaps. At the time." Alessandra smiled and Pepper suddenly realized that the other woman was making fun of her. She flushed in irritation.

"You funning me, sister?"

"Heaven forefend." Alessandra pointed at Pepper's wrists. "I thought I taught you how to get out of knots."

"Must have been somebody else." Pepper sighed and leaned forward. "Thank you."

"What?"

"Thank you," Pepper repeated, more loudly. "For saving me. Trying to save me, I mean. Thank you."

Alessandra paused in her rotations and gave Pepper a startled look. "Did you doubt I would?" she asked, in an almost hurt tone.

Pepper flushed. "No. No! I just – y'know. Thanks, is all."

"You are very welcome, Pepper."

"Yeah, well, maybe I'll get a chance to return the favor."

"You will forgive me if I say I hope not," Alessandra said, unraveling the rope tied about her wrists and dropping it into the bed of the truck. "There now. That is better." She bent and started working on the ropes around her ankles.

"You got loose?" Pepper asked, in shock.

"Of course. These knots were child's play. Henri should be ashamed of himself." She tossed the ropes from her ankles aside, and reached for Pepper's wrists. "Come, let me help you."

Pepper's pulse sped up. "So, what's the plan then? We jumping out of the truck or what?" She cast a nervous glance at the road unreeling in the vehicle's wake. She'd never jumped out of a moving vehicle, but she was pretty sure it would hurt. "Only I'm not so sure that's a good idea. Maybe we should commandeer it instead."

Alessandra smiled. "Relax, Pepper. Believe it or not, we are right where I want us to be." She began to pluck apart the heavy knots that bound Pepper's wrists. "I could swear I taught you how to do this."

"Hey, I got out of the chateau by myself, didn't I?"

Alessandra gave her a bemused look. "Did you? And how did you accomplish that?"

Pepper smirked. "The chimney."

Alessandra sat back. "Oh?"

"Right up it, just like you taught me." Pepper gestured for emphasis. "Climbed down the roof, and into the woods." She preened slightly. "Smooth as butter."

"Then why are you in the back of this truck?"

Pepper glared at her. "Well, I wasn't the one with the gun, was I?"

Alessandra sighed. "Shooting Henri would have accomplished nothing. We would have been captured or worse, and no good to anyone." She finished untying Pepper's ankles and moved back, toward the crates. "Besides, as I said, we are right where we want to be."

"Yeah, maybe explain it for the cheap seats." Pepper rubbed her wrists and ankles. "How does us staying captured help anybody, especially us?"

Alessandra ran her hands along the edges of the crates. "I have good reason to believe that whatever Henri is up to, he cannot be allowed to succeed in it. Hiding the book from him was the obvious answer, but there were other factors in play..."

"Me, you mean," Pepper said.

Alessandra paused. Then, "Yes. So, I had to show him the book. And I knew that once I did that, he would try and renege on our deal. However much he declaims about his familial honor, Henri has never let such things stand in his way when it comes to getting what he wants. So, I thought it best to go along."

"But now we're trapped," Pepper protested.

Alessandra took off one of her shoes and carefully peeled back the inside sole. "Yes. That is what he believes. But I have always found that the best time to put the knife in is while standing next to someone." She rolled back the material of the sole, revealing a hidden compartment, containing a flat piece of metal, edged in rubber. She pulled it out and put her shoe back on. She looked at Pepper. "Besides, we are not alone in this."

"We're not?"

"No. Help me with this." Alessandra inserted the flat piece of metal beneath the lid of a crate and began to lever it up, albeit slowly, so as not to alert the driver to any problems. Pepper, curious about what was in the crate, moved to help. In a few moments, they had the nails loose and the lid almost up. Alessandra peered inside – and immediately slammed the lid down with a muttered curse.

"What is it?" Pepper asked. She'd caught a whiff of something unpleasant, like rotten meat. Alessandra sat back, her expression concerned.

"A corpse."

Pepper shoved herself back from the crates. "Jeezum crow!" She hesitated. "Do you think they're all … I mean, why?"

"I do not know, and I hesitate to guess. Likely he needs them for something." Alessandra sounded thoughtful. "All the more reason to stop him, if we can. Any endeavor that requires the use of rotting corpses is questionable at best."

"I could have told you it was questionable without the stiffs." Pepper took off her hat and sat down opposite Alessandra. "So what's the plan, then?"

"Follow my lead, and try not to get killed."

Pepper laughed. "Same as always then!"

"Indeed. I …" Alessandra stiffened. "We are slowing."

Pepper peered out of the back of the truck. "I recognize these trees. At least I think I do. We're at the chateau."

Alessandra joined her. "Yes. I never thought I would come back here. Certainly not tied up in the back of a truck."

The truck carried them into the courtyard and came to a halt. A black motor car was already parked there, and several other trucks. Alessandra motioned for Pepper to sit down as the tailgate was lowered and several armed men stepped into view, rifles and shotguns aimed at the two women. Pepper swallowed thickly, but kept her expression neutral.

The Comte pushed through the line of men, using his cane to nudge them aside. "Did you enjoy the ride?" he asked, gesturing for them to get down. Swann and Selim stood behind him. Pepper thought they both looked like they had something on their minds, and neither looked happy. The Comte, on the other hand, looked downright cheerful. He had the *Cultes des Goules* nestled in the crook of his arm, safe as a beloved child.

"Not in the least. Here is your rope back." Alessandra tossed him the rope, and Pepper laughed to see the look on his face. "Why the truck, if I might ask?"

"I wanted to see what you might do." He dropped the rope onto the ground and smiled up at her. "I expected you would free yourself. But I am happy to see that you took our bargain seriously and did not try to escape." He held out his hand and after a moment's hesitation, Alessandra took it and stepped down out of the truck.

"Perhaps I am simply curious as to what you are planning."

Pepper hopped down after her. "And why you brought a load of stiffs all the way from Toulouse," she said, waving at the truck. She looked around the courtyard. It was much the same as she recalled; lots of boxes and men, lots of weapons. The ghoul's body was gone, thankfully. She didn't want to think about where.

"Every hunt needs bait, every war needs supplies," the Comte said. He turned and ordered his men to begin unloading the truck. He gestured with his cane. "Into the house. It will become intolerably busy out here in a few moments. My men have preparations to make before we begin."

"Yes, tonight is the equinox, is it not?" Alessandra asked, in an innocent tone. The Comte whirled, the edges of his coat flaring out as he stared at her. Not startled this time, but angry. Her smile could have sliced a side of beef as she continued. "Tell me, is this the event you were planning for when I stole the book in the first place?"

The Comte glared. "Yes," he said. "As a matter of fact, it was. You forced me to delay everything – all my careful preparations. Money and time wasted, because of your larcenous behavior." He stepped closer to her, and thrust the head of his cane under her chin. Pepper took a step toward him, fists balled, but Alessandra waved her back, never taking her eyes from the Comte.

"How sad for you, Henri. Would you like an apology?"

The Comte grimaced and raised his cane, as if to club Alessandra to the ground. Pepper readied herself to lunge for him. But in the end, he lowered his cane and stepped back, visibly composing himself. "Yes, actually," he said, after a moment. "Among other things." He looked at Pepper. "I would encourage you to choose your friends more carefully in the future, mademoiselle. Alessandra has a habit of making things more difficult for everyone around her."

"Pal, she ain't the only one," Pepper said, fixing him with a pugnacious look. The more she learned about him, the more she thought maybe feeding the Comte to Jules was the way to go.

The Comte turned away. "Take them upstairs. Watch them. No more escapes." He paused and gave them a lingering glance.

"Not for either of you."

CHAPTER TWENTY-NINE
Answers

The room Alessandra and Pepper were shown to was empty, save for a bricked-up fireplace. No furniture and the windows shuttered from the outside. Henri had taken precautions. The door was locked behind them. Alessandra turned in place, studying the room from every angle.

"I don't think they want us getting out of here," Pepper said, knocking on the bricks that filled the fireplace.

"Even so, I will still make the attempt," Alessandra said. "If only to allay suspicion." She glanced at the window. Judging by the light, it was midday, maybe a bit later. They had a few hours until whatever Henri was planning started. Enough time, she hoped, for Trish and the others to do their part.

Pepper made a small sound in her throat, and Alessandra turned. The young woman was crouched beside the fireplace, holding something – a scrap of cloth, she thought – in her hand. Alessandra hesitated, then asked, "Pepper? What is wrong?"

"I... nothing," Pepper said, rising slowly to her feet. Her voice was hoarse. Her hand clenched about the cloth, and Alessandra caught a flash of yellow. Quickly, she strode over and took Pepper's face in her hands. She forced the young woman to look at her. Pepper looked up, startled, and Alessandra saw the fading glimmer of fear in her gaze.

"Tell me," she said, softly.

Pepper looked down, at the scrap of cloth in her hand. Something snagged from a blanket or perhaps a shirt. Alessandra gently took it. "What is this?"

"Just a piece of trash," Pepper said. "But – it wasn't there, and then – then it was. Like someone left it for me." Her eyes slid away from Alessandra's. "But that can't be. I been… I think I been seeing things. Ever since Paris. Since Znamenski's studio."

Alessandra felt a sinking sensation in her gut. "What sort of things?"

Pepper shook her head. "Just things. A thing. I don't know how to describe it. And I – I had a dream. The first night I was here. Something was chasing me – no, *following* me. Like it wasn't worried I might get away." She swallowed, and looked at Alessandra. "Like it knew it was going to catch me eventually."

"Did you see it?" Alessandra asked intently, thinking of Arkham and of a man who was not a man, swearing vengeance in the name of his masters. *Zamacona is dead,* she thought, and almost believed it. She was almost relieved when Pepper shook her head.

"No, it's… I don't know. Like it's not ready for me to see it yet. I can almost hear it though, sometimes. Like an echo in my head." She clenched her fists, as if wishing she could pummel her tormenter. Alessandra looked at the scrap of yellow cloth – only it wasn't yellow. Not really. More orange than anything. Had it ever been yellow, or had it just been a trick of the light?

She thrust the scrap into her pocket and caught Pepper by the shoulder. "That is all to the good," she said. "It means we have time. I know someone who might have some answers, but first we must get through tonight intact." She'd come close to losing Pepper once already; she didn't intend to do so again. The young woman was her responsibility. Her friend. And Alessandra would be damned if she'd let anything happen to her.

Cinabre would know what this was, she was certain. And if not him, then Znamenski might. Whether either man would help or not – and what it might cost to secure their aid – was another matter. But she was careful to keep her worry off her face.

Pepper took a deep breath and nodded. "Yeah. We'll worry about it after we punch the Comte in his smug kisser." She straightened and looked Alessandra in the eye. The fear was still there, but Pepper had it under control.

Alessandra decided to change the subject. "How many guards on the door, do you think?" It was an old game; one her grandfather had often played with her. Give the brain something to do, so that it didn't succumb to worry.

"One for sure, maybe two," Pepper said, automatically. "Both armed."

"Of course." Alessandra looked up at the ceiling. Ceilings were weak points. No one thought about them. Cracked plaster, loose boards, all of it offered a way in or out, if one was clever enough to take advantage of it. Of course, one needed the right tools for that sort of thing. In that regard, they were out of luck. Her pry bar had been taken, and they'd both been thoroughly searched before being deposited in the room. "What else did you notice?"

"More guys here than when I left. Thirty or forty, easy." Pepper hesitated. "What's he need all those guys for? It's like a small army."

"Men for the guns, guns for the men," Alessandra murmured. "And bodies for bait. What exactly are you planning, Henri?" Nothing good, that was for certain. Swann's presence, willing or otherwise, attested to that.

"So what do we do? Just sit here and wait?"

"Think of it more as biding our time," Alessandra said.

"Until what?"

"Until the signal."

Pepper made an impatient gesture. "What signal?"

Before Alessandra could answer, the sound of the door being opened caused them both to turn. Alessandra saw the familiar, white-suit clad shape of Chauncey Swann being shoved into the room by Henri's man, Selim. The latter looked at them both, before slamming the door and locking it once more.

Swann bent and picked up his hat from where it had fallen to the floor and dusted it off. "That guy is getting on my nerves, I tell you what," he said, looking at them.

"Chauncey," Alessandra said, coolly. Swann grimaced.

"Zorzi. You look in fine fettle, if I might say so."

"You may not."

Swann held up his hands, as if in surrender. "Consider my course corrected, then."

Alessandra crossed her arms and looked at him. "Did Henri send you in here for a reason, or just to annoy us?"

Swann snorted. "No, this is my punishment."

"Punishment? For what?"

"I slipped away for a bit. Thought about making a run for it, but realized there was nowhere to go. But I did see a familiar face…"

"Oh?"

"Friend of mine. Co-worker, you might say."

"Oh?" Alessandra was careful not to react. The plan that she had been so confident of only a few moments ago was now poised on a knife-edge, depending on Swann's next words. Swann studied her. From his frown, she guessed her reaction – or lack of one – had disappointed him.

"Her name's Scarborough. Trish Scarborough. Ever run across her?"

"Not to my knowledge."

Swann smirked. "Yeah, I bet." He tapped the side of his head. "I got to thinking about it, on the way back. Scarborough said something about a plan, before Selim interrupted us. I realized, smart as she is, she probably decided the best way to get what she wanted – what we both wanted – was to walk in your shadow."

"Get to the point, Chauncey."

"You and Trish, you made a deal, didn't you?" Swann glanced at the door and then back at her. "That's why she was cooling her heels. At first, I figured you weren't thinking clearly, but then I realized that you wanted to get caught. Am I right?"

Alessandra lunged, wrapping her arm around Swann's neck before he could react. She kicked his feet out from under him, dropping him to his knees. He gave a strangled yelp, but didn't resist. Pepper hurried to the door, listening out for trouble. "Geez," she muttered. "I don't like the mook, but throttling him don't seem polite."

"I am not throttling him. This is how I get Chauncey's attention. Isn't it, Chauncey?" Alessandra crouched over Swann and tightened her hold on his neck. It was, perhaps, an overreaction, but a bit of violence was the easiest way to keep a man like Swann off balance. "While I am not certain that I can snap your neck, having never attempted such a thing, I do know that I am strong enough to give your windpipe a most unpleasant squeeze. Savvy?"

"Understood," he wheezed, hands spread. "I didn't come for a fight. I came to help."

"I do not see how, given that you appear to be as much a prisoner as I – as we – are."

"If you'll stop with the anaconda grip, I'll tell you," he hissed out, plucking at her arm. "Things are going dark. I'm seeing spots."

"Oh fine," she muttered, releasing him. He pitched forward, catching himself before he hit the floor. "Talk, and be swift, Chauncey. Or I will do my best to make your last moments incredibly unpleasant."

"And I'll help," Pepper said.

Swann glanced at her and picked himself up. He rubbed his throat and glared at Alessandra. "Like I said, I saw Scarborough. Her and that blond guy."

"Lapp," Alessandra supplied.

Swann shrugged. "Didn't catch his name." He paused expectantly, as if waiting for her to elaborate, but she made no move to reply. The less Swann knew, the better. Seeing she wasn't planning on answering, he sighed and continued, "Anyway, I saw them. Spoke to them. Told them what the score was, which they seemed happy about. Though they didn't say thank you…"

Alessandra snorted at his expression. "Did they hurt your feelings, Chauncey?"

"A little bit, yeah. And after all the trouble I went to, to find them. At significant risk to myself I might add."

"Risk – or profit?"

Swann grinned. "Can't have one without the other, right?"

Alessandra smiled, despite herself. For all his faults, Swann was a peer. He understood the game in a way people like Trish never could. But that didn't mean she trusted him farther than she could throw him. "I will give you that, yes."

"So you two are in cahoots, hunh?" he asked.

"Does that surprise you?"

"A bit." He gave her a sly look. "You know she's the one who suggested we tell the Comte where you were."

Alessandra glanced at Pepper and then nodded. "So I gathered. But she had her reasons. As you did."

"I do what I'm told," Swann said, sounding offended. "Anyway, we didn't get much opportunity to chat. Selim showed up."

"Then Henri knows about her?"

Swann shook his head and pulled a pack of cigarettes out of his jacket. "Don't worry, Selim didn't say nothing about your pals," he said, offering Alessandra the pack of cigarettes. She waved it aside, but Pepper snatched one before he could take the pack back. He frowned at her, but didn't argue. "Don't know why. Maybe he's getting cold feet."

Alessandra raised her eyebrow. "It seems as if he is not the only one, Chauncey."

Swann grunted. "I never signed up for this. Neither did my employer. Your pal Henri is crazy, and not the usual type of crazy. I can work with that kind of nut. But this… this is bad for everyone, and I do mean everyone."

"How so?"

"I'm surprised your pal hasn't told you." Swann blew smoke into the air and glanced at Pepper. "He's opening a gate, Zorzi. A door to somewhere else. And he ain't waiting for anything to come out."

Alessandra paused and looked at Pepper. "The guns, the explosives... he's launching an invasion." It sounded ridiculous, even as she said it. But what other explanation could there be? "This... gate of yours, where does it lead to?"

"Pnath, or close environs thereof." Swann peered at her. "Ever heard of it? I'd be surprised if you had."

"No." She hesitated. Mouth suddenly dry, she asked, "Is it... like N'kai?"

Swann paled slightly. "A bit further away, or maybe a lot closer, depending." He swallowed. "You had a run-in with the corpse-eaters, right?"

"Yes."

"Well, think of Pnath as the lobby of an apartment building. The ghouls, well they live in the penthouse. But Henri, he's heading for the basement. He wants to talk to the super, you might say."

"I do not understand."

"He's looking for the guy in charge of the building," Pepper said, softly. "I meant to tell you before, but I got distracted."

Swann pointed a finger at her, indicating that she was right. "Bingo. Give the young lady a kewpie doll."

"Enough of this cryptic nonsense. Who is he looking for?"

Swann leaned closed. "Umôrdhoth," he whispered. The very sound of the name made her feel vaguely ill. She swallowed thickly and tried to push the feeling aside.

"And who is that? A ghoul?"

"No. He's their god." Swann ran his hand through his hair. "And that's why this is going to be bad for all of us. I thought he was just planning a- a raid, maybe. We do that, sometimes... go a-Viking, like in the old days. Take whatever ain't nailed down. But this isn't a raid. He's planning to start a war – or maybe finish one. Only, he can't. You can't just kill a god, let alone in its own holy fane. Even your old pals from K'n-yan failed in such an attempt…"

At his mention of K'n-yan, Alessandra felt her heart speed up and she closed her eyes. In her mind's eye, she could see again that great underground city, with its firefly lights and abyssal shadows. She looked at Swann. "I assume you tried to convince him of this?"

"Lady, he ain't one for convincing," Swann said, in a disgruntled tone. He gestured. "Why do you think I'm in here with you, rather than sipping wine and reading that first edition Baudelaire I saw on his shelf?"

"*Les Fleurs du mal*?" she asked, absently. "I thought I stole that one."

Swann sniffed derisively. "No. *La Fanfarlo*. An earlier and better work in my opinion. Last time he was enthusiastic about his writing, if you ask me."

"Why Chauncey, you soppy old romantic. I never pictured you as the type." Alessandra peered at him in mild surprise. Swann had unplumbed depths, it seemed. "You are telling me all of this… why?"

He laughed and shook his head. "Ain't it obvious? I want in on whatever plan you and Scarborough cooked up. In the words of a great man, we stand together or hang separately."

CHAPTER THIRTY
Muster

Trish leaned over the bonnet of the motor car, her binoculars fixed on the distant outline of the chateau. They'd parked a safe distance away, on the other side of the thick woodland that banded the estate. Far enough to avoid the notice of any roving guard patrols, but close enough to get to it and back on foot without too much trouble. Or so she hoped.

Gnarled trees rose wild around them, and she could smell rain on the air. Birds sang sweet, sad melodies in the branches. It would have been idyllic, on any other day. She could feel an underlying tension in the air, as if the land were waiting for something to happen. Maybe it was. Maybe it could sense what the Comte was up to. Or maybe she was simply imagining things. It was hard to tell which was which, these days.

It had taken some time to follow the Comte's convoy from Toulouse, but Trish was an old hand at tailing hostile parties. So was Lapp, apparently. She was starting to be grateful that Cinabre had insisted on sending the man. Lapp was competent, if not especially sociable. She'd worked with worse, in her time.

She glanced at him. "Let's go over it once more," she said. Lapp, who'd been busy studying a map, looked up. He'd changed out of his suit and tie for outdoor gear, but it looked unnatural on him. He folded the map and tapped it against the car.

"We will begin our approach when Bera and her followers arrive. While they cause a distraction outside, we will make our way inside, where we will locate Zorzi and her associate – as well as the book – and make our departure, causing as much disruption as possible to the Comte's organization on our way out. We return to the motor car, and withdraw, leaving Bera and her followers to clean up." He looked at her expectantly. "Did I leave anything out?"

She turned back to the chateau. "No. Except for the part about how we're going to get inside." He cleared his throat, catching her attention. She lowered her binoculars and turned. Lapp silently proffered a shotgun. He had two of them, one in each hand. She took the weapon with a nod of thanks and checked it. "Ammunition?"

He set two boxes onto the roof of the car. "Of course."

"You come prepared, Lapp."

"Always." He began to load his weapon and paused, head cocked like a dog that had caught a familiar scent. "They are here."

Trish finished loading her shotgun and nodded. "Right on schedule." Not that there was a schedule. She hadn't seen so much as a whisper of the ghouls since leaving Cinabre's residence. But even so, something had told her that they'd show up right when and where they needed to.

A branch cracked behind her and she turned to see Bera, still in her dress, standing a wary distance away. Having seen how fast Bera and her monstrous kin moved, Trish didn't doubt it was more for her sake than Bera's. "Have any trouble finding the place?"

Bera's eyes narrowed. "A joke?"

Trish settled the shotgun into the crook of her arm. "Just a little one. I thought you were bringing some help." She looked around, but didn't see any of the familiar hulking shapes from the library. But the birds had gone quiet, and the forest was still. She figured that meant they were close by.

Bera smiled; an ugly sort of expression. It was like watching a tiger try its best to appear non-threatening. Amusing and worrisome at the same time. "They are close. It was discussed and decided that you might find their presence… off-putting. They do not wish to give offense, not when we are allies in this matter."

"How considerate of them," Trish said, slowly, trying to work her head around the idea of thoughtful monsters. "Alessandra is in the chateau."

"We know," Bera said, sniffing the air. "When we arrived, we discovered that someone had broken the wards that prevented us from gaining access to these grounds. An error on their part, and one we will make them pay dearly for. My cousins have already slunk about the walls, listening to the men talking in the courtyard."

"And what are those men saying?"

"They think they are on the cusp of victory." Bera's teeth flashed. "It will be our pleasure to disabuse them of that assumption."

"Are there enough of you?"

"One would be enough," Bera said, haughtily. Lapp snorted and she glared at him, but amended her statement. "Yes, there are enough for this. But we must stop him before he opens the way… else all of this is for naught."

Trish didn't need to ask why. The glint of fear in Bera's feral gaze was proof enough. "We'll do our best," she hedged. "Worse comes to worse, we'll set the house on fire."

Bera blinked. Then, nodded. "That… might be enough."

Trish didn't care for the way she emphasized "might". "We'll do our best," she repeated. Bera seemed to accept this assurance in the spirit it was intended. The ghoul-woman straightened and looked up at the sky. "It will be dark soon. We will make our move then. My people prefer to hunt at night."

Trish nodded. "Good enough. We'll start making our way down, then."

Bera paused. "Do not think to betray us, woman. It will not go well for you if you do. The book will be ours when this is done."

Trish nodded again. "Of course."

Bera stared at her for a moment, then turned away and was gone, melting into the shadows beneath the trees with animal grace. Lapp snickered. "They are going to be very angry, when this is done."

"That's my problem, isn't it?"

"Yes. Very much so. They will not stop hunting you, until they have what they want, or you are dead and filling their bellies."

Trish couldn't help but shudder at the thought. "If they want my scalp, they have to get in line," she said, trying to keep her unease out of her voice. She hefted her shotgun. "Now, what else do we need?"

"Luck," Lapp said, simply.

"We'll make our own. Let's go."

The forest was largely silent as they made their way toward the chateau. The birds, having fled the presence of the ghouls, had yet to return. They'd probably steer clear of the area until things had calmed down. Trish thought that showed they were smarter than humans. Part of her wanted to follow their example.

They stopped when they spotted the first skull on its post. One of several, scattered along to the left and the right, like a fence. She wasn't surprised. She'd expected something like this. There was always a skull somewhere, when it came to this kind of thing. "Ugly sort of fence," she murmured.

"Boundary markers," Lapp said, softly. He took out a handkerchief and wiped a muddy, red mark off the skull. He sniffed the residue. "Blood."

"Human?"

"Possibly." Lapp looked away. "I do know one thing… they were raised to keep out Bera and her kind."

"I don't think they're the type to be scared of skulls." Trish paused. "It's the mark, isn't it? Some sort of witchcraft." She knew a little about such things; less than she needed, more than she liked. Certain marks worked like "no trespassing" signs. You scratched them into a door or on a threshold and things of a certain nature couldn't enter.

"Some sort, yes." Lapp gestured. "We should keep moving. It is getting dark."

She indicated that he should take the lead. "After you."

It was late afternoon, edging into evening, when they found the boundary wall, just as Alessandra had described it. Tumbled, piled stones, nearly chest high. They stopped and Trish raised her binoculars, focusing on the chateau. It was lit up like Christmas. "Lots of movement. Lots of artillery down there."

"As we expected," Lapp said, sitting down and leaning against the wall.

Trish grunted and sat down too, her back to the boundary wall. "I didn't expect quite that many, I have to admit. There's an army down there."

Lapp was silent for a moment. Then, "They are desperate men. The wreckage of the unseen world. There are always more of them, after a war. War sharpens the appetite of the things that hunger in the shadows, but it breeds survivors. Those survivors need little encouragement to throw themselves into the fire."

"Did Cinabre tell you that?"

"He did not have to." Lapp grimaced and stared at the chateau. "Everyone has a master. If they do not, they look for one. It is our nature."

Trish paused and studied him. "Not Zorzi," she said, after a moment.

Lapp snorted. "Why do you think he is helping her?" He turned and met her gaze. "In this world, if you do not have a master, one will find you. That too is our nature."

Trish felt a chill run through her. "He wants her to owe him. Why?"

Lapp looked away. "Does it matter? You will have what you want – what your masters want – when this is done. What does it matter why Monsieur Cinabre wants Zorzi to owe him? Better for you, perhaps, not to know."

Trish stared at him, then laughed softly. "Maybe so. But you can't fault a girl for being curious, can you?"

Lapp grunted, but didn't reply. Trish smiled and settled

back. But inside, worry gnawed at her. She'd assumed she'd known the game; but what if the rules weren't what she'd thought? What if, what if, what if? That was the problem with finding patterns; sometimes the pattern was more complex than you imagined.

She wondered if she ought to warn Zorzi. Then, Zorzi probably already knew that Cinabre was after something. Given her proclivities, it wasn't out of bounds to assume that Cinabre wanted her to steal something for him. It'd be nice to know what. But that was for later. She heard a murmur of voices, and froze. She looked at Lapp and gestured. He nodded silently as she handed him her shotgun.

Trish rose silently and made her way toward the voices. Hiding was all well and good, but it limited your options. Forced you to react. Better to seize the initiative than to wait passively. At least that had always been her view.

Two armed men stood beneath the trees, looking down at a fallen boundary marker. The skull had been broken. In the dim light of the setting sun, she could tell that they both looked concerned. She coughed politely, and they looked up in startlement. They cursed in French and raised their rifles. She raised her hands, and put on a frightened expression. "Hello?" she quavered, in broken French. "I- I am lost. I need help."

"Stay where you are," one growled. He waved his companion forward. "Check her."

The second man started toward her with obvious reluctance. Trish kept her expression placid and her hands up, even as she calculated the likelihood of taking them both out with her pistol. "I- I don't understand. I just… I was hiking, and I got turned around…"

"Shut up," the first man snapped. "Remember to check the jaws, the way we were taught. They can look like people, but they can't hide their teeth."

"I remember, damn you," the second man snapped, as he reached out to take hold of Trish. She waited until she could smell the wine on his breath, and turned, stepping into his reach and stabbing her elbow into his midsection. He wheezed and bent, allowing her to drive the heel of her palm into his throat. He staggered and she snatched the rifle from his grip, shoving him aside as she did so. She had it up and aimed at the first man before the second had slumped to the ground, gagging.

"Don't move," she said, quietly. "Put your gun down, or I put you down."

He hesitated, eyes wide. Before he could respond, however, two hairy hands emerged from the shadows behind him and gripped his head. He gave a single, startled squawk as his neck was snapped. His body toppled forward.

The second man whimpered and Trish turned to see Bera crouched beside him. She traced the line of his cheek with a fingernail, drawing blood. "Don't," Trish began, without thinking. Bera ignored her, and sank her fingers into the cowering man's throat. She tore out his jugular with barely a flicker of effort. She looked at Trish as she sucked the blood from her fingers. Trish stepped back, not quite aiming the rifle at Bera.

Bera rose and gave a throaty chuckle. "Remember what I said, woman. Do not think to betray us, or we will crack your bones and suck the marrow." With that, she stepped past Trish and vanished once more into the trees. Trish heard the sound of several heavy bodies moving, then… silence.

She exhaled a shuddering breath and made her way back toward Lapp.

CHAPTER THIRTY-ONE
Ritual

Shadows were lengthening along the floor when Selim returned for them. He entered warily and Alessandra could see two other men over his shoulder. He was taking no chances. "Up," he said, looking around the room expectantly. He grunted in approval. She'd made no attempt to get them out after Swann's visit had interrupted her. "It is nearly time," he added.

"Great. I was getting impatient," Pepper muttered, as she and Alessandra rose to their feet. Swann rose as well, cigarette dangling from his lips. He took the cigarette and flicked it at Selim.

"This is a bad idea and you know it," he said, simply. Selim looked at the cigarette on the floor and carefully trod on it. Then he drove his fist into Swann's belly, doubling him over. He shoved the wheezing acquisitionist toward the two guards.

"Yes," Selim said. "I do." He looked at Alessandra and Pepper. "But he is determined. Nor is he the only one. Many here have endured hurt and horror at the claws of that folk. Many want revenge. The Comte was careful in his selection."

"Including you," Alessandra said, giving him a steady look.

Selim nodded. "Including me. I owe him. And I will not abandon the others to Hell."

"Admirable sentiments, if somewhat foolish." She sighed. Selim seemed a decent sort of fellow. Henri was utterly undeserving of that kind of loyalty, in her opinion. "I suppose he wants to preen a bit, beforehand."

Selim nodded ruefully. "He is most excited to show you what he has accomplished." He gestured. "This way, if you please."

"I can't decide whether this guy wants to kill you or kiss you," Pepper said, as she and Alessandra stepped into the corridor. The men Selim had brought were armed, and looked perfectly willing to use their weapons. Nervous, but not frightened, Alessandra thought. Soldiers, then. There were a lot of ex-soldiers about these days. Men looking for a war; any war. And Henri was apparently planning to give them one.

"He wants to do both," Alessandra said, looking at the younger woman. "I made him look a fool and that is the one thing he cannot bear."

"Sounds like a few guys I know," Pepper said. She glanced at Swann, who snorted.

"Kid, I don't mind looking the fool, so long as I get paid," he said, rubbing his midsection. "Reputation is just another currency, as far as I'm concerned. If you don't have enough, you can get it. You got too much, you may as well spend it."

"How philosophical of you, Chauncey," Alessandra said, not looking at him. "Unfortunately for us, the only currency Henri seems to be interested in is blood." There was a strange smell on the air; not of rot or mildew, or even blood. Alessandra could not say what it reminded her of, if anything. The unfamiliarity of it only added to her unease.

There were men everywhere, stationed on every floor. Servants were shuttering windows and closing internal doors, as if to trap heat for a chilly night – or as if Henri was expecting a siege. For a moment, she suspected that he somehow knew of her plan. But something about it seemed off. She would have known if he'd known. He wouldn't have been able to resist telling her. This was something else.

"What kind of ritual is he planning, exactly?" she murmured to Swann. They were approaching the narrow stairs to the attic. It was from there that she believed the strange odor emanated. Incense, perhaps.

"I don't know, exactly." Swann frowned. "Something that Mr Sanford definitely thinks is a bad idea, though. He says it could open a door that can't be closed."

"Sanford is a coward," Henri said, descending the stairs to meet them. He was dressed as if for hard travel, and had a sword belted to his side. His hand rested on the blade's pommel as he looked down at them. "He has power, but hesitates to employ it save in the most petty of circumstances."

"You seemed happy enough to take his guns," Swann said, pointedly.

Henri laughed. "What is that saying you Americans have, about gift horses?" He gestured dismissively. "In any event, the guns are mine and you will witness my triumph. Perhaps your account will lend some steel to Sanford's spine, eh?"

"You know, one of your more unattractive traits has always been your need to show off," Alessandra said, mildly. "It speaks to a lack of confidence."

Henri glared at her. "When I want your opinion, I will ask for it, Alessandra dear."

She put on a nonchalant expression. "I thought that was why I was here. To give you my opinion on this undertaking of yours. Why else would you keep me alive?"

His glare faded and he laughed softly. "Why indeed?

Come. See what wonders I have wrought, with your help." He turned and headed back up into the attic. Selim gestured for Alessandra and the others to follow.

The attic had been decorated for the ritual. Iron braziers, standing on iron claws, had been set up at the cardinal points, and fuming bowls of incense hung from the roof beams. The floor was decorated with great overlapping circles and sigils that squirmed in unsightly ways before her eyes. The haze of the incense made her eyes sting and water, and she blinked them rapidly, trying to clear them.

There were guards here as well. They had gas masks hanging from their necks, and cannister grenades attached to their belts and harnesses. In the dim light, they looked like the soldiers they had been, in another life.

Alessandra made a show of looking around. "Yes, very impressive. A drafty attic and some incense. You always did have the eye of a professional decorator, Henri."

Henri snorted. "You mock me, but Swann here knows what he is looking at." He pointed at Swann. "Tell her what she is looking at."

"A mistake," Swann said.

"Possibly. What else?"

Swann frowned. "A gate."

"Exactly. A gate. My ancestors chose this land for that reason, among others. The membrane of the world is thin here, it always has been. But over the centuries we worked our magics into the soil, and peeled back layer after layer of reality even as we raised this chateau upon the bones of the Cathars who once held it, and Umayyads before them." Henri spun, arms spread. "Oh, they had their reasons, my ancestors. Bad ones mostly. But I am grateful to them nonetheless. They paved the way."

He turned to Alessandra, his expression wild but not un-controlled. The wildness of the fanatic, not the berserker. "The right words, the right gestures, and the path will reveal itself. But first we must unlock the door and set the foundation stone."

"Meaning?" Alessandra asked, but she had a feeling she knew where this was going.

"Blood," he said, softly.

"Mine, of course," she said, lifting her chin. She'd expected something like this.

Henri smiled. "Oh no, Alessandra. I would not dream of hurting you." His gaze slid slowly toward Pepper. "Her, on the other hand…"

"What?" Pepper said.

"No," Alessandra began.

"Take her," Henri said, with a wave of his hand. Two of his men stepped forward and grabbed Pepper by her arms. She shouted and tried to pull free, but to no avail. Alessandra lunged for one of them, but Selim caught her by the neck and slung her backward into a support beam. She tried to rise, and he kicked her in the shoulder, knocking her back down. An instant later, he had his revolver drawn and aimed at her.

"Stay down," he said, flatly.

"You cannot do this," she snarled.

"He is not. I am." Henri had drawn a thin knife from under his coat and tested the point with his finger. "Selim, for all his virtues, lacks the stomach for such necessities. If I did not know him so well, I would suspect he has become squeamish."

Selim's gaze flicked to his employer, and then away. Alessandra didn't move. Squeamish he might have been, but she had no doubt he would shoot her if he had to. "Pepper, stay calm," she called out.

"Indeed, mademoiselle, stay calm. I do not need all of your blood. Merely a few drops. Hold her hand out." Pepper struggled, but her hand was forced out, so that Henri could grab it and slide the knife across her palm. Pepper yelped and snatched her hand back to her chest, as Henri turned away, holding the knife aloft like a trophy.

He held up the knife, the tip gleaming red. "Blood is the stuff of life, but also the substance of our being. Blood is the anchor that holds us fast to the world. Thus has it ever been." He flipped the knife around and flung it down, so that it embedded itself at the center of the circle. "I would have used mine, but it is unfortunately tainted. We needed blood free of the touch of the unreal." He turned to Alessandra. "Originally, I intended to use yours. But Mr Swann informed me of your recent… encounter, making you sadly unsuitable. But Miss Kelly is exactly the tonic required."

Pepper clutched her hand to her chest and grimaced. "Lucky me."

Henri glanced at her, a smirk on his face. "Yes, lucky you. It was Selim who convinced me to make use of you for this purpose, rather than disposing of you as I intended. I had planned to use a dog, or a horse, but human blood – ah. It is potent stuff. All the better for our anchor." He indicated her hand. "That said, too much is as bad as too little. Someone bandage that."

Selim lowered his weapon and stepped back. He barked an order at one of the men, who vanished only to reappear a moment later with a first aid kit. One eye on Alessandra, Selim began to bandage Pepper's injured hand.

Henri went to Alessandra and held out his own hand. She hesitated, and then took it. For an instant, she contemplated going for his sword, holding him hostage, demanding the book... but dismissed the idea almost as soon as it occurred. Henri was no pushover; he wouldn't surrender that easily. She needed to wait for her moment, when he was well and truly distracted.

He leaned close, pulling her toward him. "I hated you. I admit that. A part of me still does. But another part of me understands what you have been through of late, Alessandra." His voice was barely a whisper. "Your encounter in Arkham. Sanford saw it hiding inside you; that monstrous stowaway from a forgotten time. I too have felt the vile touch of the abnatural on my soul."

He traced her cheek with the side of his hand, and it was all she could do not to bite the offending fingers. "You could help me," he continued. "What we do today is but the first offensive in a greater conflict, the scope of which is all but inconceivable to lesser minds."

"Not including yourself in that, I suppose," she said, pulling away from him.

"No, nor you, Alessandra." He smiled and extended a hand, snapping his fingers as he did so. One of his men stepped forward, holding the *Cultes des Goules*. He handed the volume to Henri with a look of relief. Henri stepped back and turned toward the circle, opening the book as he went. Violet sparks seemed to dance along the pages and across his fingers as he flipped the pages, one by one.

"Be glad at heart, my friends. Today is the first day of the last war... a war we will win." He found the page he was looking for, and gave Alessandra a final look. "I am Henri-Georges Balfour, the Comte d'Erlette, and this I swear on the honor of my family."

Then, voice raised and back straight, he began to chant. The violet sparks rose from the book and clustered like a swarm of fireflies about his free hand as he raised it over his head, the fingers hooked like claws. In the center of the largest circle, the knife began to quiver and hum.

Then, with a great cracking and rending, the world dissolved into madness.

CHAPTER THIRTY-TWO
Assault

Night had fallen, and lights had come on throughout the chateau. More trucks had arrived, and more men. There were at least forty of them outside the chateau, opening crates and loading weapons. From a distance, it almost looked like a party.

Trish wondered where Bera was. She'd seen no sign of the ghouls since the sun had set. She glanced at Lapp, and found him staring at her. "You seem nervous," he said, softly.

"Of course I'm nervous. Aren't you?" She glanced down, checking her shotgun for the dozenth time in as many moments. Lapp had given it back to her when she'd returned, and she'd opted to use it rather than the rifle she'd acquired. She wanted something with stopping power.

"No."

Trish shook her head, not at all surprised. She'd seen combat before, during the war. She'd been shot at more than once, chased, harried. Trapped in a burning farmhouse. But just because she'd experienced it didn't mean she enjoyed it. She wasn't that sort of agent. She unraveled puzzles and broke codes. Getting in a shootout usually meant she'd made a mistake somewhere.

In this case, agreeing to the mission had been the mistake. She'd let herself get caught between powerful people, and now she was stuck. Lapp stiffened, and she pushed the thought aside. She focused her binoculars on the chateau and saw a flash of movement. Something was creeping across the lawn. Several somethings. Was Bera out there?

Trish counted to ten, under her breath. The first gunshot sounded on the eight-count. A flurry followed – crack, crack, crack. Rifles. The dull boom of a shotgun. Then, the chugging roar of a Thompson. Men screamed. That sounded like a signal to her. She looked at Lapp, who nodded.

They rose from behind the boundary wall together and took stock. Floodlights swept the estate, momentarily illuminating what looked like dozens of hunched, loping forms that seemed to bleed out of the shadows. "Good sweet god," she murmured, momentarily forgetting herself. "How many of them are there?"

"Millions," Lapp said. "We should get moving."

Trish nodded absently as she followed Lapp toward the chateau. The ghouls were everywhere, darting into every shadow or scuttling through the ornamental trees. Drawing fire, even as their kin invaded the chateau itself. It was as if they had been waiting for this moment for a long time – perhaps longer than she knew.

The Comte had managed to keep them out with his wards for who knew how long – and she and Lapp had undone it all in a single night. Created cracks in whatever mystic wall had been created, and now the ghouls were pouring in, hungry for vengeance. More of them than she'd imagined. But the overkill was the point. Bera and her kin were showing the world – or at least the shadowed parts of it – what happened when you crossed their kind. The Comte wasn't just an enemy; he was an example.

Trish had never been one to ignore a lesson, especially when it was happening to someone else. Even as she and Lapp ran toward the chateau, dodging searchlights, she was studying the attack, noting how it was conducted. The same way she'd noted the design of the sigil Lapp had erased earlier. She gathered the information instinctively, knowing it might never be used. At least she hoped it would never need to be put to use. But if it did, she – and by extension, the United States – wouldn't be caught unawares.

That went for Lapp as well as the ghouls. She watched him, and remembered their earlier conversation. As with the ghouls, she studied him, drew information from the way he moved, the way he carried his shotgun. He didn't act like a soldier. But there was something there; an experience, instinct. Maybe not a soldier then, but a warrior. Again, she couldn't help but wonder where Cinabre had dug him up.

Gunfire stitched the overgrown lawn, throwing up chunks of grass and earth. Trish swung behind a statue of a grinning and obviously excited satyr, covered in a shroud of vines, and raised her shotgun. The Comte's people were no slouches; they were forting up, taking cover where they could. But the ghouls were coming at them from every angle.

She saw one slither down a statue of a nymph and snatch a man up, snapping his neck in a single, violent motion, and felt a rumble of nausea. Another sprang over a fallen statue and tackled a man into the shrubbery, where it messily tore him to pieces. A third danced a grisly jig on the lawn as a hail of bullets chopped into its rubbery flesh.

Some of the creatures were larger than others – gargantuan

horrors fully twice the size of a man, with jaws capable of removing limbs and heads. These juggernauts of hide and sinew barreled along, howling hideously as they overturned trucks and sent gunmen scattering. Men – soldiers, some of them – were dying at the hands of monsters, and it was partially her fault. "What have we done?" she muttered.

It wasn't just guilt. From what she knew of the Comte's plan, given what Swann had said, it was one she could sympathize with. When you discover horrors in the earth, your first instinct is to dig them out. Whatever his reasons, the Comte seemed to be attempting to do that very thing. Under better circumstances, she might even have found herself helping him. But the circumstances weren't better, and the world wasn't that simple.

"Keep moving," Lapp hissed, as he plucked at her arm to catch her attention. "Before these creatures forget whose side we're on." He stepped out from behind the statue and fired at something she couldn't see. The air had a strange tang to it – an iron taste that made her sinuses pulse painfully.

She looked up and saw that the windows of the chateau glowed violet. "Lapp…" she began, feeling a sudden chill.

"I see it. He has begun the ritual." He tracked a running shape – ghoul or human, she couldn't tell – and fired. "We have to get inside. Quickly."

"Lead the way," she said. She hadn't fired once. Her shotgun felt heavy in her hand. The air swam with indistinct, gossamer shapes. Hints of things that were not there, could not be there and yet were. The sky overhead was wrong, though she wasn't sure why she thought that. The stars no longer looked like stars, but something else that reminded her of raindrops against glass. No one else seemed to notice, being too busy killing one another.

The chateau walls loomed up. The gates were open, but there were trucks parked in front of the entrance. Men fired over and under them, and she smelled the acrid odor of accelerant. A ghoul leapt onto the bonnet of a truck, and a gout of flame struck it. The creature tumbled backward, squealing in agony.

"Flamethrowers, they have flamethrowers," she hissed. "Why the hell do they have flamethrowers?"

"To kill ghouls, presumably," Lapp said. "Follow me." He edged toward the gates and the trucks. Gunfire raked the lawn again and again. Trish heard shouts and saw something dark bounce down. She was grabbing the back of Lapp's coat and hauling him to safety even as the grenade went off. A trio of nearby ghouls weren't so lucky.

Lapp looked at her, startled. "Grenades too," she said. She pushed past him and scanned the area in front of the gate. It had been turned into a hard point, simultaneously drawing the ghouls in and repelling them. She wasn't surprised Bera's people weren't tactically astute, but even they had to see it was a bad idea to run head first into a machine gun nest. Unless… a sound made her look up. Something dark crawled along the top of the wall and she nudged Lapp. He followed her gaze and nodded.

She'd been wrong. The ghouls weren't attacking randomly. They were forcing the Comte's men to congregate in one area of the courtyard, but why? She got her answer a moment later, when the dark shape vanished into the courtyard. There was a cry followed by an earthshattering explosion. Smoke vomited from inside the courtyard, wafting out over the trucks and filling the air. Men cried out in pain and shock as the gunfire tapered off.

Arkham Horror

She knew instantly what had happened. Grenades and crates full of ammunition and God alone knew what else, didn't mix. Bera was smarter than she'd thought. Maybe haunting human battlefields for centuries had taught the corpse-eaters something.

Trish gestured to Lapp and they headed for the gates. She could hear the baying of the ghouls, but couldn't see any of them. Motes of violet fire danced through the air. She boosted herself up onto the top of a truck and saw that the courtyard was full of smoke. There was debris everywhere, and bodies – not all of them human. She glanced back at Lapp as she dropped off the truck into the courtyard. "Hurry up."

A burning truck was backed up near the steps to the chateau, and Trish wondered what had been inside it. Pieces of broken crates lay scattered all around. Men were picking themselves up, going for weapons or trying to help the wounded. She didn't look like a ghoul or move like one, so they weren't paying her any attention. That ended as she reached the steps. A heavyset man, his face bloody with splinters, barked a question in French as he stepped around the burning truck. "What are you doing out here, woman? It is not safe. Get inside with the rest of the servants, idiot! Monsieur-Comte has made sure the beasts cannot get in…" He had a Mauser in his hand, but wasn't aiming it at her. Not yet.

Lapp shot him. Trish spun to look at him, met his cold gaze, and turned back. There was nothing to say. The howls of the ghouls were louder now, coming from all directions. The gunfire from outside the walls was sporadic. There was no sign of Bera. Maybe that was for the best. Trish figured having her nearby would only complicate things.

She hurried up the steps to the door and went in. Inside, it was quiet. No, not quiet. Not quite. There was a sound. A droning hum, like a thousand wasps battering themselves against the curves of a bell jar. She looked at Lapp. "Outside, before you shot him, he said that the Comte had warded the chateau itself to keep the ghouls out."

Lapp said nothing. She indicated the door. "Close it."

"They will not like that. We said we would clear the way for them."

"I don't give a damn what they like or don't like. But I've come too far to lose that book now. So close the door."

Lapp shut the door behind them, and it was if the horrors outside were nothing more than a dream. There was a faint, violet radiance to everything. Motes shimmered at the edges of her vision, and along her fingers as she twitched her hand and watched them dance.

She turned to Lapp and he placed a finger against his lips. She heard the voices a moment later. Had they not heard what was going on outside? She glanced at the windows of the foyer and saw... nothing. No reflected firelight, no shadows. It was as if they were somewhere else, far from France.

Then, a door slammed. Raised voices echoed as heavy footsteps sounded. Something snarled and gibbered. Trish waved Lapp back, and they concealed themselves behind a corner of the foyer. Eight men came into view, coming from the rear of the chateau. Three of them dragged something in their wake, bound in chains and heavy rope – a ghoul. Smaller than the others, and half-starved by the look of it. It wailed and screeched as they bullied it up the stairs, taking turns to club it when its recalcitrance got on their nerves.

When the men and their captive were out of sight, she

signaled Lapp and they began to climb the stairs. She felt nervous; afraid. There was no telling what was waiting up there for them, and only one way to find out. But she pushed the feelings down.

She had a job to do. And she was going to get it done, one way or another.

CHAPTER THIRTY-THREE
Threshold

Alessandra felt as if her eardrums might burst as the hum of vibrating metal reached a painful pitch. The knife corkscrewed in place, grinding against the wooden floorboard. The braziers rattled on their tripods and something like tar ran along the protective circle carved into the floor. She hadn't seen it poured, or where it might have originated from, but it was there now, bubbling and spurting. Globules of black liquid dripped upward, like a spill in reverse. Everything felt at once too light and too heavy.

It felt as if it had been hours, but she knew that it had only been minutes since he'd begun, at most. She couldn't hear what Henri was saying. It was as if he stood at the far end of a long tunnel, with a great wind snatching his voice away. Space distorted around him, the air twisting and stretching like indigo taffy. The wind rose, bringing with it a charnel stink. She couldn't tell where it came from, only that it had no earthly origin.

She felt almost as if she had stepped outside of herself; at once, oddly calm and terrified to her very core. The two sensations balanced one another, leaving her feeling neither fear nor awe, but something in between.

"He's doing it, he's really goddamn doing it," Swann said, as a tremor ran through the floorboards. The plaster on the walls cracked and split. She looked at Swann. His face was pale, his expression strained. How many of these had he seen, she wondered. Did the look on his face mean it had gone wrong – or horribly, terribly right?

"Doing what exactly?" she demanded. "Opening this gate of yours, you mean?"

Swann glanced at her. "He's building a bridge, from our world to theirs," he said. "He anchored it to the house; the house is the gate and the book is the key..." The rest of his words were lost to the howling wind and he turned away from her. He looked as if he wanted to run. Alessandra hated to admit it, but she felt the same.

She pushed past Selim, who paid her no mind, and went to Pepper. "Are you okay?" she shouted. Pepper nodded, her eyes fixed on the ritual. Her injured hand trembled against her chest. She was pale, frightened.

"I don't think I'm enjoying France anymore," she said, her words barely registering before the howling void snatched them away. "Can we go somewhere nicer? Like Paraguay?"

"Remind me to never tell you about the last time I was in Paraguay," Alessandra said, forcing a smile. The wind was howling now, rattling the shutters. She glanced at the window, but saw nothing but violet light, impossibly bright and painful to look at.

There was a loud crack; wood splintering, plaster ripping away from the buckling lattice. Another tremor, more violent this time. Selim shouted something, and his men took up positions. There were a dozen of them up here now. One of them hefted a Thompson submachine gun. Another was helped into a bulky cannister backpack – a flamethrower. The others had rifles, but they didn't seem to know where to aim them. None of them looked scared – awed, perhaps, but not frightened. Henri had obviously prepared them for what was to come.

The floor rippled strangely beneath her feet, as if something large were moving swiftly just beneath it. Floorboards popped and bucked, and bent upward at impossible angles, as if pulled by invisible hands. Violet light limned the cracks in the plaster, extruding soft, shimmering motes of light that coursed through the air like radiant streamers. The plaster bulged and split, running like water, drawn up and around.

A third tremor. The far wall began to crumble, as if drawn in to an immense, unseen turbine. Henri stood before it, chanting, drawing on the air with his hand. The streaming lights spun in tight circles about his fingers, shivering into what she could only describe as ornate sigils that flared and faded with each recitation of the chant.

The wall's crumbling sped up, a whirlpool of wood and plaster. The edges of the roof were slowly drawn in, as was the floor. Henri's recitation had become thunderous, his voice echoing out as over a great void.

The whole chateau felt as if it were about to fly apart. The wind clawed at them, threatening to draw them into the whirlpool. Only Henri stood unmoved against it, but his gestures had become more urgent; even frantic. Alessandra caught Pepper by the arm and sought to draw her toward the door, but Selim barred their way. "You go nowhere," he shouted, pistol aimed at Alessandra's head.

She glared at him in rising panic. She forced it down with great effort. "Are you mad? Can you not see that we will all be sucked into whatever that is if this keeps up?"

Selim glanced at the whirlpool. He clearly agreed with her conclusion, but his loyalty was stronger than his sense of self-preservation. Alessandra had resigned herself to making a lunge for his weapon when the metallic hum rose past the point of pain. She clutched at her head and cried out as a searing agony struck; it was as if her skull were full of fiery, stinging wasps. Nor was she the only one who felt it. Pepper, Selim, everyone cried out, clutching at their heads. A man fell to his knees, blood pouring from his nose and ears. The sound spiraled up and up, thinner and sharper until at last she thought she'd gone deaf.

Violet flames flickered silently at the eye of the whirlpool. Henri strode toward them, his expression rapturous. He made a pressing motion with his free hand and the flames were sucked backward, drawing the ruined wall with them. The remnants of the wall spun like a cyclone, rearranging itself into a new and impossible shape. It flexed and contorted like a living thing, but its purpose was unmistakable. A tunnel – no, a bridge, just as Swann had said, Alessandra realized. But to where?

The wind faded to a dull moan. Henri exhaled a shuddering breath and turned. In the gleam of the guttering lights, his skin looked waxy. "It is done," he said.

"No going back now," Swann said, in a hollow voice. "You just rang the dinner bell."

"Yes, and the first course will be lead," Henri said, gesturing to his men. He looked at Selim. "Did you send Francois and the others to collect our guide, as I asked?"

Selim nodded. "Yes, m'sieu. Just before you began." Even as he said it, the door to the attic banged open and a group of men entered, dragging a chained ghoul behind them. The creature yowled in what might have been fear as it saw what awaited it. Pepper caught Alessandra's forearm and squeezed. Alessandra looked at her.

"Jules," the younger woman said, softly.

Alessandra studied the thrashing creature more closely. It was starveling thin and its hide was brittle looking, rather than rubbery. It clearly lacked the strength of the other ghouls she'd encountered, either because of its age or condition, but even so, Henri's men clearly had difficulty restraining it.

"Let him go," Henri boomed.

Selim made to protest, but Henri cut him off. "I said let him go, damn it!" he roared. He shifted the book into the crook of his arm and curled a finger in a beckoning gesture. "Come, cur. Your master awaits."

Selim gestured, and Jules' captors released their hold on the ghoul, unlocking its chains and letting the ropes fall slack. The creature sprang for Henri's throat without hesitation. But even as it launched itself toward him, he drew his sword and caught the creature a clout on the side of its head with the flat of the blade.

The ghoul fell, whimpering. Henri quickly stepped forward and placed the sword's tip beneath the ghoul's chin. Henri raised his blade and forced the scrawny beast back onto its haunches. "You will listen to me, beast, or I will cast you into the outer dark myself. Do you understand?"

Jules cowered back, hands raised. "I- I understand," it – he – croaked. Selim made a gesture at the sound of the creature's voice – protection from the evil eye, Alessandra thought. "Wha- what do you want?" Jules went on, peering up at Henri.

"A guide," Henri said, swinging his sword away from the ghoul. "Someone to take us across the Sea of Bones and into the Vale of Pnath – the first step on our route to that liminal in-between vault where the Devourer Below resides. You know of whom I speak, and I know that all ghouls regardless of age know the way. It is bred into you. So – up." He indicated the slowly coruscating bridge of wood and mortar. "There is our path. You will show us the way."

"You will not survive," Jules quavered, somewhat hesitantly. "Few humans have ever traversed the underworld and lived to dream again. There are worse things than my kind in these depths, and even Umôrdhoth cannot control them."

"Why control, when I can kill?" Henri motioned to Selim. "Go. Have the men start bringing everything up. I want the gas up here first. We may need to employ it sooner rather than later. In the meantime, we will establish a bridgehead and wait for the rest of you." As Selim headed for the door, Henri looked at Alessandra and smiled. "Are you impressed?"

"Yes, it is a very nice hole in the wall," Alessandra said, in a burst of almost hysterical flippancy, and almost laughed as his face fell. The fear she'd felt earlier was dimming, or maybe she was simply past the point where she noticed its presence. "Surely you do not intend for us to go with you?"

"What she said," Swann added, quickly. "There's no reason to take us. We'll stay here, out of the way."

Henri laughed and approached them. "Perish the thought, m'sieu. I would have you both with me to witness my triumph." He looked back and forth between them and then, swiftly, extended his sword so that the flat rested on Pepper's shoulder. "Particularly you, Alessandra. And just to ensure that you do not get any funny ideas, I must insist that Mademoiselle Kelly accompany me." He guided Pepper toward him with the sword. For a moment, she looked as if she were considering putting up a fight. Alessandra prayed the young woman would think better of it, at least for the moment.

Thinking quickly, she said, "On second thought, it seems an awfully great adventure." She stepped forward, past a startled Henri. Perhaps he'd been expecting more protest. Or maybe he was simply suspicious. She tucked her hands in the pockets of her jacket and stood before what she could only think of as a gaping wound in reality. "Where are we going, exactly?"

Henri came up behind her. "The Vale of Pnath, which is the deepest point of the vast underworlds which stretch beneath Earth's Dreamlands."

"The Dreamlands…?" She glanced at him. "I have never heard of them." Even as she said it, she knew, somehow, that it was a lie.

"You have," Henri said, almost gently. "Everyone has. Everyone has visited the Dreamlands, whether they know it or not. Celephais, Hlanith… Kadath, of the Cold Wastes. All these places and more."

"Hlanith," she repeated. Cinabre had mentioned such a place. Henri nodded.

"We are near none of them, of course. I thought it best to keep our path short, though it is more dangerous. Time is of the essence, you see. We have this night and no more. When the sun rises – or the spell is ended – the bridge will collapse back into itself. The gate I have thrown open will slam shut."

"And what do you intend to do in this place, Henri? You keep talking about a war. Swann mentioned some nonsense about a god. Who is your enemy, Henri?"

"Umôrdhoth," he said, and as she had before, Alessandra felt a pang of revulsion at the sound of that name, though she could not say why. "The charnel god; lord of the corpse-eaters.

Arkham Horror

The source of my family's damnation." He tapped the *Cultes des Goules.* "This book contains the secrets my ancestor learned after joining the cult of Umôrdhoth. In later editions, many of those secrets – the most dangerous of them – were bowdlerized. But this edition is perfect. I will use the knowledge within to strike a blow against my enemy… the enemy of all mankind."

"How?"

Henri's smile was cold and savage. "By killing his children of course. Every filthy one of them." He sheathed his sword without flourish and gestured to his men. "Bring our hostage along – and our guide. It is time to cross the Sea of Bones."

CHAPTER THIRTY-FOUR
Standoff

Trish knew they were too late when everything began to shake. The chateau felt as if it had been hit by cannon fire, and she half expected to see the walls start to crumble. But instead, the rumbling faded almost as soon as it had begun. Now there was only silence. She looked down at Lapp, standing several steps below her. "I think we're late to the party," she said, her voice sounding impossibly loud in the stillness.

"You can leave if you wish," Lapp said.

"I didn't say that." She paused. "Maybe we should have let a few of Bera's pals in with us. Just to even the odds."

"You are the one who wanted to keep them out," Lapp replied, pointedly.

"A girl's allowed to have second thoughts," Trish muttered. She started back up the stairs. Her shotgun hadn't gotten any lighter, and she was starting to regret accepting it. Weapons narrowed the available options too much for her liking. And she had a suspicion that a shotgun wasn't going to be much help against whatever was waiting on them upstairs.

She was halfway to the top when she spotted Selim on the landing above her. He was coming down, his body language conveying hurry. His eyes widened as he noticed her, and his hand fell to his revolver. Her shotgun bobbed up, but she hesitated. "Don't," she warned. But Selim did. He snatched his revolver free and snapped off a shot, taking a chunk out of the plaster near her head. She ducked back and nearly fell down the stairs.

Lapp, just behind her, leveled his weapon and fired, shattering a porcelain urn standing in a corner of the landing. Selim scrambled out of sight, shouting for reinforcements. Lapp hissed a curse and made to shove past her. She caught his arm. "Wait."

"He will bring the whole chateau down on us," Lapp said, shaking her loose.

"Like you firing a shotgun won't?" Trish snapped, meeting his glare with one of her own. She looked past him, back down the stairs. Nothing showed itself. And no sound of reinforcements coming down from the attic. She waved Lapp back down to the landing below. No sense waiting out in the open. "We've got a chance here," she murmured, as they descended. "Let's not blow it."

"What do you mean?"

"We met him back in Toulouse, remember?" She set her weapon down and took off her hat. "He didn't look very happy about what was going on. We might be able to use that."

"Might being the operative word," Lapp said.

She looked at him. "There're at least five other palookas up there, all armed. And no telling what'll come through the gate that the Comte's opening. And that's not even taking Bera and her bunch into account. We're going to need every gun we can get."

Lapp hesitated. "You intend to betray Bera," he said.

It was Trish's turn to hesitate. "I have my orders," she said.

Lapp shook his head. "It will not go well for you." But he settled back against the wall, his shotgun across his lap. "But I am not your keeper. I am here to ensure Zorzi survives – not you. Do as you like. Worse comes to worse, I will shoot him while he is distracted."

"Thank you for your confidence," Trish said. She stripped off her coat, exposing the pistol holstered under her arm. She briefly considered dispensing with it, but discarded the idea. Selim was going to be suspicious regardless. She took a deep breath and called out, "I want to talk!"

Silence followed this entreaty. Then, "Come out where I can see you."

Trish hesitated, weighing the odds one last time, and then followed her gut. Something told her Selim wasn't the type to shoot someone in cold blood. Especially a woman. Hands raised, she stepped into the open. "We just want to talk," she repeated.

"You," Selim said. He stood at the top of the landing, his pistol aimed at her.

"Me. Us." She gave him a smile. "You don't seem surprised to see us."

"You should have known better. You are in danger here." Selim glanced toward the attic. "We are all in danger."

"Is that why you were leaving, then?" she asked, though she doubted he'd been doing any such thing. To his credit, he looked insulted by her accusation.

"I was going to alert the others."

"They're a bit busy right now," she said, taking another step up toward him.

"What do you mean?"

"We didn't come alone," she said, rising a second step. The barrel of his pistol twitched in response.

"Stop. No closer. Explain."

"You had an army. It seemed only fair that we bring one of our own. Of course, they had their own reasons for wanting a piece of your boss. Something about a hostage…" She smiled slyly, as his stoic expression crumbled.

"No," he said, hoarsely. "You did not, could not…"

"Desperate times," Trish said. "Wasn't my first choice, I can tell you that. But it was necessary." She paused and gave him a hard look. "I'm sure you know all about that, though, don't you?"

Selim blinked. "What we do is a great thing," he said, but he sounded like he was having trouble believing it. Trish nodded in what she hoped was a friendly fashion.

"That's what he told you, right? Did you believe him, then? Or did you have doubts, like you have doubts now?"

"I- I do not doubt him," he began, but faltered as a sudden banging sounded from below. Trish didn't turn.

"The ghouls have realized that we shut them out," Lapp said, from behind her. "They do not sound best pleased with us."

"I don't give two hoots," Trish said, not taking her eyes off Selim. "They've done their bit. And I bet Selim here doesn't mind all that much – do you, Selim?"

"I warned him," he said, absently. "I told him this would happen."

Trish sighed. "I bet you did, didn't you? I bet you warned him every step of the way. But he didn't listen. They never do. Believe me, I know." She kept her eyes on him, ignoring the commotion from below. If the ghouls broke in now, that was the ballgame – Selim would start shooting, and she couldn't blame him. But he was close to the tipping point. If she could get him on side, they had a better chance of success. "I know what it's like to argue against a course of action and be ignored, because your boss thinks the ends justify the means. Only sometimes those ends are worse than anyone realizes. Sometimes you can't just follow orders."

"I…" Selim hesitated. He shook his head. "What do you want?"

"Your help," she said.

"You want the book," Selim said.

She nodded again. "Yeah. But stopping your boss is more important, don't you think? Before this whole situation gets any worse."

The pounding from below grew more urgent. Trish paused, wondering if she had the gumption to simply shoot Bera and spare herself the trouble later. Windows rattled. But no breaking glass, no splintering doors. She looked at Selim. "Might want to think quickly. Those doors don't sound like they'll hold for long."

He ran a shaking hand over his bald pate. "The Comte warded the chateau as well as the grounds. Their sort is barred from entering, so long as the magics hold. Unless they are invited. I was not certain it would work in conjunction with the rite, but…"

"Lucky us," Trish said.

"Not so lucky for those outside," Selim said. He stared down at the doors, as if contemplating what might be happening. He fixed Trish with a flat gaze. "By letting those creatures through our defenses, you have as good as condemned them."

"What does it matter where they die?" Lapp interjected. "In this world or the other – it makes no difference." He started toward the attic, but Selim moved to bar his way.

"I have not said yet that I will help you."

Lapp pointed his shotgun at the other man. "As she said, I suggest you decide."

Trish gently pushed the barrel of the shotgun aside. "I think he's already decided; he just doesn't want to admit it. Isn't that so, Selim?"

Selim looked at her and then away. After a moment, he sighed and gestured. "Follow me. They've likely already gone through, but we may be able to catch up to them."

"And after that?" Trish pressed.

Selim didn't look at her. "After that… we will see."

Lapp didn't look happy with that, but Trish was satisfied. She had a feeling that Selim wanted this to be over as much as they did. They started up into the attic. The air took on a greasy pall as Selim opened the door, revealing the impossible vastitude beyond the collapsed wall – it looked like a cavern, but not like any she'd ever seen.

It was too big, too dark. Things that might have been mountains rose up in stretches of white, higher than the edge of the attic. Something told her, however, that they were not mountains, not as she knew them. She paused, unable to reconcile what she was seeing with her understanding of reality. It was like looking into the eye of God – or rather, a god.

"Jesus," she murmured. It was almost a prayer.

"He had nothing to do with this," Lapp intoned.

Looking around, Trish had to agree. She had seen similar sites before, but never one where the rite had actually worked. A weird wind whistled through the eaves and violet wisps floated on the air. If she squinted, she could make out vague shapes writhing through the air around the rupture. They weren't very nice to look at, so she tried to ignore them.

She'd once been sent to interview a scientist named Tillinghast. He hadn't known who she represented, of course – he'd thought she was a journalist – but he'd espoused a theory about overlapping planes of existence. She wondered if there was some connection here. Had Tillinghast been right? She'd considered him a lunatic, and had reported as such to her superiors, but what she was seeing now made her reconsider. But if she'd been mistaken about that, what else had she gotten wrong?

The thought caused her to seize up, just for an instant. What if it wasn't just her, but everyone? What if every decision she and the rest of the Cipher Bureau had made to date had been based on erroneous information? What if they'd taken half-truths and confabulations as factual statements?

Trish forced the thought aside. For good or ill, the decision had been made and it was well out of her hands. Hers was not to reason why, and all the rest of it. She looked at Lapp. "What do you make of it?"

"Why ask me?"

"I assumed Cinabre would have tried something like this, at least once."

"He knows better than to be so sloppy." Lapp shook his head. "The Comte is a fool. He might as well have sounded a cannonade to announce himself. Did he not understand that there are better ways of getting there?" He glanced at Selim, as if seeking an answer.

Selim grunted. "He knew and discounted them all. He wants them to know – to see. What good is it to defeat an enemy, unless they know who conquered them?"

Lapp rounded on the other man. "He will conquer nothing! Not even the high kings of Sarnath could... never mind. It does not matter." He turned to Trish. "We must follow them."

Trish nodded. "I know. The question is, where are they going?"

"To the other end of the bridge, but no farther." Selim swallowed and wiped sweat from his eyes. His expression was haunted, as he stared at the shimmering portal and the impossible vista beyond. "They will attempt to establish a bridgehead somewhere stable. He will be expecting reinforcements."

"Then he's going to be disappointed," Trish said. She looked at the others. "Ready?" Lapp and Selim nodded. Lapp extended a hand.

"Ladies first."

Trish gave him a brittle smile, and raised her shotgun. "Delighted to."

CHAPTER THIRTY-FIVE
Sea of Bones

Alessandra stared out into the darkness beyond the shifting debris of Henri's mystical bridge. She could just make out immense stalagmites and stalactites meeting like great ligaments of stone. But she could not see where they rose to. And the ground below was a pallid expanse of something like sand; or so it seemed, from where she stood.

Ahead of her, she could see the swirling endpoint of the bridge. It was still stretching, building itself, as they traversed it. Henri's magics were impressive, and she wondered how much of it was him, and how much was the book. She glanced back, toward the hole – the gate – and could make out the chateau attic beyond.

Pepper stayed close, her eyes wide. "What the hell is this?" she murmured, not for the first time since they'd entered. She still held her bandaged hand to her chest.

Swann, slouching alongside them, lit a cigarette with trembling hands. "You got it right the first time – it's Hell. Or a suburb thereof." He blew a thin stream of smoke from his lips and looked around. "I do not get paid enough for this."

Alessandra forced a chuckle. "Cheer up, both of you. How

often does one get to see an alien world?" But despite her attempt at reassurance, what she saw past the edges of the bridge reminded her of K'n-yan and N'kai. Of the dreams that had plagued her nearly to death in Arkham. And yet, despite the similarities, there were some differences.

The firefly glow of K'n-yan was nowhere to be seen, here. The only real light, aside from the violet aura of the bridge, came from beyond the closest ligaments of rock; a distant spine of what she could only describe as mountains – a sawtooth ridge that rose out of the dark and ascended into the same, with peaks and valleys lit by an eerie radiance.

Henri noticed her looking and said, "The death-fires of Throk. Beautiful, in a vile sort of way. Like the phosphorescent glow of a rotting corpse." He stopped and turned, gesturing to the distant glow as he did so.

"What are they?" she asked.

"Mountains."

"We are underground," she protested.

"No, we are in the Underworld. The flipside of the Dreamlands – the shadow of man's dreaming, where numberless nightmares crawl through lightless canyons." Henri seemed pleased by this bit of hyperbole. Alessandra shook her head in annoyance. He'd always been prone to poetry at the most inconvenient times.

"I thought you French types liked the Riviera," Pepper said.

Henri ignored her. "The Underworld, Alessandra. The gateway to the fane of the Devourer. For years I sought a route here, never realizing that my ancestors had mapped it for me." He patted the *Cultes des Goules* affectionately. "But once I did, I knew it was a sign that this was my destiny."

"As destinies go, it seems a tad morbid," Alessandra said.

She peered down at the irregular landscape far below, dimly lit by the phosphorescent glow of the mountains. "What is that, down there? Sand? Or is it ... snow?"

"Bones, I should think."

Pepper blanched. "Bones?"

"Yes. A millennium of morbid refuse. A sea of ghoulish leavings." Henri laughed softly. "Which puts us exactly where I hoped to be, near the bottom of the Crag of the Ghouls – is that not so, Jules?" He snapped his fingers at the hunched figure of the ghoul prowling ahead of them, to the length of the chain that bound it to one of Henri's men.

The creature paused and turned, yellow gaze simmering with hatred. "Your bones will soon join those below," he growled. "My people will kill you, Henri-Georges Balfour. That I promise you."

"I think not," Henri murmured. He gestured and the man holding Jules' chain gave it a sharp yank, nearly pulling the scrawny ghoul off his feet. "I think whatever waits below will soon know better than to cross my path."

"So what's the plan, then? Because while I'm all for sightseeing, I do have other places to be," Swann called out. "You keep talking invasion, but all I see is a handful of guys who should know better. Where's the artillery I scrounged for you? Hell, where's that mustard gas?"

Henri gave the acquisitionist an impatient look. "It is coming. But first, we must establish a perimeter. These brave men will see it done – with fire and shot, the way our ancestors did." He indicated his followers. There were twenty of them now, all armed to the teeth. Two bore the heavy flamethrowers that had no doubt seen use in the trenches. Several were armed with Thompson submachine guns, while others carried rifles

and shotguns. All had grenades and extra ammunition clipped
to the military harnesses they wore.

There was no denying that they were kitted out for war. The
thought filled Alessandra with revulsion. She had experienced
the war firsthand, and had difficulty believing that anyone
might throw themselves back into such a conflagration – let
alone one in another world.

Besides weapons, several carried heavy crates of unknown
equipment. Alessandra wondered what was in them. Likely
whatever it was, Henri judged it necessary for his "bridgehead".
"And how do you intend to do that?" she asked. "Where does
this bridge lead exactly, Henri?"

"Let us ask Jules his opinion on that matter, eh?" Henri drew
his sword and laid the tip beneath the ghoul's chin. "This is
why you still live. Your people know this sea, and its dangers.
I want solid ground – an island. Some place with access to the
heights as well as the depths. Only a ghoul can identify such a
spot in these lightless depths."

"I will not help you. You want to kill my people," Jules spat,
in contrast to his earlier resignation. Alessandra wondered
if perhaps being here had given the ghoul access to some
newfound reservoir of strength.

"I do. Every one of them. But I know that is a dream with
scant chance of becoming reality. Your kind are vermin, with
the tenacity that entails. Some of you will inevitably survive;
chastened, but alive. Now – do as I say and you might be
among them."

Jules growled softly, but turned away and shuffled to the
edge of the bridge. After a moment, he pointed to a spot below.
One of the great ligaments of stone, Alessandra saw. They were
close enough to it that she could see that it was covered in what

resembled pinholes. "There. Down there. That is what you want, and may it serve you ill."

Henri nodded, sheathed his sword and began to walk toward the spot the ghoul had indicated. He gestured as he did so, and Alessandra felt a faint tremor run through the bridge, as if it was gradually shifting position. There seemed to be no end to the raw materials Henri had available. She looked at Swann. "You would think he would have run out of house by now," she said, softly.

Swann snorted. "Shows what you know. This is magic, Zorzi. He's not using the house to make this bridge; he's using the idea of the house. The memory of it, the dream that his ancestors built. That's what he's using for raw materials. He's made himself a ghoul-road, the canny bastard."

Alessandra shook her head in puzzlement. "I do not understand."

Swann laughed, and there was an edge of hysteria to it. "It's the Dreamlands, lady. Just like he said. You can't walk a solid road into this place. You got to do it like the ghouls do. You got to use paths made out of smoke and dreams." He looked around, face tight and jaw clenched. "Only people from the waking world aren't meant to come here like this, not awake and in the flesh. There's no telling what'll happen now that he's done this."

She shook her head again, not quite following the logic. Then, maybe that was her mistake, in thinking logic applied to such things. "Can he find this god of his?"

"Maybe. Or maybe he's hoping it'll come looking and save him the trouble."

With a booming crunch, the bridge slammed down against a ledge of rock. Alessandra and the others stumbled, and nearly fell. Writhing beams of wood pressed against the stone, anchoring the bridge in place, though it swayed unpleasantly.

The ledge was roughly the size of the attic, and jutted from the lip of one of the pinholes she'd noticed before; in reality, the hole was a deep cave that wound back up into the ligament of stone. Henri was the first off the bridge. "Francois, the flare," he said. One of his men raised a flare gun and fired. The hissing light rose over the sea of bones, casting a pale glow over everything.

Sword in hand, Henri waited. Jules sat on his haunches and let out a gibbering shriek, despite his handler's attempt to stop him. It was echoed from within the cave. Henri motioned with his sword. "Form a firing line," he called out.

Half of his men hurried down, including the two carrying flamethrowers. The others arrayed themselves along the bridge. The shrieks and howls grew louder. Jules began to caper. "I warned you," he howled. "My kin are hungry and you have provided them a feast!" He fell silent as his handler struck him in the back with a club.

On the ledge, Henri raised his sword. "Ready yourselves," he shouted. The ghouls came in a rush even as the words left his mouth. There were dozens of them, loping out of the darkness from all directions.

"I told you," Swann shouted, holding onto his hat. "I told you!" Alessandra tensed, ready to flee back along the bridge with Pepper, the surrounding gunmen be damned.

Henri barked an order, and the pair with the flamethrowers stepped forward. Bright jets of fire erupted from the nozzles of the weapons and scythed across the line of approaching creatures. The smell struck Alessandra like a fist, and her eyes immediately teared up. Henri shouted again, and the two men cut off the flames and retreated. Their fellows stepped forward in a rough firing line.

Gunshots sounded like whipcracks. Burning ghouls spun and fell. The survivors of the rush scrambled back in messy disorder, yelping and screeching. Jules set up a mournful howling until his handler struck him on the snout, silencing him. Henri flourished his sword as a single ghoul, greasy hide aflame, burst through the fusillade and barreled toward him. He gracefully sidestepped the pain-blind creature, and removed its head with a single stroke. Alessandra turned away, sickened.

Henri gestured and his men advanced in a tight phalanx, pushing the retreating ghouls back, farther and farther, until the last of them had squirmed back into a crack in the rock and vanished from sight. Henri turned to those men who hadn't been in the firing line. "Quickly! The wards! While they are in disarray."

Crates were opened and sandbags marked by sigils were flung down in a large semicircle, marking the line where the ledge became the cave. Another crate was broken open, revealing some unfamiliar contraption. Swann grimaced. "Livens projector," he muttered. "Forgot I got him one of those."

"What is it?" Alessandra asked.

"It fires poison gas shells," Swann said, gnawing on a thumbnail.

"Indeed it does," Henri said, as he sheathed his sword. "I saw them used during the war. Not very accurate, but perfect for filling tunnels with chlorine or mustard gas." He smiled in satisfaction. "One will not be sufficient for the task at hand, of course. But it will do until Selim gets here with the rest." His gaze strayed to the bridge and he frowned. He reached for his pocket watch and Alessandra smiled.

"I do wonder what is keeping him," she said.

Henri snapped his pocket watch shut and looked at her. "He will be along soon enough. In the meantime, we will begin." He turned back to the cave. "The gas will fill this rats' nest; every warren and tunnel will be choked with the dead before we leave here this night. More, I will scatter poisoned corpses for the survivors to gnaw upon, and perish in their turn. I will have made my point, and the corpse-eaters will know that the line of d'Erlette is avenged upon them."

"They will hunt you in your dreams and the waking world for this blasphemy," Jules hissed. "You will not be allowed to escape." He jerked at his chains, as if trying to fling them off. "We are not man's enemies!"

"Not man's, no – mine." Henri drew his sword and pricked Jules' muzzle with it, causing the ghoul to cower back. "But I welcome their attempt. My chateau is warded, and my men hardened against the terrors of the dark. Let them come – let it be war between us. And finally, when your foul god has had enough, and rises from his lair, I will be here to meet him. To cast my defiance into his teeth, and set my flag upon the ruins of his temple. I am the Comte d'Erlette, and I will be victorious."

"Very inspiring," Alessandra murmured. Henri had always talked a good game, when it suited him. Like a matinee idol, he'd no doubt rehearsed for this moment. She didn't know whether to applaud or to laugh at the absurdity of it all.

Before Henri could reply, a sound intruded. Barks and howls drifted down from the surrounding pillars of stone – or perhaps up – in a quaquaversal symphony. Hundreds of voices, echoing across the Sea of Bones. Henri's men looked around nervously, weapons at the ready. Henri cleared his throat and began to sing. His men picked it up, one by one, some of them more haltingly than others.

"What are they singing?" Pepper asked, as she flexed her injured hand.

"The national anthem," Alessandra said, her eyes on the nearest of Henri's gunmen. The man had a revolver holstered on his hip, and it was within reach.

"Doesn't sound like it to me," Pepper said, with a frown.

"You are thinking of the wrong nation. They are singing 'La Marseillaise'." She looked at Pepper. "How is your hand?"

"Hurts. But I got another one." Pepper was alert now. "What's the plan?"

Alessandra thought quickly, calculating the variables. "Do you think you can make it across the bridge, if we get the chance?"

"Yeah, but what about them?" Pepper jerked her chin at the men.

"I think they will be preoccupied." Alessandra looked at Swann, who was eavesdropping but trying to look otherwise. "Do you agree, Chauncey?"

Swann nodded. He shuffled toward them, one eye on Henri. "I'm with you, Zorzi. You hear me? You start running, I'm going to start running too."

"Good to know that you will have my back, Chauncey," Alessandra muttered sardonically. The howling grew louder, drowning out all attempts at conversation. All eyes were fixed outward. Now was the time, for there might not be another opportunity.

Then – a gunshot. The ghouls fell silent as a man spun and fell, face a red mask. Alessandra turned and saw a familiar trio –

Lapp, Trish and Selim – poised at the edge of the bridge with their weapons leveled. Lapp's weapon smoked. Trish spoke up, in the sudden silence. "The book, Comte. Hand it over."

Henri stared at them in shock. "Selim … ?" he began.

"It is over, m'sieu," Selim called out. "This madness must end. We must retreat. The house is under siege. The others–"

Henri shook his head. "Damn the others! This is my destiny!"

Trish cleared her throat. "Whatever you want to call it is your business. My business is that book. Toss it over here, if you would."

Henri peered at her. "And who are you, then? It seems to me that I ought to recognize you, woman."

"I have one of those faces," Trish said. "The book. Now."

"Or what? You will shoot me?"

"One of us will," Lapp said. While everyone was preoccupied by that threat, Alessandra stepped forward and snatched the gunman's revolver from its holster. He whirled, swinging his Thompson around toward her, startled, and she clubbed him in the face with the butt of the weapon, knocking him sprawling.

She spun, leveling the weapon at Henri, who had only just then realized what was happening. "Zorzi, no," Trish began. Henri opened his mouth to shout – and Alessandra shot him. It was instinctual, but a long time coming all the same. She felt no sense of triumph or even satisfaction, however, as he stumbled back into one of his men, the *Cultes des Goules* tumbling from his grasp.

"The book," Trish shouted. "Get the book!"

Confusion reigned. Men swung their weapons toward her, but hesitated as Trish and the others started shooting. Out of the corner of her eye, Alessandra saw Pepper go for the gunman's fallen Thompson.

Alessandra rose, ready to dive onto the book while she still had the element of surprise. But she froze as a thunderous clattering sounded, drowning out the gunfire. The carpet of bones below the ledge shifted and rolled away as something awful and immense slowly rose from the depths, casting its shadow across the ledge and those who occupied it.

Then, all at once, a great, serpentine form, covered in a shroud of shaggy slime, larger than anything Alessandra had ever seen before or hoped to see again, broke the surface with an ear-splitting roar.

CHAPTER THIRTY-SIX
Dhole

Pepper barely saw Alessandra make her move. She still wasn't used to how quickly the other woman could spring into action when she put her mind to it. The pistol went off – the Comte went down – and then it all went to hell as Selim and Trish and a man she didn't recognize started shooting.

She didn't look up. She didn't want to see what it was rising out of the bones that shrouded the ground below. Instead, she went for the fallen gunman's weapon. Not his pistol, because Alessandra had that, but the Thompson he'd dropped. She scooped it up quickly and swung it around to cover the Comte's men. Even as she did so, she realized that she needn't have bothered. They were all too busy staring up at the newcomer. Slowly, against her better judgment, she looked up.

At first, she couldn't say what she was looking at. It was too big, too unbelievable. It was the size of a skyscraper or nearly such, with a mouth like an open blossom, studded with sharp teeth. Its hide was slimy, and forest-like patches of mold clung to its flanks. Dully, she realized that only a small portion of the creature was visible; the equivalent of a giraffe stretching its neck over the top of its enclosure.

She wondered, in the tiny part of her that wasn't struggling against the urge to scream, if this was Umôrdhoth. If this was the god the Comte had hoped to challenge. If so, it looked as if he'd underestimated his enemy's willingness to mix it up.

It rose up and up over the ledge, and the air throbbed with the stink of it. It was so big that it was simultaneously too close to be ignored, and too far away to be an immediate danger. It swayed for long moments, studying the small things scuttling about on the ledge, though she could see nothing that she recognized as an eye. Was it curious? Hungry? Pepper couldn't even hope to guess.

Its mouth irised open, triangular mandibles unfurling – stretching – quivering. Teeth glinted in the witch-light of the bridge. A hollow groaning echoed from within it, accompanied by a battlefield stink.

Men gagged and whined like whipped dogs. Only the Comte seemed unafraid, but he also didn't look like his usual confident self. Then, the bullet in his shoulder might have had something to do with it. "The sigils – the wards, the wards will protect us… retreat. Fall back," he croaked as he hastily pressed a handkerchief to his wound, but none of his men were listening.

One of them, braver than the others, lifted his flamethrower and sent a gout of fire streaking upward to splash against the slimy hide, even as the Comte cried out, "No!" The thing, whatever it was, emitted a screech that made Pepper's teeth ache in her jaw as it reared back, away from the ledge. For a moment, she hoped it would leave. But instead, it just swayed above them, screaming.

The sound was so loud, so piercing, that she instinctively squeezed her eyes shut against the force of it. It filled the vast space, deafening her for a moment. Her heart spasmed, and she wanted to run. It didn't matter where to, just away. Away from the thing, away from the noise, away from all of it. But she forced the impulse down, burying it deep in the pit of her soul. She'd seen worse; lived through worse. Maybe that was true, maybe it wasn't, but it was enough to steady her nerves.

Someone caught her arm, and she nearly shot them. She saw Swann, a look of panic on his face. "We have to go, kid! Now!" She jerked her arm free of his grasp. As she did so, the rest of the Comte's men opened fire on the creature. Most of them, anyway. Some of them simply stared up at the wormlike monstrosity. A few were just… screaming. She didn't blame them. Ghouls were one thing; giant worms were another altogether.

"Where's Alessandra?" she demanded. She'd lost sight of her in the confusion, and didn't see the other woman anywhere. Swann shook his head.

"She can look out for herself. Let's get to the bridge and your pals and get out of here! If that thing wasn't looking for a fight before, it's sure as hell looking for one now."

"You go if you want," Pepper said as she stepped back, unwilling to abandon Alessandra. Swann stared at her for a moment in obvious disbelief, and then shoved past her, heading for the bridge as quickly as his feet could carry him. She considered calling after him, but dismissed the thought almost immediately. Swann would be of no help. Better not to have to worry about him at all.

She tried to ignore the looming horror, and focus on her surroundings. The bridge was behind her – Selim and the others were falling back along its length, shooting at the new arrival with no appreciable effect. A quick sprint, and she'd be heading back to the chateau with them. The cave was ahead of her, but there was no telling what sort of reception she'd get in there. The ghouls might not be inclined to make a distinction between one human and another, especially after the way the Comte had slaughtered a bunch of them.

The thought made her seek him out. He was standing amid a large knot of men, shouting orders and waving his sword like a tinpot king, despite his injury. She realized that he'd probably forgotten all about her and Alessandra in his haste to keep the worm away from the ledge. She raised the Thompson almost unconsciously, instinctively judging him a bigger threat than the worm. A hand pushed the barrel down before she could pull the trigger.

"No. Much as it pains me, he is our best chance at getting out of here," Alessandra said, not looking at Pepper. Her face was pale, her voice strained. Pepper realized she was afraid. That made her feel better. If Alessandra was scared, then things were definitely bad. "Did you happen to see where the book went when he dropped it?"

"Book?" Pepper asked, her mind still trying to catch up with what was going on.

"The *Cultes des Goules*," Alessandra said. "He dropped it when I shot him. I – ah! There!" She pointed, but Pepper couldn't see anything past the shuffling feet of the Comte's men. "I need to get that book," Alessandra continued. "Can you cover me?"

Pepper shook her head in disbelief. "Who cares about the book? We should get out of here while we can!" The creature shrieked again, and Alessandra was already up and moving before the sound had faded, without waiting for Pepper's reply.

Pepper tried to follow, but a man stumbled into her path, his face contorted in fear. He was screaming, but without sound. It looked like a painting Alessandra had showed her. The sight shook her and she watched him stumble toward the cave, clutching his head. Men were running in every direction, firing up at the creature, reloading, trying to move the sandbags. The Comte was shouting like a battlefield commander, trying to stay in control. And something else – a flash and flicker of tattered yellow.

She froze. There was a shape in the crowd, prowling through the confusion. A pale death mask bobbed on an impossibly long neck, above a stretched frame. It was at once smaller and taller than the men around it, changing size with every step. The blind eyes of the death mask were fixed on her with marrow-curdling intensity. She heard... something; words, whispers, just at the edge of her hearing. They grew louder but no more intelligible as the apparition drew closer.

Something jostled her, breaking the spell. She blinked, but the yellow shape was gone. She realized she'd been bumped by the man acting as Jules' handler. The ghoul was thrashing – straining at his bonds. He lunged in the direction of the Comte, but was jerked back by his handler.

Pepper watched as the ghoul was beaten to the ground by the man holding his chain, a club thudding into his head and chest. Before she knew it, the Thompson was roaring and the chain split. Both man and ghoul seemed surprised. Then Jules was up and pouncing on his tormentor with a triumphant howl. The man went down, screaming.

Good deed done, Pepper turned and spied one of the Comte's men drawing a bead on Alessandra, who was heading for where the Comte's book must have been. She popped off a burst at the gunman, stitching shots along the ground with an inexperienced hand. In general, she knew how to fire a weapon, but she'd never handled a Thompson before. The gunman ducked away, yelling. No one heard him. Everyone else was too busy with the creature looming above them.

Fire and shot might have served against the ghouls well enough, but the thing – the worm – was too big for either bullets or flames to be much more than an annoyance. The creature's head dipped toward the ledge, the blossom-like mandibles flaring out. She gagged as a fetid wind washed over her, and she hurried to get out of the way. Others had the same idea, however, and she was nearly trampled by the exodus.

She was knocked to one knee by a panicked man, and it was all she could do to keep hold of the gun. The shadow of the thing engulfed her and she felt its weight overhead, like the slow collapse of a building.

Something grabbed her, yanked her aside as the great head scraped the ledge. For a moment, she thought it was Alessandra. Instead, Jules grinned at her, all teeth and yellow eyes. "Hello, Pepper," he meeped. "You should stay out of its way."

"Is that thing your – you know, your god?" she asked breathlessly as the worm raised its head, mandibles contracting about a screaming figure. One of the flamethrowers, she thought. There was a muffled whoomph and the creature shrilled in pain as fire spilled out of its maw and crawled along its head. It whipped away from the ledge, shaking itself.

"That?" Jules snorted. "No! That is a dhole. Very dangerous, but hardly a god. The smell of death must have attracted it." He plucked at her sleeve. "You should go, Pepper. It is too dangerous here." He paused. "Come with me. I will take you to my people. They will protect you."

"Not without Alessandra," she argued, looking for the other woman. Something told her she could trust Jules, though she wasn't sure why. She spotted Alessandra's dark hair. The book had been kicked toward the tip of the ledge, right under the dhole, and Alessandra was darting toward it.

Unfortunately, the creature had chosen that moment to lunge down at its tormentors once more. Pepper felt the world slow as she realized that Alessandra was right in the creature's path. Its mouth opened wide – pieces of its last victim still caught on the thorns of its teeth – as it descended.

She cried out "Alessandra!" and ran toward the other woman, ignoring Jules' barks of entreaty, the dull thunder of gunfire, the stink of the dhole's breath, everything, save that awful maw getting closer and closer. Alessandra had paused, her hand on the book, her eyes drawn upward. She'd raised her weapon, but it seemed impossibly small next to the threat of the creature's approach.

Pepper elbowed the other woman aside, and raised the Thompson. She fired until the drum clicked and the weapon became a dead weight in her hands. The thing – the dhole – retreated, ichor raining from its open mouth. It whipped around, segmented body slamming into the rocky pillars. Clouds of dust and splinter-rains fell, causing the Comte's men to scatter. She tossed the useless gun aside and turned, searching for Alessandra. She kicked something – the book, she realized, belatedly.

The dhole shrieked and came for them again, throwing up waves of bones in its haste. Gunfire erupted from the ledge, as a few men, those with more self-possession than the rest, flung lead at the approaching horror in an effort to turn it aside. Pepper turned away – spotted the book, laying where she'd kicked it. Instinctively, she dove for it.

She caught it – and a boot slammed down on her injured hand. She cried out in pain and looked up. The Comte glared down at her. "That belongs to me, I think." He kicked her viciously in the ribs, knocking her aside, and reached down. A revolver snarled, and sent the book skidding out of his reach.

"You should really learn to be nicer to your guests," Alessandra said. She aimed the smoking pistol at the Comte. "Step back, Henri. I will not ask twice."

Before Pepper could scramble away, the Comte caught her by the back of the neck with his free hand. He dragged her to her feet, and pressed the edge of his sword to her throat. He glared at Alessandra.

"Nor will I, Alessandra. I want my book, and you want your friend. Get me my book, or I will cut her open and leave her for the dhole!"

CHAPTER THIRTY-SEVEN
Escape

Alessandra cursed herself silently. The book was within easy reach, but she knew Henri well enough to know he had no intention of playing things fairly. Not now. His sanity, already debatable, looked to be hanging by a thread. Behind him, his men fired at the thrashing monstrosity, trying to drive it away. But it only retreated a slight distance before returning to attack again. She wondered if the wards he'd set up were somehow keeping it at bay. If so, she couldn't see it working for long.

"I do feel sorry for you, Henri," she said, keeping her pistol steady. If the sword so much as twitched, she would fire. She focused on him, blocking the rest of it out, albeit with some difficulty. "All that preparation and look what has come of it. You must be quite disappointed."

"Disappointed is an understatement," Henri said. "You did this. I know it. You somehow sabotaged my men, prevented them from coming across the bridge. I do not know how, but I know you. You let me capture you." He laughed bleakly. "I should have known you came along too quietly. I fooled myself into thinking your concern for this little wretch had made you careless. But you always did have an eye for the main chance."

"Yes. But you did help. You wanted so badly to gloat." Alessandra sank slowly into a crouch and fumbled for the book. The ledge was shaking from the creature's paroxysms. Men were screaming. The roar of a flamethrower sounded. The creature was being kept at bay, barely. Pepper had managed to hurt it, somehow. Or maybe it was simply thinking better of what it had assumed was an easy meal.

Henri exposed his teeth. "Can you blame me? Stop stalling, Alessandra. Pick up the book and hand it to me. Otherwise, we will all be food for that creature. My wards were meant to hold back ghouls. They will only stymie that thing for a few moments more, then it will scoop us all off this ledge. With the book, I stand a chance of stopping it."

"Is that so?" Alessandra hefted the book. "Then you must want it very badly indeed, Henri. Let her go, and I will toss it to you." She caught a flash of movement over his shoulder. A lean form – Jules. The ghoul was free and creeping toward Henri, unnoticed by anyone. "In fact, I will hand it to you and gladly. But she goes free first."

"You are bargaining with me?" he hissed, in evident disbelief. "Here? Now?" The ledge shook as the great worm brushed against it. Fire crawled up its foul hide and ichor fell like rain. It screamed again and Alessandra winced; it was as if someone had inserted an icepick into her ear canal. The worm looped around, trying to come at the ledge from another angle. A man was scooped up and swallowed before he could even scream. A grenade burst against the side of the creature's head, causing it to flinch away.

"When better?" Alessandra said. Jules caught her eye, and

tensed, ready to leap. Henri grimaced and, with a snarled curse, shoved Pepper to the ground.

"Fine. Now give me the– Ahh!" Jules sprang, claws and teeth sinking into Henri's arms and shoulder, respectively. He yelled as the ghoul clambered onto his back, gnawing and gibbering. Alessandra tried to get a bead on Henri, but he was thrashing about too much.

"Pepper, get over here!"

Eyes wide, Pepper scuttled toward her. The young woman snatched up the book as she stood and turned. "We got to help him!"

"Which one?" Alessandra asked.

"Jules!"

"Jules looks as if he can handle himself. Come on, we need to get out of here!" Alessandra caught Pepper by the back of her jacket and bodily shoved her toward the bridge, ignoring her protests. She didn't know anything about magic or other worlds, and she wasn't sure how long Henri's bridge was going to last under these circumstances.

She heard a shout from behind her and glanced back to see Henri fling Jules to the ground. The ghoul scrambled away from Henri's sword, yelping. Henri looked up – spotted her – and started after them. The ledge was shaking now, as the immense worm slammed into the rockface, as if trying to bring it down atop its attackers.

"Keep running," she shouted, shoving Pepper ahead of her. Up ahead, she could see Trish and the others hurrying back toward the gate. Scarborough was no fool; neither was Lapp. They knew there was little they could do against such a monster. "And whatever you do, do not lose that book!"

They reached the bridge a moment later and she turned to

find Henri charging after them, a look of wild fury on his face. She fired at him, and though the shots plucked at his coat and trousers, he did not stop his headlong rush.

Henri's sword slashed down, clipping buttons from her jacket and knocking her sprawling onto her back. She heard Pepper call out, but had no time to respond. Henri came at her again, cursing wildly, and she booted him in the stomach. He staggered back, mouth open. She rolled over, hauled herself to her feet. Saw Pepper, staring – not at her, not at Henri, but past them. Then, there came the shivery crack of splintering stone.

The bridge shuddered like an injured animal. Chips of stone and dust fell from overhead. The ledge shifted, dragging the bridge sideways. Men were screaming, running. But too late. The worm screamed in frustration and raised itself upward, pulling the ledge free of the pillar in the process.

It happened so suddenly. The ledge, and the men on it, were there one moment and gone the next. The bridge snapped like a bullwhip, and it was all Alessandra could do to stay upright. She shouted wordlessly and heard Pepper scream. Henri was still holding on, thanks to his sword. He'd buried it in the end of the bridge, and was gripping it for dear life.

The magics flowing through the bridge seemed to contract, and cracks ran through its surface. It was coming apart, maybe from the attack; maybe the sun was rising; Alessandra didn't know and didn't care. All that mattered was getting herself and Pepper back across it and to safety. She pushed herself up, fighting for balance, and reached for Pepper. The younger woman had all but flattened herself against the bridge in an effort to hold on.

"Climb," Alessandra shouted. "Go – now!"

Pepper nodded and started to climb, as the bridge thrashed

and shuddered. Alessandra heard a shriek and caught a flash of movement out of the corner of her eye. Not Henri – the worm. It had noticed the bridge and was coming to investigate, or to attack. The bridge was shrinking rapidly, pulling just out of the creature's reach, but it pursued, jaws spread wide as it arrowed upward after its prey. There was no way to say which was faster.

Alessandra concentrated on following Pepper, pushing everything else to the back of her mind. There would time enough for fear later. The closer they got to the attic, the more stable the bridge became. But it was still crumbling and contracting. Soon, it would be coming apart under their very feet. And the bones were very, very far below.

"Alessandra!"

Henri's cry alerted her an instant before his sword chopped down, catching the barrel of her revolver and tearing it from her grip. She spun away, striving to put as much distance between herself and Henri as she could.

Pepper stopped and hesitated. "Countess…?"

Alessandra didn't look at her. "Go! Do not wait for me!" She faced Henri on the bucking bridge. He had shucked his coat, but still held his sword. Blood streaked his sleeve from his injured shoulder and his face was pale. "Do not be a fool, Henri. We can both survive this…"

"No, my dear Alessandra, we cannot. This is your doing. You have ruined my plans, killed my men, and stolen my book, *for a second time*." He extended his sword. "*En garde*, Alessandra Zorzi." He leapt forward, blade looping out. She narrowly avoided the deadly stroke but found herself tumbling along the broken edge of the bridge. She caught something that might once have been a floorboard and ripped it loose, whirling around in time to interpose it between her skull and the edge of the sword.

Henri forced her back, against the shifting side of the bridge. Chunks of plaster and broken brick struck her back and shoulders. The solidity beneath her feet was falling away as she fought to stay upright. "When I found out where you were, I should simply have sent gunmen to kill you," he growled. "I should have put you down like a wild beast. But I will not make that mistake again. I will kill you, and then take my book back from your little helper."

"You want your book back, fancy-pants?" Pepper called out from behind him. Alessandra saw Pepper hanging onto the edge of the attic wall, holding the book in one hand. "Here you go!" She flung the book away from her, down the remaining length of the bridge. Henri turned, pulling his sword away from Alessandra as he dove after the book.

Alessandra hesitated, torn between going for the book and leaping to safety. Pepper called out, "Come on!"

Henri snatched up the book with a yelp of exultation. But it was quickly drowned out by the roar of the worm as its flanged maw snapped shut on the end of the bridge. Henri flung himself back as the maw opened again – and snapped shut, erasing more of the bridge.

Propelled by equal parts fear and adrenaline, Alessandra turned and sprinted over the unraveling surface toward the attic and Pepper's outstretched hand. She leapt. Their hands slapped together, Pepper's fingers snapping around her own in a vise-like grip. The bridge crumbled away from her and she fell with a lurch as something caught her ankle. Pepper cried out, trying to hold on. Alessandra looked down and saw the bridge crumble away to nothing – and Henri's terrified face.

"Selim! Selim, help me!" Henri shrieked. Alessandra looked up and saw Selim peering down, over the top of Pepper's head. The bald man's expression was rueful as he considered his employer. Then, his eyes widened and Alessandra turned to see the worm rising up beneath them.

"Get them back in," Trish shouted, as she and Lapp fired down through the gap at the approaching monstrosity. Selim hauled Pepper back, but her hand was sweaty and her grip on Alessandra began to slip.

"Countess… I can't hold on …" she said. Alessandra reached for the floor of the attic, straining against Henri's weight. She wasn't going to make it. Henri was going to drag her into the abyss with him. There was only one chance – one way to save herself. Guilt warred with terror as she closed her eyes – and drove her foot down, into Henri's face. His cry was cut short. Selim shouted, and Henri's grip on her ankle went slack.

"I am sorry, Henri," she murmured under her breath as she accepted a helping hand from Trish and was hauled up, back into the attic, alongside Pepper. She immediately turned to peer back through the gap, but could see nothing of Henri; only the razor-toothed maw of the worm as it shot toward the gap.

It slammed into the gate, the force of its approach knocking them all back. But it was too big to get through, and the gate was already shrinking as the magics that had summoned it faded. It gave a frustrated shriek and dove away, back into the Sea of Bones. As it did so, Alessandra looked down, toward where the ledge had been. A solitary ghoul crouched in the mouth of the cave, and raised a hand in what might have been farewell.

"I told you he could look after himself," Alessandra said, as she and Pepper helped each other to their feet. She looked at Trish and the others. "And where have you been?"

"We came to rescue you," Trish said. She watched the gate shimmer closed.

"How courageous of you," Alessandra said, shakily. She felt wrung out and hollow.

Trish looked at her. "You're welcome. Where's the book?" she asked. It was phrased idly, but it was nothing short of a demand.

Alessandra hesitated. "Henri had it."

They all looked toward the gate or, rather, where the gate had been. There was only a vague violet gleam to the now unbroken wall. Trish made to speak, but was interrupted by the sound of the door to the attic crashing inward.

Bera stepped through, her dress torn, and her hands wet with blood. She gave them a yellow-eyed glare, that was matched by the ghouls who squeezed into the attic behind her, growling and gibbering.

"Where is my son?" Bera snarled.

CHAPTER THIRTY-EIGHT
Morning

"Where is my son?" Bera demanded again.

Alessandra stepped between the others and the ghouls. "Safe on the other side," she said, quickly. "The last we saw of him, at any rate. Someplace called Pnath, I believe. You should be proud of him – he saved our lives."

"Why would he do a foolish thing like that?" Bera asked. Her expression was one of simultaneous relief and frustration. Her followers meeped and gibbered quietly behind her, until she silenced them with a sharp gesture. She fixed Alessandra with a narrowed eye. "It does not matter. You locked us out. You were trying to betray us."

"I do not believe I locked anyone out," Alessandra said. She glanced at Trish and Lapp as she spoke, and added, "And if it did happen, I am certain it was nothing more than an accident." Trish met her eye with a bland expression, and Alessandra felt a flicker of annoyance. She'd expected Trish to try something, obviously, but had hoped she'd restrain herself until after the situation was resolved.

"Not an accident. Treachery." Bera flexed her fingers, as if imagining them digging into Alessandra's throat. "Where is the book?"

Alessandra glanced at Pepper. "Gone."

"Gone?"

"Lost."

"Where?"

"The Sea of Bones, I believe it was called. Henri had it, but I doubt it did him much good, seeing as he was tumbling into the gullet of a rather large worm at the time."

Bera hesitated. "What?"

"A dhole," Lapp supplied. "It rose out of the Sea of Bones when we confronted the Comte's people. I doubt it left any of them alive."

Bera blinked. "A dhole? Truly? If so, you are lucky that any of you survived. Dholes can and will devour whole packs of ghouls – and even gugs, should they get the opportunity." She shook her head slowly. "But that does not settle things between us."

"I believe it does, actually," Lapp said. He handed Selim his shotgun and straightened the knot of his necktie. "You wanted the book removed from the hands of humans. It has been swallowed by a dhole. An object cannot get much more removed than that. And your son is safe in the Dreamlands. You have no reason to be angry." Lapp raised a finger to interrupt as Bera made to protest. "Also, need I remind you that Monsieur Cinabre would frown on any violence done to this woman." He indicated Alessandra with a languid gesture. "Or, by extension, these others. All of whom are under his protection."

"You think I fear Cinabre?" Bera asked, darkly.

Lapp shrugged. "Some wariness, at least, might be advised. But your affairs are your own, I am sure."

Bera hesitated, and one of her ghouls leaned forward to discreetly grumble into her ear. She waved the creature back and snapped her teeth in irritation. "Fine. It is acceptable."

"Oh, well, that is nice," Alessandra murmured, hoping her relief wasn't as obvious as she suspected. A thought occurred to her and she looked around. "Where is Chauncey?"

"Swann?" Trish asked. She turned. "I thought he was up here with us."

"He is not here now," Lapp said.

"And did anyone see where he went?" Alessandra asked, looking at the others.

Trish gestured to Bera. "Maybe her bunch caught him."

Bera grunted. "We saw no one."

Alessandra laughed softly. No doubt he'd fled to safety, to report back to Sanford what had happened. "That sounds like Chauncey. He always did know when to make an exit. It is not important, I suppose. Whatever his employer wanted out of this, I cannot imagine that he got it." She looked around the attic until her eyes came to rest on Selim. He looked lost – out of sorts. "What now, monsieur?"

As if suddenly reminded of Selim's existence, Bera growled. "I know this one. He served the Comte. He is one of the ones who took my Jules. He belongs to us." She gestured and two of her ghouls padded toward Selim, their eyes alight with malice.

"Lapp…?" Alessandra began. She didn't care for the way this was going.

Lapp shook his head. "Monsieur Cinabre's protection does not extend to him, I am afraid. He is on his own."

Selim's face hardened and his hand inched toward his revolver. Pepper stepped between them with her arms spread.

"Selim is an OK joe, no matter who he might have worked for. You ain't taking him nowhere, lady."

"Who are you to deny me?" Bera spat.

Alessandra was about to speak when she heard a sudden faint scratching at the walls. Bera and the others heard it as well, and paused with their heads cocked like those of attentive hounds. The sound came from everywhere and nowhere, growing louder until a chunk of plaster fell from the attic wall. Then another chunk, and another, followed by broken lattice and crumbles of brick, until a hairy arm emerged. It was followed by a rounded shoulder and then a familiar, narrow head.

"Jules!" Bera cried, as Jules tumbled awkwardly out of the wall. There was no sign of where he'd come from, save a few tufts of hair caught on the lattice. Bera helped the ghoul to his feet and stroked his canine head with maternal affection. "You are so thin – they must have starved you!" She glared at Selim again. "It is only fair you be allowed to devour this one. It will be justice!"

"You hard of hearing?" Pepper said, still standing between Selim and the hesitant ghouls. "I said nobody is taking him." Bera turned to snarl at her, but was startled by Jules slouching over to join Pepper. He set a clawed hand on Pepper's shoulder.

"I am afraid I must stand with her, mother." He glanced at Selim, and his lips curled back from his teeth. "As much as it pains me."

Bera hesitated and looked at Alessandra, as if seeking support. Alessandra stepped back, at once bewildered and slightly repulsed by the scene before her. "He is your son, madam."

"She is a ghoul-friend, mother," Jules said quickly, before Bera could reply. "I tried to devour her, and yet she spared my life, and freed me." He gave Pepper a fond look – or maybe a hungry one; it was difficult for Alessandra to tell. "When she dies, it will be my great honor to suck the marrow from her bones."

"Truly?" Bera asked as she looked at Pepper as if seeing her for the first time.

Pepper blanched. "Y- yeah?" Alessandra wondered if she were stuck on the marrow-sucking bit. Alessandra knew that she would have been, in the young woman's place.

Bera snorted and waved her followers back. "Very well. It seems I am to be denied both the book and vengeance."

"But you have your son," Alessandra said, softly. "That must count for something, surely." She put her hand on Pepper's other shoulder. "I know it does for me."

Bera met her eyes and nodded, after a moment's hesitation. She gestured, and her followers left the attic with a great rumpus and racket. She held out her hand, and Jules took it, enfolding his mother in a loose-limbed embrace. Bera looked at Alessandra over the top of his head. "You are not a ghoul-friend, Countess. But you are known to us, now. And we will treat you with the respect you deserve." She glanced at Lapp, nodded in something that might have been gratitude, and departed.

Jules hesitated. He growled softly at Selim, and then shyly handed Pepper something – her hat. Alessandra realized that the young woman had lost it at some point during their flight. "You dropped this," he said. Then, with something that doubtless passed for a smile among ghouls, he followed the others out of the attic. In moments, even the sound of them had faded. Alessandra wondered whether they'd gone out the door, or simply... vanished back into the Dreamlands.

"Either way, exit stage left," she murmured.

Pepper looked down at her hat and then at Alessandra. "He said he wanted to eat me." She didn't sound startled so much as perplexed.

"After you die," Lapp said. "It is considered a great honor among those folk." He looked down his nose at Pepper. "You must have impressed him."

Pepper blinked and looked at Alessandra, as she hiked a thumb at Lapp. "Who's this palooka? He looks like a bank teller, or maybe a butler."

Alessandra laughed at the offended look on Lapp's face. "An ally."

Lapp looked as if he might disagree, but instead nodded in acceptance if not agreement. "This place, does it have a telephone?" he asked Selim. The other man nodded.

"Downstairs, in the study. I can–"

Lapp waved him back. "I will find it. I must inform Monsieur Cinabre that we have been successful." He bowed stiffly. "If you will excuse me?"

Trish watched him go. "I don't suppose I have to warn you about owing favors to guys like Cinabre, right?" she asked.

Alessandra shook her head. "No more so than I have to warn you about working with people like Carl Sanford and Chauncey Swann." She paused. "Speaking of which, I am afraid you did not acquire what you came for."

Trish frowned and looked down at the shotgun in her hands. "I ought to shoot you for losing that book," she said. She tossed the weapon to Alessandra. "But maybe it's for the best." She tapped the brim of her hat and started for the door. "Be seeing you, Countess."

"You are just going to leave? After all this?" Alessandra called after her. She wasn't sorry to see the back of the other woman, but she was somewhat surprised to see her leave so quickly. Then, like Swann, perhaps Scarborough knew when to make an exit.

Trish paused at the door. "Maybe I can catch up with Chauncey. Bum a ride back to civilization. Failing that, I'll borrow a car. There's plenty of them out there and some of them aren't on fire. It's not like anyone around here is going to complain." She glanced back at Alessandra and gave a smile. "Like I said – be seeing you."

"I look forward to it," Alessandra said, and was surprised to find that she meant it.

Then, Trish too was gone, leaving only Alessandra, Pepper and Selim in the attic. Pepper rubbed the back of her neck and looked at Alessandra. "What now? We gonna follow her example and get out of Dodge?"

"Perhaps. Though perhaps there is no hurry, as yet." Alessandra had the glimmerings of an idea. "We have no place to be, after all."

"What about Znamenski and that tablet of his, the one we promised we'd get for Armitage?" Pepper asked. Alessandra waved this aside.

"We know where Znamenski has gone. And while I wish to speak to him about his part in luring us into a trap, I am in no hurry to do so." She smiled. "I think we are due a bit of a rest, after all of this palaver."

Pepper blanched. "Here?"

"Why not? I doubt Selim will argue the point, will you… Selim?" She turned to find that Selim had gone to the widow's walk and stepped out. Alessandra followed him, leaning against the door frame. She watched him for a moment and then said, "It could not have been easy. Turning on him."

"Easier than it might once have been," Selim said. "The man who first employed me was not the man who died today. That man would not have been so blinded by pettiness ..."

"I hate to tell you this, but Henri was always petty. He was a man driven by equal measures of spite and arrogance. That is why it was so easy for me to steal that damned book in the first place." She paused. She felt regret, of course. But Henri had made his choice, and she had made hers. "You never answered me before. What do you intend to do now?"

Selim grunted. "The servants will be wondering what has happened, if they have not all fled. And there will be survivors from the fight to see to." He leaned on the rail and looked down into the courtyard. Alessandra resisted the urge. She'd seen enough carnage for one lifetime. But she could still hear the crackle of flames and the moans of injured men.

"And you?" she asked.

Selim glanced at her. "My former employer is currently in the belly of a giant worm. I suppose I must find a new one." He sighed. "We all must."

Alessandra pulled out her cigarettes. The idea percolating in her head had solidified now, into something workable. "Tell me ... did Henri ever move that cache of valuables from the loose flagstone in the cellar?"

Selim frowned. "I know of no loose flagstone."

Alessandra offered him the pack. "Well then, you and I should have a look before we go. If he has not moved that one, well – I doubt he moved any of the others. Or his will, for that matter."

Selim waved the cigarettes aside. "His ... will?"

Alessandra stretched and selected a cigarette. "Mm. Yes. For a brief moment, I was his designated heir. I expect that has changed, but it is a simple matter to make another adjustment. I know a fellow in Rheims who would be delighted to help, for a slight fee."

Selim stared at her. "What are you talking about?"

Alessandra lit her cigarette. "Once upon a time, I might have been the Comtesse d'Erlette for my sins. I see no reason to let a good title and fortune go to waste, do you?" She smiled brightly, realizing that she'd found a solution for her money woes at last. "And, of course, as the new comtesse, I will see fit to maintain the employment of my predecessor's staff." She blew a smoke ring toward the rising sun. "I have a need for a good hunter, you see."

"Oh?" Selim asked, in a neutral tone.

"Yes. I need to find an artist in Milan."

Selim snorted. "Better to ask me to find a rock in a river." But he sounded interested. Alessandra thought he would go along with it. He was a pragmatic fellow, despite it all.

Alessandra laughed. "Yes, well, this artist's name is Znamenski. He has something of mine." She paused and looked at Pepper. The young woman stood in the center of the attic, hat in hand, her face half in shadow. It was as if she was listening for – or to – something. Alessandra could only imagine what it might be.

She stared at the young woman, worry gnawing at her. She would need to speak to Cinabre – and Armitage, at Miskatonic. They might be able to shed some light on what Pepper was experiencing; and more importantly, how to stop it. Before it became something more than bad dreams.

As if sensing her concern, Pepper looked up, and met Alessandra's gaze. For a moment, the younger woman's face seemed nothing more than a pallid mask, blank and empty of life. Then, "What?" she asked. "I got something on my face?" She brushed briskly at her cheek with a sleeve.

Alessandra shook her head. "Nothing," she lied. "Just a trick of the light."

EPILOGUE
The Game Continues

Cinabre set the telephone down and looked at his guest. "Well, as you predicted, the book is lost. Lapp is quite certain that our little thief did it intentionally." Lapp's call had been expected, if somewhat disappointing. He'd assumed the book would not be returning to his possession, and considered the loss a fair price for what had been accomplished.

"Intentionally, or opportunistically?" Carl Sanford asked, with a hard smile. The head of the Silver Twilight Lodge sat comfortably in Cinabre's sitting room, sipping from a cup of coffee. "From what I know of the woman, she's one of nature's born tacticians. A quick thinker where it counts, but not one to waste time crafting an elaborate plan."

"Debatable," Cinabre murmured. He suspected Zorzi was a more capable planner than Sanford cared to admit, but he said nothing. That Zorzi had survived was unsurprising; he had plans for the esteemed countess. But not ones he would be sharing with his guest. He sat down opposite Sanford and retrieved his own coffee. "The owner of the book has been lost as well."

"Shame," Sanford said, in an amused tone. He'd arrived the

night before, accompanied by a distressing red-headed woman named Van Shaw. The woman was outside and had been since the early hours of the morning; something about Cinabre's home seemed to disagree with her.

"In a sense it might be. The Comte d'Erlette was a potent piece on the board."

Sanford gestured dismissively. "A loaded gun is only useful if it's aimed in the right direction. Our friend Henri hasn't been pointed the right way in more than a year. He was a wild card, and we don't need any more of those running around."

"Says the man who employs nothing but wild cards," Cinabre said, pointedly. "Madam Van Shaw for instance, or your pet thief, Swann."

Sanford smirked. "A wild card in the hand is an advantage. It's when they're loose in the deck you have to worry about them." He took a sip of coffee and studied Cinabre over the rim. "Besides, don't tell me that he wasn't keeping your pals in the Red Coterie awake at nights. Him and that crazy idea of his."

"Is it so crazy?" Cinabre asked. Sanford paused – frowned.

"Maybe not," he admitted. "But the way he went about it…guns and gas and the like. That's not the way, and we both know it." He leaned forward. "Real change – effective change – that requires a less mundane arsenal. Bullets and leftover artillery aren't going to put a dent in the hide of what's waiting on the other side of the curtain. Your people know that; that's why you have your agents racing around, collecting all the artifacts and talismans you can lay your grubby mitts on."

"As if your organization is any different."

Sanford accepted this statement with a shrug. "I'm not denying that. We know where we stand, our two groups.

Occasionally at odds, but mostly we stay out of each other's way. That's how it's always been."

"Until now," Cinabre said. He set his coffee aside. "We both wanted Henri off the board. You dangled the bait, I set the hook... and human nature took its course."

"We did a fine job of it, if I might say so." Sanford looked around. "Say, I heard you had quite the library. Only this place doesn't seem big enough."

Cinabre paused. "Big enough for my purposes, at least."

"You don't exactly live in luxury, do you?" Sanford continued, slyly.

"As I said, it suits my purposes."

Sanford nodded, as if he had expected as much. "I understand. I'm a simple man, myself. I just want a little plot to call my own. That's what all this hoo-ha is about, in the end. About taking what's mine – what's ours – and holding onto it, despite the designs of others. Something we can only do together."

Cinabre sat back, hands folded across his stomach. "A very pretty speech, Mr Sanford. But I am not a gullible socialite or an occultist desperate for a monied patron. I do not need you. We do not need you."

Sanford paused. "Need is a funny word. Like all the best words, it's got its layers. You don't need us and we don't need you. Our two organizations can happily sail past one another, like ships in the night. But at the same time, we do need each other. Every sailor knows the law of the sea, monsieur. You see a ship in trouble, well, you're obliged to help. And that's what I'm saying. It's not about the here and now, but the maybe later."

Cinabre studied Sanford as the latter continued his well-rehearsed pitch. He planned to agree to whatever proposal the other man laid out, of course. He was speaking only for himself, though Sanford didn't know that.

Nor did he seem to realize that the Red Coterie was less an organization and more a collective of individuals with similar goals. A society of dilettantes, rather than a cult. What Sanford did know was that the members of the Coterie had access to a number of useful talismans, totems and tomes. In the hands of the Coterie such items were so much more than their appearance and history suggested; they were keys to enlightenment. To immortality. To survival. But to Sanford, it likely seemed nothing more than an arsenal of the occult – one he desperately wanted access to.

It was much the same with the American Cipher Bureau. The Black Chamber wanted the knowledge the Coterie could provide. Knowledge that Cinabre and others had parceled out in dribs and drabs, when it suited their purposes. In return, the Black Chamber sought those artifacts that had escaped the Coterie's own agents.

Cinabre doubted the Silver Twilight Lodge would be so accommodating. No, Sanford was not looking for an equal partner so much as a patsy. He'd offered to play the sacrificial goat, largely out of boredom. Through him, the Coterie would discover what Sanford's endgame was – and whether it was in the best interests of the Coterie to allow it to proceed. If not, Cinabre would be well placed to disrupt whatever scheme Sanford had in mind.

In theory, at least.

The truth was, Cinabre suspected that Sanford was well aware of the possibility of betrayal and had planned accordingly. Granted, that only made it more exciting. And some excitement was what he was in search of, these days.

The problem with a long war was the interminable stretches of inactivity between moments of frantic activity. Waiting for the other side to make a move was wise, but dull. Especially when they measured time in epochs.

Playing the patsy for Sanford would enliven the tedium, somewhat. It might also get him killed if he wasn't careful. But what was the point of playing a game if there were no stakes involved?

Sanford finished his pitch and sat back, every inch the American huckster. A snake-oil salesman, selling eldritch tinctures to the gullible and the mad. But that was only a mask, covering the true darkness beneath. There were shadows in Sanford's gaze, and an echo of power that beat on Cinabre's senses like the reverberations of a hammer.

Some among Cinabre's fellowship – the Claret Knight, for instance – would have seized the opportunity to remove Sanford's head while it was poking up out of its hole. He would not have blamed them for it either. But Cinabre had never been one to kill a snake when he could tame it instead.

With effort, the Silver Twilight Lodge might be turned to a useful purpose, much like he intended to do with Alessandra Zorzi. If not, it would have to be destroyed. No doubt Sanford was thinking the same about the Coterie. But that was a concern for the future. Right now, it was simply a new game.

Cinabre smiled. "You are proposing an alliance, then?"

Sanford nodded. "Of convenience only, I assure you. Tit for tat, and a bit of a helping hand in our diverse and necessary works. A rising tide lifts all boats, as they say."

"Indeed."

"So. What do you say?"

Cinabre's smile didn't waver. "Why, Monsieur Sanford, I say that this looks like the beginning of a beautiful friendship."

ABOUT THE AUTHOR

JOSH REYNOLDS is the author of over thirty novels and numerous short stories, including the wildly popular *Legend of the Five Rings, Arkham Horror, Warhammer: Age of Sigmar* and *Warhammer 40,000*. He grew up in South Carolina and now lives in Sheffield, UK.

joshuamreynolds.co.uk // twitter.com/jmreynolds